THE BAY PHANTOM

CONFEDERACY OF DEVILS

AIRSHIP 27 PRODUCTIONS

The Bay Phantom-Confederacy of Devils
© 2014 Chuck Miller

Published by Airship 27 Productions
www.airship27.com
www.airship27hangar.com

Interior and cover illustrations © 2014 Zachary Brunner

Editor: Ron Fortier
Associate Editor: Charles Saunders
Marketing and Promotions Manager: Michael Vance
Production and design by Rob Davis.

ISBN-13: 978-0692308349 (Airship 27)
ISBN-10: 0692308342

Printed in the United States of America

10 9 8 7 6 5 4 3 2 1

THE BAY PHANTOM

CONFEDERACY OF DEVILS

by Chuck Miller

PROLOGUE ONE

"Our time is coming soon," said the man in the purple robe. "And that means yours is, too. You know how it has to be. The night you didn't die, I knew you had a power, and that it had been delivered into my hands. Since then, I have learned much from you. You are the key, and you will be used to unlock the door."

His speech was monotonous, measured and mechanical. He sounded like a priest reciting a particular passage of Scripture for the ten thousandth time. He stood in front of a large metal cage, addressing the stooped and broken man who sat inside it.

"Those who stand in our way will fall," he continued. "When they do, we shall rise again. Our memory has been perverted and our world has been all but destroyed. A spark remains, however. It never went out, and it will be fanned into a flame that will burn away this blasphemous new age before it gains any more ground. It will be better for all of us, your people and mine. I am convinced that the time is upon us. I am waiting for more signs. They will come. I will be ready to do my part."

The man in the cage gave no sign that he heard what was being said. This did not discourage the speaker.

"It won't be long now. I have a strong feeling about this. You will finally pay for what you did to my brother, and it won't be mere revenge on my part. It will have a purpose. The door will be opened and that which went wrong will be set right. Your people and mine will rejoice because the natural order will be restored."

The man in the cage looked up. His eyes were empty. He had less self-awareness than a dog or a cat.

"Soon you'll be free from this clay," said the man in the purple robe. "That will be nice. And the world will be what it was always meant to be."

No light of understanding appeared in the caged man's vacant eyes.

PROLOGUE TWO
MOBILE, ALABAMA
1931

"They say this place is haunted," said Mirabelle Darcy. "They say it may be the most haunted house in the entire South."

"I certainly hope that's true," said Joe Perrone. "I paid enough money for it. If there aren't at least three ghosts in there, I've been swindled."

Perrone was a tall, dark-haired man in his 20s, seemingly quite average in every way; a thoroughly unremarkable fellow if you went strictly by his appearance. His companion, also in her 20s, was five and a half feet tall, with hazel eyes and very dark skin. She was slender, though not quite petite.

"I can't tell if you're being serious or not," Mirabelle said. "I know you have a strong interest in that kind of thing. Y'know, I thought it was us darkies that were supposed to be the superstitious ones; afraid of haints and all that."

Perrone winced. "I wish you wouldn't use terms like that in reference to yourself. I realize you're being flippant, and I understand, but..."

"With all due respect, Mister Perrone," Mirabelle said firmly, "I don't think you do understand. You've never been on my side of the great divide."

He thought about that for a moment, then shrugged.

"Granted," he said. "We don't need to go into that now, I suppose. At any rate, I'm completely serious about 'that kind of thing,' and I'm not afraid of 'haints.' Indeed, I welcome them. I would love to have my own private laboratory in which to study them."

"More like a game preserve," Mirabelle observed.

"I suppose so. Of course, it isn't my primary purpose in acquiring this property. The house is perfectly situated to make my work a great deal easier."

"Right," said Mirabelle, in a voice devoid of inflection. "The 'work.' I have to tell you I've got my doubts about the wisdom of the whole thing."

The two of them were standing on a patch of land on the edge Mobile Bay, a few miles south of downtown Mobile. The place had a feeling of remoteness about it, though it was very close to the city. If you crossed the road and got as close to the water as you could and looked to your left, you could see the lights of downtown. Step back a couple paces, you were in the middle of nowhere.

Joseph Perrone had recently acquired the land and the large, old house that stood on it, a dark, blocky, formidable-looking pile of wood and stone that struck Mirabelle Darcy as not exactly sinister, but a place where nothing ought to be taken for granted. She and her employer, Perrone, would be in residence here within a few more days, and the *work* would begin. She knew he would never be dissuaded from it. Right now, she would limit herself to urging him to proceed with great caution. Beyond that, she would just have to wait and see, and hope that what she saw was good.

Perrone had known Mirabelle when they were children; her parents had worked for his family. Six months ago, she had been unexpectedly reunited with him, and he had offered her a position as his housekeeper. He had waited until she accepted, and got used to the arrangement, before dropping the bomb on her. Joe Perrone was not what he seemed. Of course, neither was Mirabelle Darcy. Perrone couldn't have cared less whether or not he had a housekeeper; he needed someone who could help him in his strange avocation. Mirabelle, he believed, was uniquely suited for this role.

"The house dates back to the late 18th Century," Perrone was saying. "This was a rather desolate area back then. It was built by a character called Seamus Gregory. He called it Tull House; nobody knows why. Gregory was from Ireland or Scotland or some other place. He made his living as a smuggler over there, among other things, and he continued those activities here.

"There are other reasons I chose it, aside from the ghosts. It was outfitted as a smuggler's den years ago, and I can renovate all the secret passages and things. And, with just a little blasting and digging, I can link up with Doctor Piranha's tunnel system, just fifty yards to the west. That gives me covert access to places all over town. My particular favorite is a tunnel that terminates in the Church Street Graveyard. It's time to close down Gulf Bay Manor for good. That place has too many of the wrong kind of ghosts."

Mirabelle just nodded. She stood now with her back to the house, staring out over the dark waters of Mobile Bay, listening to the waves lapping the shore across the road.

After a while, she said, "The problem is, that kind of ghost tends to follow a person around, no matter where he goes."

On the surface, Joseph Perrone was one of the idle rich; heir to his family's successful commercial fishing operation in Bayou La Batre. He was the sort, everyone thought, who never would have amounted to anything if he hadn't come from money. But he was something of a tragic figure, too. His parents and older brother had died in a house fire when Joe was ten years old. The fire had been deliberately set by burglars who had broken into the house, thinking the family was away. Someone, probably Joe's father, had surprised them in the act. That was when things turned lethal. Within a very short time, Joe Perrone was an orphan. This fact allowed people to view him more charitably than they might otherwise.

But there was more to the story than anyone knew. The tragedy had affected Joe Perrone deeply, which was common enough in such cases. What was not common was the way in which he responded to it.

To cut a long story short, Joe had created for himself a new persona, a strange figure that lived outside the law and prowled the night, administering his own brand of justice to those who had it coming. For almost two years, in the mid-1920s, the Bay Phantom had cut a swath through the criminal underworld of the Gulf Coast, matching wits with bizarre criminal masterminds and besting them every time.

Joe Perrone had never intended to call his "other" self the Bay Phantom. In the beginning, he had simply thought of his masked identity as "Mister Zero" or "Nobody." He had not wanted or dared to give a name to his obsession. But someone, probably a reporter, had dubbed him the "Bay Phantom," and the name had stuck. In time, it had grown on him, sort of, though he still wasn't completely comfortable with it.

He supposed that the regional pride implied by the moniker helped make him a symbol around which the citizenry could rally, when necessary. Things had gone well for the first few months. He saved some lives and taken some very dangerous characters off the streets. He felt that he was making the sort of difference he had set out to make.

And then came Doctor Piranha.

From the beginning, the Doctor Piranha case had been different. Whereas the Bay Phantom's earlier opponents had been motivated by profit, the mysterious Doctor's aims were more obscure. His crimes were more like pointless vandalism on a large and diabolical scale. The man was a terrorist without a cause. He never made a penny from any of his crimes, but the loss of life and property had been appalling.

For the first time in his life, Joseph Perrone, the Bay Phantom, had lusted for the blood of another. He wanted to kill Doctor Piranha. He managed to stop himself in time, but the experience had been wrenching, and had poisoned the part of his spirit that had created and sustained the Bay Phantom. After Piranha had been locked away, Perrone put the Bay Phantom away too, and swore never to unleash him again.

But things change. The worm had burrowed too deep and could not be dislodged...

CHAPTER ONE
COVERING THE WATERFRONT

This has got to be the low point of my career, thought Louis Rickert. He'd been doing this kind of work since he was fourteen; more than twenty years. He was more than capable, though not particularly brilliant or inspired. Even so, he wasn't the kind of guy you'd leave outside on lookout duty, while less-experienced guys who hadn't cracked half as many safes as he had were inside pulling the job. It was wasteful, an inefficient allocation of resources.

The management has it in for me, he thought sourly. *That damn Karl Volker. What the hell is his problem, anyhow?*

Rickert was of average height and build, with slicked-back blonde hair and watery greenish-blue eyes. He was thrity-five years old, though he could look much younger or much older, depending on his mood.

He walked around the perimeter of the building, an old brick warehouse close to the river, and saw nothing out of the ordinary. He wasn't expecting anything. The cops wouldn't be out here. He was pretty sure Volker's little gang was working for the Carter family, and if this was something the Carters wanted done, the cops would have been paid to stay away. The gang had been hired to break into this warehouse and steal something they would find in a certain safe in a certain office. The warehouse belonged to a businessman named Hector Sams. Sams had recently announced his candidacy for mayor against the Carters' candidate, Simon Brickell. It wasn't hard to see why there would be bad blood there.

Rickert consulted his watch. The crew had been in there fifteen minutes already. If he'd been on the inside team, they'd have been finished long ago. *Well, if Volker doesn't give a damn, there's no reason for me to.* He needed to quit worrying about the stupid things Volker did and said, or he was going to give himself ulcers or a stroke.

Rickert moved around to the back of the building, leaned against the wall, and lit a cigarette. He stayed there for quite a while, imagining the things he'd like to say to Karl Volker. He was well into a very eloquent and vitriolic diatribe when he noticed something odd. A very dense ground fog had moved in from somewhere and was spreading rapidly over the back lot, bearing down on him like a silent, horizontal avalanche, blotting out everything. It reached him and engulfed him, and, suddenly, he couldn't see two feet in front of his face.

Rickert stood up straight, turned around, and placed his palms against the warehouse wall. He began moving to the right, toward the rear door, groping the bricks as he inched along.

"How old are you?"

The voice came from somewhere nearby, no more than a yard or two behind him. He whirled around but couldn't see anything through the fog.

"Who's there?" he said in a low voice. "What's the gag? Are you a cop?"

"No," came the voice. Rickert didn't recognize it. It had a strange timbre, sounding both deep and insubstantial at the same time. "I'm not with the police. I asked you a question. How old are you?"

"Old enough to bust your head wide open," Rickert snarled. "If I could see you," he added.

"I doubt that. The reason I asked about your age is because lookout duty usually goes to the youngest and least experienced member of a crew. You're thirty-five at the very least."

"You've got three seconds to tell me what this is about," Rickert blustered. "I'm not out here to play with you."

"I guess I'll have to take some kind of action, then." Now the speaker was behind him once again. He hadn't heard any footsteps. He whirled around, straining his ears. His heart sank into his stomach as his pistol was snatched away from him by an unseen hand. He lunged forward, arms stuck out in front of him, groping blindly for his tormenter. He tripped over something and landed on his face in the grass.

"Aw, shit," he said morosely.

"Be of good cheer," said the voice. "And please remain on the ground for the moment. I have two guns now, and I wouldn't want this to get out of hand. I've actually done you a good turn. I entered the building shortly after your friends did. I saw you tear the rear door open with that crowbar totally by chance, believe it or not. I didn't want to alarm you, so I slipped in through an upper story window while you were on the opposite side of the warehouse. They were going to do their business in the office, come back down, knock you out, and phone in an anonymous tip to the police.

I heard them talking about it. Have you any idea why they would do such a thing?"

"What? Are you telling me the truth?"

"Certainly. What would it profit me to tell you a lie?"

Rickert thought about that for a minute. He couldn't answer the question. "But… that's crazy. Why would they do that? I know everything about this operation. They would have just croaked me if they wanted me out of the way. I could have spilled the whole thing to the cops. It just don't add up."

"It *is* curious," the voice said thoughtfully. "You seem to be a man in trouble. This is most fortuitous. I seem to have stumbled across something interesting this evening. I'd like to discuss it with you. Perhaps we can figure it out if we put our heads together."

"Okay," said Rickert. What other choice did he have? He was at the mercy of this unseen individual. Might as well play along and hope for the best. "You're no cop. I don't know who you're working for, but you might want to be careful. Do you know you're screwing around with a crew that's backed by the Carters? You know what that means?"

"Not exactly, but it sounds intriguing. You can fill me in once we're away from here. Your treacherous friends have been subdued, and the police *will* be here very soon. Come along with me, I have my own transportation."

Rickert sighed. Whoever this was, he held all the cards. And what he was saying did have the ring of truth. There was such a thing as honor among thieves, but it was more the exception than the rule.

"What the hell," he said, "you're probably on the level. You know, I *thought* that sonofabitch Volker had it in for me! Can I stand up now? Thanks. So, where are you parked?"

"On the river," the voice replied as Rickert got to his feet. "I know it isn't very manly, but if you'll take my hand, I'll lead you down to my boat."

"Sure," Rickert said resignedly, reaching out toward where he thought the voice was coming from. He felt a gloved hand slip into his own. "Lead on Macduff."

"That's a misquote, actually," said the voice. "*Macbeth, Act Five, Scene Eight.* The line is, *Lay on, Macduff, And damn'd be him that first cries, 'Hold, enough!'* Macbeth is challenging Macduff to a final duel, you see. It's his last line in the play, as Macduff kills him shortly after."

"Oh."

"Don't worry. My voice is not in my sword tonight, and I believe *you* are the one who has suffered a betrayal. You very nearly became a tragically wronged man, and you may still be a marked one. Perhaps we can do something about that."

By this time, much of the thick fog had dispersed, and Rickert was able to make out a tall man, dressed in a dark suit and a wide-brimmed slouch hat. He also seemed to be wearing a cape, which was something you didn't see every day.

"At some point," Rickert said, removing his hand from the stranger's grasp, "are you going to tell me who the hell you are?"

"My apologies. I am the Bay Phantom."

"The Bay *what*? Is that an actual name? I don't think I... Oh, hey, wait a minute! You're the guy that busted that nut Doctor Piranha three years ago. Yeah, I remember. I figured you were dead. What happened to you?"

"Quite a bit. I had things to do that could only be done elsewhere. But I'm back now. Watch your step. We'll have to wade out just a bit, you may want to remove your shoes and roll up your trouser legs."

The strange fog was almost gone now, but Rickert still couldn't see very well. Some clouds had moved in and hidden the moon. He waded carefully toward what appeared to be a small, flat motor launch of some kind, gently bobbing up and down on the muddy water. The Phantom waded along beside him, though he hadn't bothered to take off his shoes or roll up his pants. They climbed into the boat, which must have had a very low center of gravity, as it barely tipped to the side as they clambered up and over. Rickert took note of several squat canisters attached to the deck, from which a few wisps of dark smoke still issued. This must have been the source of the weird fog.

"Yes, I activated that pseudo-fog machine by remote control," said the Phantom, apparently responding to Rickert's unspoken thought. "Come up front here and sit down."

As they lowered themselves into a pair of bucket seats near the prow of the craft, the moon became visible again, and Rickert saw that his strange companion was wearing a black full-face mask, with blue-tinted goggles over his eyes.

"Jesus, I guess you really *are* him " Rickert said, as he rolled his pants legs back down and replaced his socks and shoes. "You look just like that picture. Well, I mean, you can't really *recognize* a mask; *anybody* could be behind it, I guess. But who the hell else would want to? I didn't mean that as an insult, by the way."

The Bay Phantom chuckled as he pressed a button on what must have been the dashboard. The motor started up. It was very quiet, an oddly comforting low hum. Rickert could feel the little craft vibrating in a subtle, controlled way. It must have had plenty of horsepower, but it didn't feel the need to show it off.

"I know how you meant it," said the masked man. "No offense taken. Let's go somewhere less perilous, and you can tell me all about what went on tonight. It strikes me that your comrades intended to leave you there, alive, so that you would tell the police everything you knew or thought you knew."

"What do you mean?"

"I'm not sure, but we can discuss it."

The Bay Phantom pulled a lever and worked a small steering apparatus, and the little boat moved toward the middle of the Tensaw River, out into the current, and sped off south, in the direction of Mobile Bay.

CHAPTER TWO
FOUR BAD ENDS

Karl Volker and his gang hit the street at three o'clock the following afternoon, having spent the previous night in the city jail. "Some lawyer posted your bail," said the officer who processed them out. "I didn't recognize the guy. He left you a note. That's all I know. You have a court date, and you'd better show up for that."

Volker assumed the lawyer was connected to the man who had hired them for the warehouse job. Before they were escorted out of the building, the officer handed Volker a folded piece of paper. Written on it was a phone number none of them recognized, and nothing else.

Volker found a pay phone, fed it a nickel, and dialed the number. He had a brief conversation while the others stood around him.

"We're gonna meet our go-between," Volker said after he hung up. "He gave me some directions. Out in the open, on D'Autremont Road. We're supposed to be there at eleven o'clock tonight. I thought we screwed the job up, but the guy said he was gonna pay us off. But keep your eyes open tonight."

They spent the day making the rounds of their usual haunts, trying to track down Louis Rickert, without any luck. They visited Rickert's shabby apartment, but it looked as though he had moved out.

They arrived at the rendezvous point at exactly eleven p.m. It was a residential area north of downtown, a well-to-do section, with large houses widely separated by huge lawns and plenty of foliage. Most of the houses were dark, and there were no streetlights. The only illumination came from the three-quarter moon.

They pulled off the road near a small wooded area, as the voice on the phone had instructed. Four minutes later, someone emerged from the clump of trees. The figure moved toward the car, but stopped a few feet away, remaining in the shadows cast by the trees.

Volker, in the front passenger seat, rolled down the window.

"Are you our guy?" he asked gruffly. "What the hell's going on, anyhow?"

"Here's your money," said the man, tossing a large brown paper envelope through the open window. His voice sounded muffled. "What happened last night?"

"I wish I knew," Volker said. "There was some character wearing a mask and a cape, he busted in on us, sprayed some kind of gas, and trussed us up. I don't know what happened to that idiot Rickert. Basically, the whole damn production went down the crapper. We didn't say a thing to the cops about any of it."

"Well, that's good," said the man. "The less they know the better. But what about this man in the mask and cape? Who was he?"

"Hell, I don't know!"

"That much I can believe," said the man. "You've been kept in the dark about a lot of things. I think it's time you got the straight dope. First, go ahead and count that money, so you'll know I'm on the level."

"Okay, fine," Volker grumbled, tearing open the package. Several bundles of bills tumbled out into his lap. He picked them up one by one and riffled through them.

"Jesus," he said, feeling a little light-headed. "These are all hundreds! There must be... This is more than we were promised. A *lot* more..."

"Well," said the man, "I believe in rewarding success."

"Yeah, but we... We didn't..." Volker said haltingly. He was having trouble getting his thoughts together. "I mean, we did everything you told us to. The thing is, we didn't do everything you *hired* us to do, even though it wasn't our fault, and..."

"Never mind all that," the man interrupted. "You did well enough. Now, here's what's going on: For one thing, I'm not the guy who hired you. For another, the guy who *did* hire you wasn't who you thought he was. He was working for another guy, and that guy was working for another guy, and so on. I've been keeping an eye on the guy at the top, that's how I traced the whole thing down to you. You guys are working for the person I've been keeping an eye on."

"Who do *you* work for?" Volker wanted to know.

"I wouldn't say I work *for* anybody. I'm my own creature and I have never been formally employed by anyone. But I need cash to indulge my expensive and esoteric tastes, so I sometimes do favors in exchange for cash considerations. And I am very thorough. I know more about your mystery employer than you do. And I know something very important about all of you that you aren't aware of."

"Like what?" Volker said hoarsely. He was starting to feel ill.

"There was more than money in that package," said the man matter-of-factly. "It also contained an airborne nerve agent which you breathed in. You fellows are paralyzed now; everything but your autonomic nervous systems. You'll keep breathing and your hearts will keep beating... until they stop."

Volker tried to reply to this statement with a bit of bluster, but found that he could not speak. He couldn't move at all.

The man stepped forward, into the moonlight.

He was wearing a long, white lab coat and he had something covering his face. It was white and shiny, like a Mardi Gras mask, but there was no color in it.

The man reached behind his back and brought something into view. Volker didn't know what it was, but it looked a bit like the harpoons he'd seen used by whale hunters. It was about three feet long, slightly bigger around than a broom handle, and it tapered off to a sharp point.

"This is my thing," said the man. "I've killed with guns and knives and ropes and even my bare hands on occasion, but this gimmick here is my favorite. I invented it myself." He opened the car door and bent down.

Volker felt a bit of pressure near the bottom of his ribcage, followed by the disconcerting sensation of something moving up into his chest. The man had pierced his torso with the rod. Then he twisted it a bit, very gently, as though adjusting it to his liking. Volker thought he saw a black rubber hose attached to the handle of the rod, looping around behind the masked man's back.

"There," he said from behind the weird mask. His voice sounded a bit huskier than before. "The apparatus will have just barely pierced your right ventricle, if I've done my work properly. You won't feel any pain, thanks to my nerve agent."

He reached behind his back again. There was a faint click, followed by a rhythmic chugging sound. Volker felt a horrible coldness spread through his body, starting in his chest and radiating outward.

"Perfect," said the masked man. "Just a couple more little details and you'll be on your way to hell in fine style, old sport!"

He reached into his lab coat and drew out a large stainless steel scalpel.

"Watch this, boys," he said cheerfully to the other motionless occupants of the car. "Don't worry, I'll get to all of you. Relax and enjoy the show!"

CHAPTER THREE
PLANS

"**S**omething is going on," said Perrone. "That attempted burglary at the Sams warehouse was not at all what it appeared to be. Rickert was misled by the rest of the gang he was with. He was set up to be captured. There is a reason for that."

"And what is that?" Mirabelle asked.

"I can't say just yet. But I'm keeping Rickert somewhere safe. He may not know anything at all, he may be totally unimportant. But, on the other hand, he may be the key to... something."

"What if he isn't?"

"He can still be useful. And if that sounds cold and manipulative to you, let me assure you that I have taken a personal interest in Mister Rickert. I believe he is a good man at heart, and I think he can be reformed."

Mirabelle sighed. "Do you remember when you were a kid and you found that dog with rabies?" she asked. "Remember how you trapped him in that orange crate and hid him in the barn, thinking you could nurse him back to health?"

"Mirabelle, I was eight."

"Yes, and you were damn lucky to make nine, pulling stunts like that. So, where have you stashed this noble savage of yours?"

"Well... At first, I set him up in that little safe house of mine in Chickasaw. But after the crew he'd been working with turned up dead, I... Well, I..."

"Oh, no," Mirabelle said. "You *didn't*! You *did*! You trapped him in your orange crate, didn't you? Where is he?"

"Downstairs," Perrone said. "In the catacombs. I blindfolded him before I brought him here, you needn't worry about that. He doesn't know where he is or who I am. I just want to keep him safe until I know what's going on."

"How long are you going to keep him here?"

"Not much longer. I think it unlikely that he is in any danger. I believe he knows less about that warehouse job than the men who were killed, and has no connection to whoever was behind it. He was just unfortunate enough to have somehow aroused the ire of Karl Volker. I'd like to place him back into his element as soon as I can. He can be a great help to me."

"You just said you didn't think he knows anything."

"Oh, he knows quite a bit. But there is a great deal more that he doesn't know. However, he can provide bits of mismatched information, and the gaps can be filled in. There's more going on in this town than I was aware of."

Perrone, as the Bay Phantom, spent several hours with Louis Rickert, picking his brain for mismatched scraps of information on a wide variety of topics related to crime on the Gulf Coast. When they were finished, he had quite a collection. Later on, when he had time, he would make a wall chart and start trying to connect dots.

For now, Louis Rickert, having been properly tagged, would be released back into the wild. Arrangements were made for ongoing contact, and a regular "salary" was agreed upon. The Bay Phantom now had a "mole" operating on the fringes of the underworld.

He blindfolded Rickert for the drive from Tull House back into town, to his small apartment on Dauphin Street. The small-time grifter thanked the masked man for the substantial advance he had been given and promised to stay in touch. The Bay Phantom headed back to his new sanctum, pleased with the progress he had made.

"You got your pet crook all nice and comfy?" Mirabelle asked Perrone when he returned.

He was about to reply when the phone in the living room rang.

"Ah!" he said, "Our first phone call! I wonder who it might be."

"I can find that out by lifting the receiver and speaking into it," Mirabelle said dryly. "It's really a fascinating process. Watch."

She lifted the receiver, put it to her ear, and spoke:

"Hello? Yes, it is! I'm flattered you remembered me. Of course I know who you are. Your voice is every bit as distinctive as... well, everything else about you. Yes, I'm fine... Uh-huh, we're all moved in now... Yes, he's sitting right here, wondering who the hell I'm talking to. He just made a face; he doesn't like it when I curse. Ha! That's true! You have what? Oh, that sounds intriguing. I sure will. Here he is."

She handed the receiver to Perrone. "It's Mister Fort," she said.

"Charles, how are you?" said Perrone. "How's the new book coming?"

"Slowly but inexorably," said the man on the other end of the line. "Its advent can hardly be prevented, I fear. I should be ready to unleash it within a year or so. I finally came up with a title. I'm calling it *Lo!*"

"*Lo*, what?"

"Well, that's the question, isn't it? The book is another catalog of effects with no conceivable causes. The title is *Lo*, followed by an exclamation point. The implication being, *Lo and behold this accursed data that could tell us so much if we only understood the language.*"

Charles Hoy Fort was an interesting character, and something of a fanatic or obsessive at the very least. And his obsession was with what some people termed the unknown. Of course, the things Fort pursued, the information he collected, the enigmas he enshrined without unraveling, were *not* unknown. They were there for all to see: Frogs and fish falling from clear skies, houses apparently infested with invisible entities that delighted in flinging objects about, strange-looking airships, and other such anomalies. Perrone had known him for several years, and had shared with him the secret of his double identity as the Bay Phantom.

"I sometimes think you would be sorely disappointed if you ever discovered the answers to all of your questions," Perrone said wryly.

"Oh, it would kill me, no doubt about that. It's rather like a game of Russian Roulette, I suppose. But I have just come into position of some information which may interest you, as it is in your neck of the woods, more or less. And this is a contemporary affair... ongoing. Knowing of your, ah, *hobby*, I thought you might be interested."

"Tell me what you have."

There was an eagerness in Perrone's voice that Mirabelle found hard to fathom as she listened to his end of the conversation. Much as she liked Mister Fort, she saw little value in his "work." He often said that he was a collector of data that science refused to accept. To Mirabelle, he was a collector of unsubstantiated anecdotes that *had* to be rejected by science.

"In my new book, I deal with the subject of phantom dogs who slaughter sheep in England. Something similar has cropped up in New Orleans, it seems, but the victims are human, and the marauder is, so a number of witnesses swear, a *werewolf*."

"What?"

"A werewolf. You won't have heard about it. Eight victims so far, Joseph. The killer strikes only on nights when there is a full moon. The gentleman who passed me the information tells me that much of it has been kept away the press thus far. But, in the absence of details from the authorities, rumors abound, and many of them have found their way into the newspapers."

Perrone scowled. "And why does someone think a werewolf is to blame? Do real werewolves even exist?"

"I sincerely doubt it, but the witnesses are adamant. I've mailed you copies of all the information I've been able to gather. My contact in New Orleans seems to know more than he should, but I don't ask any questions. You should receive my package within the next day or two."

"This is one of those things, Mirabelle," Perrone said over dinner that evening. They were seated at the table in their new kitchen, eating red beans and rice. "Somebody is killing people in New Orleans and getting away with it. This is the kind of thing the Bay Phantom exists to deal with."

"So you're going to stop it," she said. "Catch it or kill it or whatever you think you need to do."

"I don't plan on using lethal violence unless there is absolutely no other option. I want to preserve lives. People are dying. If I can stop that without causing any further casualties, that's what I shall do. But we don't have to worry about it until the next full moon. In the meantime, I'll get a private detective to see what he can turn up."

"Okay, Mister Gandhi," said Mirabelle, with a funny little smile. "How many items will you need from that huge arsenal of deadly weapons in the cellar to go practice your nonviolent conflict resolution skills?"

"Mirabelle..."

"And what if it does turn out to be a real werewolf?" she continued. "There isn't any such thing, but what if there is?"

"I'll take precautions for that eventuality as well."

Perrone leaned back in his chair, apparently deep in thought.

"Oh, by the way," he said after a while, "I know you were being flippant, but it happens that I spent some time with Gandhi when I was in India. The Mahatma and I had several deep conversations over a six-day period. After the Doctor Piranha affair, it was my intention then to hang up the Bay Phantom for good. I set out on a journey to cleanse my soul. I see you smirking, Mirabelle, but I mean that. It was the Mahatma who first awakened in me the feeling that the Phantom's work might not be done, though he would have to act more responsibly."

"You have guns," Mirabelle said. "Many, many guns. Did you and the Mahatma do a lot of skeet shooting?"

Perrone shrugged. "I have not reached a state of total enlightenment, nor will I ever. I do not aspire to perfection. There will be times when, in order to save innocent lives, I will have to shoot someone, possibly to death. The principles of nonviolent conflict resolution are lost; I'm afraid, on the majority of career criminals and homicidal maniacs. If I must employ violence, I want to be very, very good at it. Make no mistake; the Bay Phantom is an expression of violence. He was born from trauma, and that is what he knows, how he operates. And I have come to believe that it is necessary.

"Gandhi said something to me the night before I left him. It was rather curious, and I remember it word for word:

" 'Do what you think is right, for you must trust yourself above all, though your judgment is very, very far from infallible. Keep your mind clear, and people in trouble will find you, or you will find them. Seek opportunities, but be especially alert for the *unsought* opportunities that arise, for they are the truly important ones. There is an order to the Universe. Relax, and be its agent.' "

"It has a kind of mystical ring to it," Mirabelle said, "though Gandhi isn't a mystic, as far as I know. I think I get what he meant, and I'm sure you do too. If you're comfortable with the metaphysical implications..."

"I am," Perrone said with a nod. "And it does indeed seem to work. There is a design, though we cannot perceive it."

They were silent for a while. There was more to it than Perrone had told Mirabelle. During and after his time with Gandhi, he had discovered other things about himself, things he was still coming to terms with. He wanted to speak of them, but feared that their weight might be too much for Mirabelle to bear. She was having enough trouble dealing with what she already knew.

They continued their conversation as they strolled around the grounds of their new home.

"You are a genius, Mirabelle," he said. "Very literally. I don't mean you're clever or above average or even brilliant. You are almost unbelievably intelligent and accomplished. Sigmund Freud himself says you're one of the nine smartest people in the world, and I believe him. You've mastered a dozen different scientific disciplines on your own, in total obscurity."

"It wasn't until I was almost an adult that I found out just how smart I really am," Mirabelle said. "I mean, I always knew I was smarter than anybody around me, but that's not saying much in this town. And I was treated like any other colored girl. I finished the third grade in a crummy little church school, then I went to work. I was considered to be a very poor student because I never paid the slightest attention to anything the teacher said. I learned on my own. By the time I left school, I could speak and read four different languages."

"How many now?" Perrone asked.

"Eighteen. Twenty-four if you count different dialects."

"You should be proud."

Mirabelle shrugged. "It's not like I had much choice in the matter. I wanted to know as much as I could about as many subjects as possible. It was a compulsion. And I was able to absorb everything I read, understand it completely, and never forget it. I played it close to the vest, but it was risky. I stole books, fortunately for me, I was smart enough to get away with it every time and I studied them at night. You know, I miss the stealing part sometimes. It was a challenge."

"Well, you're better off without it," Perrone said rather primly. "It isn't a good idea to indulge in situational ethics; a very slippery slope, Mirabelle."

"That's an interesting attitude coming from someone who wears a mask and breaks the law damn near every night."

"It's a totally different thing. I'm upholding the law when the law can't uphold itself."

"Which is *against* the law," Mirabelle pointed out.

"It's against the *letter* of the law, yes," he admitted. "But not the *spirit*, Mirabelle."

She closed her eyes and sniffed the air.

"What are you doing?" Perrone asked.

"Oh, nothing. I thought I caught a whiff of some situational ethics. Maybe it was just dog poop. Be careful you don't slip in it."

"We will do good works," said Perrone, "that's what's important. Perhaps we should both leave ethical nitpicking to the philosophers."

"You're the one that started it, Mister Perrone."

"You don't have to call me that," he said, a little too casually. "*Joe* would be fine, you know. How long have we known each other?"

"Quite a while," she allowed. "But I have never in my life called a white man by his first name. That kind of black-white protocol has been hammered into my head by my family as far back as I can remember. I just can't do it. A total mental block. I have what amounts to a self-conferred PhD in psychology, so I know what I'm talking about. I've corresponded with Doctor Freud for many years. He's the one that persuaded me to take that damn Stanford–Binet intelligence test, which showed me just how badly cursed I am. I've got way too much brainpower for a little Alabama pickaninny. That kind of thing can get you killed, and I mean that literally."

"I know, Mirabelle, but you're with me now, and you have resources you didn't have before. You can break those chains; the ones in your own mind, I mean."

She laughed bitterly. "I helped Doctor Freud fine-tune some of his ideas about psychotherapy, you know but I make a very poor patient. Beyond that... Well, you just don't know what it's like for us, Mister Perrone."

He sighed. "I suppose I don't."

"My cousin Lula is light-skinned enough that she can and does pass for white. Now, I am truly as black as the proverbial Ace of Spades. That option has never been open to me. Not that I would do it even if I could, because it's morally reprehensible, but still..."

"There's not much sense trying to be something you're not," said Perrone.

Mirabelle gave him a look. "Then how come you wear that mask half the time, if you believe it's better to be yourself?"

"That's *why* I wear it."

Mirabelle shuddered.

CHAPTER FOUR
THE CAGED PIRANHA
UNITED STATES FEDERAL PENITENTIARY
LEAVENWORTH, KANSAS

On the books, he was "John Doe." Nobody knew his real name. He had been exhaustively investigated by the United States Secret Service and the Bureau of Investigation, and they had come up with nothing. He had no name, he had no past. His fingerprints were not on record anywhere. He seemed to have appeared from a void, fully formed, and done his awful work before being apprehended, tried, sentenced to seventy-five years with no possibility of the slightest glimmer of a hint of a hope of parole, and locked away here.

Piranha had been at Leavenworth for almost three years.

He was not a troublesome prisoner. He was cold and quiet and there was something in his eyes that gave pause to hardened prison guards and violent, incorrigible convicts alike. Everyone gave him a wide berth.

He was Doctor Piranha, and nobody here doubted that he was one of the most dangerous men alive.

He was currently being held in solitary confinement. This, the warden said, was for his own protection, though Doctor Piranha hardly needed protecting. The move had resulted from an incident that Piranha had not started but had most decidedly finished. He had been in Leavenworth for a year, and was considered a model prisoner. He never bothered anyone.

Unfortunately, one day during the previous spring, another inmate decided it might benefit him to be the man who took down the infamous Doctor Piranha. This inmate, a crude and rather generic bootlegger, white slaver, and murderer from New Jersey named Blinky Horden, had been sentenced to life imprisonment. Leavenworth would be the only world he would inhabit for the remainder of his life, and he saw an opportunity to establish himself as top dog by knocking off the cold and silent man who was perhaps the most infamous criminal of his generation.

It came on a Saturday morning in the exercise yard. The scheme was a simple one. Blinky would approach Doctor Piranha, where he stood, alone, next to the heavy chain-link fence, and slip a shiv into his heart. There was no reason for it other than the prestige he was sure it would earn him.

That was the official take, anyhow. There were some who said that Blinky had actually been a paid assassin, acting at the behest of the powerful Carter family. Nobody would ever know for sure.

The shiv had gone in. Later, some would say it had missed Piranha's heart by half an inch; others would maintain that it had pierced the organ dead center. Blinky knew his business, after all. The doctor, who did not cry out or utter a word, had calmly plucked the shiv from his chest and tossed it away, before taking hold of his assailant's throat and squeezing. Blinky Horden had attempted to fight back, landing a dozen or more blows on Piranha's head and body, but it had availed him nothing.

Piranha had crushed the man's windpipe, then snapped his neck. The doctor had accomplished these things with a few swift movements of his left hand alone; his records said he was right-handed, but he was, in fact, completely ambidextrous. Blinky had not died immediately, and would not pass away for another fifteen minutes. That quarter of an hour would be pure hell for the hapless attacker.

The first hint the guards on the yard had that something was wrong came when one of them, a man named Seymour Pallas, noticed that Doctor Piranha's gray prison-issue shirt and trousers were soaked down one side, from chest to ankle, with what appeared to be blood. The guard noticed the dying Blinky sitting on the ground at the doctor's feet, twitching and gasping, his eyes bugging out alarmingly.

Piranha had what might have been a very slight smile on his face. He nodded politely at the guard and spoke:

"I believe I should go to the infirmary," he said calmly, "as I seem to have sustained a deep puncture wound. This man sitting at my feet inflicted it with that homemade knife on the ground there. I have killed him. He's still alive, but he only has about thirteen minutes to go, and you won't be able to save him. Now, I would be obliged to you if you would get me some medical attention. You won't need to hold that gun on me, Seymour. If you'll just give me a hand here, I'll be very grateful."

Piranha had been taken to the prison hospital and patched up. As soon as he was released, he was taken to solitary. He did not appeal this decision, or even acknowledge it in any way. Shortly after, Seymour Pallas had been transferred from the yard to the solitary wing, with no explanation given by the warden. The substantial increase in salary Seymour had noticed on his next payday was similarly unexplained.

That had been a year ago, and things had been quiet since then. Seymour, a man who knew how things worked, had assumed that a bribe to the warden had been responsible for his transfer, and he had been waiting for Doctor Piranha to start asking him for favors. Frankly, Seymour intended to grant those favors, unless they were just too unreasonable, but very few requests had come. The doctor seemed perfectly content with his solitude, his books, his newspapers, and his note pads. Once or twice a week, he would engage Seymour in long conversations on a wide variety of topics; science, history, religion, philosophy, current events. Seymour had grown to enjoy and look forward to these discussions, and he made a point of educating himself on subjects that seemed to interest the doctor.

One such subject was Mobile, Alabama. It was known, or at least assumed, that Doctor Piranha had some kind of personal connection to the port city, since he had tried to wipe it off the map three years previously. The nature of that connection was completely unknown. Somewhere in the back of his mind, Seymour nurtured the hope that he might solve this mystery. What he would do with the information once he discovered it, he was not sure. It would be unwise to betray Piranha, he knew. But maybe a smart operator could get away with it.

Maybe.

But that was for some future time. For today, Seymour would be Doctor Piranha's friend. It was helpful that he genuinely liked the doctor, even if he did fear him. There was something about the man that inspired both reactions simultaneously.

On Sunday mornings, it was Seymour's custom to take Piranha a stack of newspapers from Mobile and New Orleans. Seymour's sister, Wendy, who lived on the Gulf Coast, bundled them up every week and sent them to Leavenworth. They generally arrived with the late mail on Saturday, and Seymour carried them to Doctor Piranha's solitary cell as a Sunday morning treat. He made a habit of glancing over the front pages while he was in transit, so he could engage the doctor in meaningful conversation.

"All kinds of things going on in the old hometown," he said jovially as he passed the stack of newspapers through the wide tray slot in the thick iron door of the cell. "Mayoral election coming up, I see, and it's down to the wire between this Hector Sams character and Mayor Brickell."

"Brickell is a moron," said the doctor. "And Sams is a fool."

"Hm," said Seymour. He was unable to go into the subject any deeper, since all of his knowledge was limited to what he could quickly glean from the headlines.

"And then there's those weird murders in New Orleans," he said, just to be saying something. "People getting sliced up. A couple of witnesses

"I believe I should go to the infirmary."

swear the killing was done by a werewolf! Can you believe it? The werewolf angle has been kept out of the news, but my sister works for the paper in Biloxi, and she's heard all kinds of stories."

He waited for the doctor to speak again, but all he heard was the shuffling of newsprint. This went on for several minutes.

"Well, now," came the voice of Doctor Piranha. "Here's something interesting. A group of men were apprehended while attempting to burgle a warehouse owned by Hector Sams. They were released on bail the next day. That evening, they were all found dead. That's suggestive, I daresay."

Seymour wondered if he ought to say anything. The doctor sounded like he was talking to himself.

"It doesn't say how they died. That's rather curious," Piranha continued. "The bodies were found in an automobile parked on D'Autremont Road. That's a rather exclusive area. I believe several of the Carters live out that way. I wonder if…" His voice trailed off.

Aside from the tray slot, the only other opening in the cell door was a very small, square, barred window. It contained no glass, just fine wire mesh on both the inside and the outside, with two vertical bars in between. Seymour squinted through this, wanting to make eye contact with Piranha.

All Seymour could see was the back wall of the cell, just ten feet away.

"Doc," he said softly. "Are you okay? You need anything?"

He jumped back when Piranha's face suddenly appeared in the small square space. The irises of the doctor's eyes were a very dark green, indistinguishable from the pupils in the poor light.

"As a matter of fact, I do," Piranha said. His voice might remind one of the purring of a very large cat, if one ignored the razor-sharp edges. "I appreciate the interest you show in what you call 'the old hometown.' I realize that you only do it to get on my good side, but that doesn't make it any less pleasant. I know you want to learn as much about me as you can, in the hope that it may one day enable you to turn some sort of a profit. I can't say I resent that, either. In your position, I would no doubt do the same thing.

"The future is the future, Seymour. What you may or may not do a week or a month or a year from now does not concern me at this moment. I do not render moral judgments. I merely assess threats and address them appropriately. Currently, you are an asset, and I expect you to behave like one."

"D-doc, I'm on y-your side," Seymour stammered. "You know that."

"Mmm-hmm. That's good. You have work to do. There are three small stories in this week's newspapers that caught my attention. You won't have seen them. Three crimes in progress were interfered with by a man wearing a cloak and a black mask. Do you know who the Bay Phantom is, Seymour?"

"Y-yeah. I mean, yes. He was the guy that... Three years ago, when you... The Bay Phantom, he, ah..."

"Three years ago," Piranha purred, "the Bay Phantom apprehended me and turned me over to the authorities after I attempted to wipe the city of Mobile from the map with several large caches of explosives. You needn't be shy about mentioning it. I know exactly what I did. I thought the Bay Phantom had considered his work complete when he caught me. Things got a bit ugly, frankly, and he seemed not to have the stomach for it. I want you to use whatever contacts you can muster to compile as much information as you can on this masked crime fighter. Your sister in Biloxi would be ideal for this task. I would also like any data she can scrape together about this New Orleans werewolf. Facts, rumors, innuendo, hallucinations...*everything*. She will be generously compensated for this service, and so will you."

"Sure, Doc," Seymour said, relieved to be handed such an innocuous chore. "Anything else I can do for you?"

"Arrange for me to make a few phone calls. Very private ones, at odd hours."

"I can make that happen," Seymour said.

"See that you do. Otherwise, I might have to make your wife a millionaire."

"Huh? What do you mean?"

Piranha's mouth twitched. "What I mean is that your wife and child are blameless and cannot be held responsible for your conduct. If you do anything that would call for your death, honor would compel me to compensate them lavishly."

It was the strangest threat Seymour had ever received. Also the most genteel and that was what made it truly frightening. He decided to put any prying into Piranha's past on hold.

Indefinitely.

There is a very expensive, very exclusive hotel on the Gulf Coast, halfway between Mobile, Alabama, and Biloxi, Mississippi. It doesn't have a name, as such. It is owned by a dummy corporation that is owned by a dummy corporation, and so on. If one were able to wind his way through the maze of ownership, he would eventually reach Caleb Carter, scion of the powerful Mobile family. Caleb is the ultimate authority in the family, and has been ever since his father died and his older brother Jeremiah went on an extended "sabbatical" in Europe three years ago.

The hotel is patronized by wealthy individuals from all over the United States. These individuals have two things in common: a very great deal of money, and utter disdain for the law. Here, they are free to indulge their appetites for liquor, gambling, drugs, illicit sex, and many other things that the law dared to deny them.

In an office in a penthouse atop the six-story edifice, two men sat on either side of a large, mahogany desk. The room was decorated with expensive paintings and tapestries, and a small wet bar squatted discreetly in one corner. A set of large French windows afforded a beautiful view of the Gulf of Mexico.

"It looks like this Bay Phantom character is back, and I don't like that," said Caleb Carter, the man seated behind the desk. Caleb, son of the late Abelard Carter, brother of the absent Jeremiah. He was thin and clean-shaven, with cold blue eyes and auburn hair that was starting to show some grey.

"Why not?" said Hillyard Parnell. "He did us a good turn three years ago, you know. That lunatic Doctor Piranha seemed bent on wiping out everything we had."

Parnell, a portly forty-five-year-old, was a lawyer who had worked for the Carter family for many years. In a just, righteous world, he would have been disbarred long ago and consigned to a cell in the state penitentiary. In this corrupt reality, he was a wealthy man who enjoyed a certain amount of power. He had his own ideas about how things ought to be done, but he kept them hidden in a dark place in his soul.

"He almost *did* wipe us out," Carter said. "He put us right on the brink. If we hadn't reorganized the way we did, we'd have been finished. The only bright spot is the fact that Piranha killed my father and traumatized my brother. They had no idea how to function in the modern world, and they never could have done what I have. And now our reorganization has put us firmly on the wrong side of the law. We have to keep the boys in Chicago happy. I don't care much for Capone personally, but he's done us a lot of good these past two years. It's a nice working relationship. The point is, Hillyard, that we are *criminals*. This Bay Phantom fancies himself a crime-fighter, and I don't think we can buy him off."

"That makes it difficult," the lawyer agreed. "He *is* a wild card."

"That he is. He doesn't worry about the law, he does whatever he pleases. I'm afraid it's just a matter of time before he gets wind of our activities and decides to shut us down. We can't sit by and wait for that to happen."

"So what do we do?" Parnell wanted to know. "You have ideas?"

"Well, we have our...*special guest*. I'm sure he could do something if he could find this Phantom."

"You mean the lunatic you hired who murdered those men practically on our doorstep?"

"Yes. It would have been better had he not done that. He is difficult to control. But it did no real harm, and we might need that lunatic. Someone is gunning for us. I saw this coming six months ago, when Hector Sams announced his candidacy. He wouldn't have done that if he didn't think he could beat us. I hired the Embalmer then."

"Why him?"

"Because he's good. He's also loony and ruthless. Since I didn't know how deep this goes, I figured we'd need somebody who would stop at nothing."

"Where did you hear about him?"

"Penny. She knows all kinds of oddballs. But that's not the point. Listen: That thing at the Sams warehouse was a set-up. Somebody wants to bring us down publicly, I think, but we can deal with him in our own way. We've done similar things before. But if that do-gooder Bay Phantom is back, and he knows or suspects what we've been doing since he disappeared, he'll probably come after us eventually. People see him as a hero, and he'll have all kinds of support. So what we have to do is change that."

"How?"

"Oh, that's easy," said Carter. "If that business at the warehouse is what I think it was, there's our idea right there. We'll do the same thing, only we'll crank it up a little bit higher. And I can get Mark Marvel to print anything I want him to. We tie the Bay Phantom up with our real enemy in the public and official minds, then we smash them with a single blow."

"Right. And then there's that other problem: What are we going to do with that girl?"

"You mean Penny." Carter sighed. "I have no idea. My sister cannot be controlled at all. Maybe we could have her committed."

"Committed to a six-foot hole out in the woods," Parnell said sourly. "Otherwise, she could ruin everything we've built up. The way she chases after men!"

"I know. She hasn't had a regular boyfriend since she was a teenager. She dated some creep that worked in a mortuary. After that... But she's family. I'll think of something."

There were a couple of things Carter did not dare say to Parnell. For instance, the fact that Penny had come up with the scheme he was getting ready to implement. Penny took little or no active part in most of the family's activities, but she was a veritable idea factory. A certain native cunning ran in the Carter family, and Penny had received more than her fair share. Her nimble brain could spin the most convoluted schemes imaginable, and they were always perfect.

Her apparent lack of a conscience was also an asset. One day, though, it would become a fatal liability. Caleb just had to do his best to stay one step ahead of her until then.

"One day, you're going to be sorry you didn't do something about her when you had the chance," Parnell predicted.

Carter sighed. "Yes, I probably will. But she's family. You have to make concessions. Up to a point..."

CHAPTER FIVE
THE HOT DOG MASSACRE

"The so-called Bay Phantom has got to go!" said Mayor Simon Brickell. The audience cheered because it seemed like the kind of statement one ought to cheer, especially since it was followed by a dramatic pause. But the cheering was desultory and subdued a matter of form rather than conviction. Brickell, pale, balding, running to fat, and past fifty, was a deadly dull speaker, even when he was crying for someone's head.

Except for one man. A tall, dark-haired, well-dressed fellow standing close to the speaker's podium clapped his hands loudly and shouted, "Hear, hear! Good show, Mister Mayor."

Brickell acknowledged the praise with a nod and a smile.

Joe Perrone nodded back and looked around. Bienville Square in downtown Mobile could be a beautiful place, given the right conditions.

Today, those conditions were present in spades. The weather was unseasonably warm for this time of year, but a chill was creeping in as the sun got closer to the horizon.

Two or three score citizens had gathered here for a rally in support of the candidacy of incumbent mayor Brickell. It was almost a foregone conclusion that he would win, and that was the unusual thing about this election. In years past it would have been a forgone conclusion, plain and simple. This year it was an "almost," thanks to challenger Hector Sams.

Sams was a bit of a wild card. Perrone knew Hector in the way that all well-to-do people seemed to know one another, but they were not friends. The man had no history of political involvement or ambition, though his family had been in Mobile for generations. They were old money, and they had always avoided the spotlight.

The only thing resembling a scandal that had ever touched the Sams family was the disappearance of Hector's brother Gerald many years ago; not long before Joe Perrone's family had been killed, in fact. The lad's fate remained a mystery. No trace of him had ever been discovered. The Sams family had maintained a low profile since then, becoming almost reclusive.

Hector Sams was a most unlikely politician, and Perrone wondered why he had suddenly decided to challenge the established order. The election was still months away, but things were already heating up.

"If the Bay Phantom has indeed returned," Brickell droned on, "he must be put on notice. We appreciate what he did in the past, with Doctor Piranha. But this is not the Old West. This Phantom appears to be trying to usurp the legitimate duties of the police force! This is nothing short of anarchy. He has subdued several muggers and a gang of burglars. How many convictions will arise from his actions? Possibly none. The District Attorney's office declined to prosecute three of the cases, and the rest are up in the air. The charges may have to be dropped."

Of course, thought Perrone, *the victims of those muggings are still alive, but that doesn't seem to be much of a consideration.*

Brickell launched into a mild diatribe against crime in general. The mayor vociferously denounced most of the nefarious activities he secretly facilitated and promised to eradicate them during his next term, just as he had promised in every campaign since 1912.

Perrone was a bit surprised that the Bay Phantom had suddenly become a bone of contention. His recent activities had been low-key, and had generated little public interest, even in the newspaper. But an editorial had appeared in the *Press* this very morning. More vociferous than eloquent, it had been supported by nothing in the way of facts. Mention was made of the Volker gang, who claimed to have been subdued by someone who might have been the Phantom, before they turned up dead in a parked car on D'Autremont Road. There was no demonstrable connection between the Phantom and the murders, which had not prevented the editorial writer from making insinuations.

Perrone scanned the crowd again. He had chosen to attend this rally in order to keep up appearances. He didn't want to be thought of as a recluse. And being seen as a supporter of Brickell's campaign, and the inevitable administration that would follow it, might give him access to information the Bay Phantom could use.

Standing off to the side were a harried-looking young man and a fierce-looking young woman. The former was a stranger to him, but he recognized the latter. She was Penelope Carter, better known as Penny. The pair seemed to be involved in a one-sided conversation. Penny was doing the talking, and she didn't seem pleased.

She should be attractive, Perrone thought, if you went strictly by her looks. She was tall for a woman, almost six feet, with red hair and freckles. But there was something about the way she carried herself, and the look in her pale gray eyes, that overrode physical appearance and made her rather fearsome, not to say loathsome. Like Cassius, she had a lean and hungry look.

Perrone had an uncanny danger sense, and Penny Carter, even from a distance and oblivious to his presence, was causing it to light up like a busy switchboard. Judging by the look on his face, she had the same effect on the young man she was talking to. Perrone wondered who the poor sap might be, and what he had gotten himself into.

And then he noticed something odd. Seven hot dog wagons, all of them identical in appearance, had converged on the Square, taking up positions around the perimeter, roughly equidistant from one another. The operators were dressed in white smocks and dark trousers, and they all wore sunglasses. The truly odd part was that they all seemed to be turning away anybody who attempted to make a purchase.

As if by a prearranged signal, the operators swiveled their wagons around so that the prows were pointing toward the bandstand. Something was about to happen, and he wasn't going to be able to stop it. He raced toward the bandstand, yelling as he went:

"Get down! Everybody get down on the ground!"

The spurious hot dog vendors had all crouched down behind their wagons. As Perrone neared the bandstand, all eyes were on him. Nobody else noticed the outer shells of the hot dog wagons falling away to reveal seven large, belt-fed machine guns. A few people had dropped to the ground as ordered. Most of them were men of a certain age; Perrone figured they must have been in the Great War and still had their battlefield reflexes. Most of the other spectators simply stood gawking at him as he ran.

Just as Perrone reached the bandstand, the guns opened up. He threw himself at Brickell, striking him square in the chest and knocking him to the wooden floor. The red-white-and-blue bunting hanging around the stage was chewed up by bullets.

"Get down!" Perrone shouted at the rest of the dignitaries at the rear of the small stage. One of them, a former city comptroller, had caught a slug in the head. The survivors dropped to their hands and knees.

The noise from the machine guns was deafening, almost but not quite drowning out the screams of the wounded and the merely terrified. How many were dead already? Bullets smacked into the bandstand from all sides. Perrone crawled rapidly to where a knot of special guests lay cowering. One of them, a sheriff's deputy, was so busy whimpering and keeping his head covered that he seemed to have forgotten he was armed. Perrone snatched the revolver from the man's belt holster, rolled a few feet to the left, and got to his feet, taking hasty aim at one of the wagons. When something that looked like the head of the operator bobbed up from behind the machine gun, Perrone fired. His shot caught the man high on the forehead, and he went down. Perrone hoped the man wasn't dead, though he had made no effort to be merciful. He was interested only in putting a stop to this carnage, and if the perpetrators had to die in the process, so be it.

And it appeared that he wasn't the only one who had come to that conclusion. The young man he had observed arguing with Penny Carter had drawn a revolver of his own. Crouched down behind a trash can, he fired three shots at the murderous hot dog vendor nearest to him. Two of them struck the man in the chest and he fell back onto the sidewalk.

Two down, five to go. As Perrone attempted to draw a bead on another gunner, he caught a flash of movement in his peripheral vision. He squeezed off two shots, both of which missed his target. Dropping back to a low crouch, he glanced to his left and saw Penny Carter racing toward the hot dog wagon that had been orphaned when the young man shot its operator. *What on earth does she think she's doing?*

When she reached the wagon, Penny delivered a savage kick to the head of the corpse in the white smock. Swinging the prow of the wagon around to her left, she took hold of the firing mechanism and started shooting. Her first barrage cut through one of the remaining four wagons and chewed its operator to bits. As she swung the wagon slowly around, sending a stream of hot lead into another wagon and the killer behind it, her eyes gleamed and her lips drew back into a wide grin. When she reduced her third target to shredded meat and splintered bone, she laughed out loud.

My God, thought Perrone, *she's enjoying this!*

That left only one assailant still standing. Penny took aim and pressed the trigger, but nothing happened. She was out of ammo. She cursed loudly and smacked the gun with her fist several times.

The last echoes of the shots died away and a tense silence descended. Perrone vaulted over the railing of the bandstand and raced toward the surviving gunner, who had stopped firing after Penny Carter perforated his comrades. He was crouched down behind the wagon, covering his head with his hands. As Perrone approached the man, the eerie silence dissolved first into murmurs, then screams. Three police cars and two ambulances careened around a corner six blocks away and headed for the Square.

The gunner uncovered his head, looked around, and stood up. He was an overweight fellow with yellowish eyes and a bushy black moustache. He seemed hardly able to believe his luck. Nobody was paying any attention to him. He tore off his smock and sunglasses and tossed them into a convenient storm drain. He reached into the bottom section of the hot dog wagon and took out a green hunting cap, which he put on, pulling the brim down over his eyes. Looking around one more time, he sprinted for an alleyway across the street, huffing and puffing all the way. He was certainly not in any shape for shenanigans like this.

Perrone followed at a distance; confident in his ability to catch up to the killer should it be necessary. For now, he wanted to see where the fellow was going.

The alley, running between two tall buildings, was quite dark. Perrone stuck his commandeered pistol into a side pocket. Then he removed his Bay Phantom mask from a large extra pocket he had sewn into his jacket and pulled it over his head. The specially-treated lenses of the built-in goggles would enable him to see better in the gloom.

The man in the green cap was half a block ahead of him, moving quietly and carefully in the deep gloom. He had almost made it to St. Michael

Street when someone stepped out of a recessed doorway, grabbed him by the throat, and slammed him against the opposite wall. Perrone slowed almost to a halt and held his breath, creeping forward slowly and silently.

"Where are you going, loose end?" came a weird, sibilant voice, just barely audible from where the Bay Phantom stood.

The newcomer cut a very peculiar figure indeed. Of average height, he was decked out in a bizarre ensemble consisting of a long, white lab coat, black gloves, and something that looked like a gas mask. The latter covered his entire head. Strapped to his back were two vertical metal cylinders, each about a foot and a half high and six to eight inches in diameter. They were fastened to a harness on this individual's back. A hose ran from one of them to a long, wand-like apparatus he was holding in the hand that was not occupied choking the gunner. It was a slender rod about three feet in length, made of stainless steel. The last few inches of its length tapered off to a sharp point.

"Never mind," came the voice again. "It doesn't matter at all. You know you cannot be allowed to run free now. You'll talk. Don't shake your head at me! I know your type."

The Bay Phantom knew what was coming. He broke into a run, but there was no way he could reach the two men in time. The man in the lab coat drew back his strange wand and jammed it into the gunman's torso, thrusting upward and at an angle under the ribcage. It must have gone directly into the struggling man's heart. As he raised his gun to fire, the Phantom became aware of a wheezing, mechanical sound.

"You!" the Phantom shouted. "Stop right there! I'm armed, and I'll shoot you if I must!"

The man turned his masked head in the Phantom's direction.

"I know who you are," he said. "Hang on just a moment, and I'll place myself at your disposal."

As the Bay Phantom closed the gap, the lab-coated man twisted the wand deeper into the gunman's body, as though to secure it, then shrugged out of the harness, letting the cylinders drop to the floor of the alley. The Phantom saw the source of the rhythmic mechanical noise: a little electric motor attached to what appeared to be a small pump. The gunman was released and he slumped to the ground. His eyes were wide and his mouth was twitching violently, but no sound came out; his windpipe had probably been crushed.

"Now," said the weird figure, turning to face the oncoming Phantom, "let's see what you've got!"

The Phantom slowed down and leveled his gun at the man's head.

"I've got a few bullets," he said, "and I'll use them before I'll risk taking you on hand-to-hand. Please just remain still and explain to me what's going on here. What did you just do to that man? I assume that he is beyond medical help at this point."

"I like you," said the other. "You're very well-spoken, even in a tense situation like this. That says a lot about a man. You're that Bay Phantom, aren't you? I'm called the Black Embalmer. I'm not actually black; the name is meant to reinforce the air of foreboding I like to project. It's nice to meet someone else with a mask fetish!"

"It isn't a fetish," snapped the Phantom. "It's a necessary tool."

Moving closer, the Phantom saw that what he had thought was a gas mask was something else entirely. There was a close-fitting hood made of what appeared to be pale, grayish leather. Affixed to the front of it was a queer, lifeless depiction of a human face, made of some material that looked like porcelain. No... not porcelain. Some sort of glaze had been applied to it, but he was sure it was ordinary plaster. *That*, he realized with a start, *is somebody's death mask*!

The features were so poorly-defined that he couldn't tell if it was a man or a woman. Holes slightly larger than silver dollars had been cut out around the eyes and fitted with tinted lenses, not unlike the ones the Phantom himself wore.

"Okay, okay!" said the Embalmer, holding his hands up in the air. "No need to get tetchy, Miss Mary. I'm just making conversation."

As he continued to advance, never taking his eyes or his gun from the weird apparition, the Phantom became aware of a strong chemical odor: formaldehyde. That's what had been pumped into the gunman's body. It was plain that the man was dead and his suffering was over. It had been brief, but it must have been intense.

"Good God!" he gasped. "What kind of a monster are you?"

"I really don't know how to answer that question," replied the Black Embalmer, sounding very chipper and bouncing up and down on the balls of his feet. "I don't think of myself as a monster, but of course I wouldn't. I take it you've never embalmed anyone alive before. You probably frown upon it."

"Was this man working for you?"

The Embalmer shrugged. "Yes and no. It's complicated. It would take too long to explain."

"I've got time," said the Phantom, jiggling the pistol for emphasis.

"No, you don't. Because my friend behind you is about to hit you over the head with something heavy. Oh, I know what you're thinking, of course. But sometimes it really is true."

"You don't expect me to…" the Phantom said. That was as far as he got before something very solid collided with the base of his skull and everything went black.

When he came to, no more than five minutes later, the Embalmer was gone. So were the victim, and the strange equipment that had done him to death. Perrone was relieved to find that his mask was still in place, but that was all the comfort available to him just then. He removed the mask, stowed it away, and headed back to Bienville Square.

The police were there in force, along with the fire department and various other rescue workers. Four people had been killed, innocent bystanders all, and sixteen had injuries serious enough to require hospitalization. Perrone told a harried-looking police sergeant that he had pursued the surviving machine-gunner for several blocks, but lost him on North Conception Street.

Among the many people milling about, Perrone spotted the young man who had been arguing with Penny Carter; he had a badge clipped onto the breast pocket of his jacket, and was deep in conversation with the Chief of Police. A detective, then.

"That'll do for now, Detective Dart," the Chief was saying as Perrone joined them. "You'll have to make a full statement later, of course."

"Hello, Chief Peller," Perrone said affably, shaking hands with the man. "Dreadful business, eh?'

"You said it," Peller replied. "I understand you handled yourself pretty well. You're the kind of guy we could use more of on the force. You ever given it any thought?"

"Oh, no, Chief. I'm flattered, but I'm hardly police material. I was just flying by the seat of my pants, propelled by panic and adrenaline, I imagine. I had no idea what I was doing."

"You looked like you did!" came a voice from behind him.

"Oh, *shit*," Tom Dart whispered, closing his eyes and shaking his head.

Perrone turned around and saw Penny Carter ambling along the sidewalk in their direction, swinging a large handbag, smiling. She might have been at an amusement park. Her cheeks were flushed and her eyes shone.

"So did you," Perrone said flatly.

"Well," she said, "I guess I was in the same boat you were in. When the shooting started I sort of went blank. Pure self-preservation. Must have been in shock or something."

No, you weren't, Perrone thought. *You knew exactly what you were doing, and you got a huge kick out of it.*

Out loud, he said, "One never knows what one is capable of until one is backed into a corner."

"Why don't you call me some time," she said, handing him a calling card. "Here's my number." She ran her tongue all the way around her lips. It was rather shapely, as tongues went, but God alone knew where it had been.

"Yes, certainly," he said. "I will make sure I do that." *Just as soon as Hades freezes over.*

Penny gave her statement to a police stenographer who had been brought to the scene of the carnage. The Chief made it plain that no charges would be brought against her for the deaths of the gunmen she had cut down. *Self-defense and defense of innocent persons.* She thought that was cute. Tom Dart had killed one of the men, too. He'd probably get a medal for it. He evidently thought he was better than she was; she saw how he was looking at her. Well, he'd come around eventually. If he didn't, he'd wind up having difficulties.

After two or three hours all the excitement had died down and people started trickling away, to their homes or their offices or wherever they went.

Tom Dart went back to his office, she supposed. She'd ask Caleb to have a talk with Chief Peller about him. Put on a little bit of pressure, he might respond favorably.

As she walked back to her car, alone, she looked around, searching faces. Joseph Perrone was long gone, but she thought he might have come back. Apparently not.

Before she reached her roadster, Penny stopped in front of a public waste bin. She opened her handbag, removed a large brick, and examined it under the street light. It had cracked almost in half. She dropped it into the trash and got into her car.

That Joe Perrone is hard-headed, she thought as she started the engine. *I'm glad. So am I.*

CHAPTER SIX
ETHICAL CONSIDERATIONS

"Look," said Gladys Turnbull. "How can we run a story blaming the Bay Phantom for that business in Bienville Square when we have no indication that he was involved?"

Gladys, a blue-eyed blonde with bobbed hair, was a reporter for the Mobile *Press*. Editor-in-chief Mark Marvel had called her into his office to discuss a "new slant" on the previous day's events in Bienville Square. She already knew the answer to her question, and she knew that Marvel knew it, too. She also knew he was going to lie about it.

"There are *sources*," he fibbed with a straight face. "We have tips from confidential informants. Hector Sams may be involved, too."

"Where is this coming from?" Gladys asked skeptically. "According to the police, none of those machine-gunners can be identified. They seem to have come out of nowhere. Nothing has been traced to anybody."

"I told you, *informants*," Marvel said. "I'm putting you on this. I want you to focus on the Bay Phantom. And I want you to establish a connection between him and Hector Sams."

"What if there's no connection for me to find?"

"I didn't say *find*, I said *establish*. Do you understand me?"

My God, he was asking her, no, *ordering* her, to fabricate news! *The dirty sonofabitch*! She knew he was dirty, that he was in the Carters' pocket, but *this*!

God only knew how Marvel had managed to become a newspaper editor, or why. He had no instinct for news, no ability to coordinate the activities of a busy newsroom. Most of his duties were permanently delegated to others; they quietly did the jobs Marvel was being paid to do, without any recognition or recompense. He was blustery, aggressive and confrontational. Everything about him seemed artificial. Even his voice sounded terribly affected; he spoke like a radio announcer, in a deep baritone that didn't sound right coming from someone who looked like him.

Gladys was pretty sure that if she told him to stick it, she'd end up unemployed. She couldn't afford that. She was lucky to have a job at all in the middle of a Depression. The fact that her father had been a genuine journalistic legend in the Port City counted for exactly nothing.

"Okay," she said in a neutral tone. "Sure, I get you." She wasn't going to make a fuss about it.

"You can do that? You're okay with that, then?"

"Sure."

What the hell, she thought. *Everybody does it. Who knows, there may even be a connection. Right now, just begin the investigation. Worry about all this other stuff later.* She had the feeling that this assignment would either make her career or break her for good.

"Listen, Gladys," said Marvel, in a voice she'd never heard him use before. "I like you. I want to see you get ahead here. But you have to understand the way things work."

She had also never heard him use her first name, nor had he ever told her that he liked her, and she didn't believe it for a second. She didn't care for the smile he was giving her, either. There was *something* he liked, sure, but it had little to do with her as a person or a reporter. Her stomach twisted itself into a knot. So this was what it came down to, eh? If she could make herself "understand," she could get ahead.

Well, maybe she wouldn't have to. She could string Marvel along, put him off, until she got some real dope on the Bay Phantom. She wasn't going to sleep with Marvel in return for the privilege of writing fabricated stories, she knew that much. But she wasn't sure exactly what she was going to do instead, and she needed to get the hell out of here so she could give it some serious thought.

"I see what you mean, sir," she said innocently. "I want to do a good job. I'll get started right away. Thank you, Mister Marvel!" She tossed the last four words over her shoulder as she dashed out into the newsroom, grabbed her handbag from her desk, and made for the door, barely pausing to snatch her hat from the rack and clap it on her head. Out on the street, she went east for two blocks, then north for three, ducking into a little speakeasy on Royal Street. When she was settled at a rickety wooden table with a glass of gin in front of her and wondered just what the hell she was going to do.

Louis Rickert was feeling woozy. Not dizzy; the feeling wasn't in his head, nor was it physical. Rather, he was extremely disoriented and uncertain about his future. At the moment, he was taking a little walking tour of the illicit gin joints that infested every block of downtown Mobile. They were very poorly camouflaged. He wondered why they bothered pretending to be hidden. Whoever owned them had the fix in with the cops and the city government. In fact, most of the clientele in most of the hooch parlors were wearing blue uniforms; they were either tying one on after a shift, or getting ready to begin one.

He knew they wouldn't bother him if he didn't draw attention to himself, but there was something about drinking in a room containing even one uniformed cop that made him nervous. He had passed on three of them before finding one on Royal Street that was pleasingly devoid of bulls.

He tottered up to the bar and ordered a shot of whiskey with a beer chaser. The bartender, a tall man with reddish hair and a walrus moustache, looked askance at Rickert. The small-time hood produced a shiny silver dollar and tossed it onto the bar.

"And keep 'em coming," said Rickert, "Because there's plenty more dough where that came from."

He got onto a stool and gulped down the whiskey, but he took his time with the beer. He had a lot of thinking to do, and it was his belief that his mind worked best when he was drunk. Maybe it sounded screwy, but he was convinced that the loss of inhibition enabled him to make logical leaps that proved advantageous. Nobody ever got far in this life by being careful. Rickert was cursed with a persistent pragmatism that sometimes needed to be short-circuited.

The Bay Phantom had saved his bacon. That was a fact. He wasn't one to experience gratitude for its own sake, though. The Phantom was a stand-up guy, but not the kind he felt like giving up everything, or anything, really, to follow. He didn't mind helping the masked man out, but all that talk about reforming and being a good citizen was strictly from hunger. I've *been a criminal my whole life*, he reasoned, *and I don't know how to do anything else, even if I wanted to. Which I don't.*

And there was no telling what the Phantom might want from him. He might expect Rickert to rat people out, and he didn't want to do that. After all, this guy was kind of a cop, in a way, and cops always wanted you to rat someone out. Rickert hadn't been raised that way. His pop always told him there was nothing lower than a rat. Of course, that might have had something to do with why the old man spent more than half his life in prison...

The idea of skipping town was looking very attractive. In fact, Rickert realized that he had more or less decided on it. A couple or ten more boilermakers, and he would head home and start packing.

Having made his decision, Rickert felt a little better. He swiveled himself around on the stool and sat with his back to the bar, surveying his fellow drinkers. He shared this dark, narrow saloon with a couple of slightly threadbare guys and a cute little blonde number who was playing around with a glass of gin and staring blankly at one wall. Something must have been bothering her. She was nicely-dressed and her makeup was immaculate, so she probably wasn't a lush.

Rickert finished his beer and ordered a fresh one, along with another shot of whiskey. He turned back around and did not look at the blonde. When he had finished the shot and the beer, he glanced back at her table. She had finished the drink he had seen her with before and started on another one, and she was still staring at the wall. His curiosity was piqued, and he was drunk enough now to do something about it.

He attempted to slide gracefully off of his stool, and almost ended up on the floor. He quickly but clumsily regained his balance and sauntered over to the blonde's table.

"Say," he said, "do you mind if I sit here?"

She gave him an arch look. He just smiled back.

"Oh, what the hell," she said. "Go ahead. If you're trying to pick me up, you're wasting your time. But if you want to talk, that's okay."

He sat down in the chair opposite hers.

"I'm not trying to pick you up," he said, a bit sloppily. "I just thought you looked like something was bugging you, and I…"

"… and you thought you could take advantage of that to worm your way into my good graces?" she finished for him. "That's awfully chivalrous of you. But I've got problems you can't help me with. Still, you can listen to me talk, and maybe bouncing this off of you will help me. See, there's something I have to do, and I'm not comfortable with it at all. The thing is it's got to do with work."

"Really?" said Rickert, raising his eyebrows. "Hey, I know what you mean. I got the same kind of thing going on myself right now."

"Sure you do," she said, rolling her eyes.

"No, I mean it. I met this guy a while back, and he wants me to work for him. It would be a pretty good deal, but there's something about it that kind of goes against my grain. Morally, this guy and me are on different levels, you know?"

"I'll be damned," she said wonderingly. "Maybe you *do* know what I mean. My thing is exactly like that. What my boss wants me to do… I don't think I'm the kind of person that would do it."

"I hear you, sister, I hear you."

"It would do me a lot of good if I did it," she said, holding up an index finger. "But maybe I can sort of pretend like I'm doing what he wants me to, but then really be doing something different. I thought that right away, and I've been trying to think how I could work it."

"That sounds interesting," Rickert said. "I never thought of that. It isn't a bad idea at all. Pretend like you're doing what he wants. Yeah, that's pretty sharp. Maybe that would work for me, too."

She took a deep breath and blew it out. "The problem is, I'm getting nowhere. Maybe I'm not devious enough. Hell, maybe I should just quit the damn job and forget the whole thing."

"Aw, you don't wanna do that. You don't look like a quitter to me."

"What the hell does a quitter look like?" she asked.

This puzzled Rickert. He thought about it, and couldn't come up with anything, so he jumped to another track.

"My old man had a code, you know?" he said. "He lived by it, and he was strict about it. It really sank in. You could say it's a part of who I am."

"It was the same with me and my dad," said the blonde, nodding. She raised her glass to her lips and seemed surprised to find that it was empty. She waved at the bartender for another.

"This guy I'm talking about," Rickert continued, "the one that wants me to work for him, isn't like me or my old man. His beliefs are totally different. Really, he doesn't have any business asking me to do something I'm morally against. Why, it's...it's un-American!"

"That's how I feel," said the blonde. "Exactly! He oughtta know better! This sonofabitch I'm working for? To hell with him! I say he deserves whatever he gets. I'll string him along somehow, and do exactly what I want to do! I'm *gonna* do it. Just like I said. I don't know how, but I'll figure it out."

"Me too," Rickert agreed. He felt great enthusiasm stirring within him, like he was at a patriotic rally or a revival meeting.

"I'm not gonna quit," said the blonde.

"Me neither!"

"What I'm gonna be," she said, slurring her words ever so slightly, "is somebody that never quits and that beats all the bastards out there at their own games!"

"You and me both, sister!" Rickert declared.

The blonde had a wild look in her eyes now, and the grin on her face might have been described as somewhat maniacal.

"That's exactly what I'll do," she said, sounding very self-satisfied. "To hell with making up phony connections. I'm gonna find out who is behind that damn mask!" She brought a fist down on the table and stood up.

"That's right," Rickert said. "I... Uh, wait, *mask*? What are you...?"

The girl bent forward, a little unsteadily, and ruffled Rickert's hair. "Thank you, mister," she said cheerfully. "I'm gonna get started right now!" She slung her handbag over her shoulder, put on her hat, turned on her heel, and left the speakeasy. Rickert, nonplussed, remained where he was.

"Mask?" he said to the empty chair across from him.

CHAPTER SEVEN
MIRABELLE

Back home at Tull House, Perrone made a phone call to an individual recommended by Louis Rickert, and learned that the machine guns used in the Bienville Square attack had been stolen from a nearby army depot more than three years previously. Nobody had any idea who had stolen them or where they had been since then. Was it just a coincidence that the weapons had turned up missing right in the middle of Doctor Piranha's reign of terror?

Of course, Perrone couldn't be sure the information he had just received was reliable. He really needed to develop some better contacts.

He hung up the phone and went looking for Mirabelle. He found her in the cellar, in the room she had fitted out as an armory. She had affixed to the door a sign she had probably swiped from some public place. "COLORED ONLY," it said in neat Gothic lettering. He tsk-tsked and pushed the door open.

Mirabelle was seated on a stool in front of a long work table, bent over some strange contraption with a screwdriver in one hand and a pair of calipers in the other.

"What are you doing?" he asked.

"Tinkering around with something you might find useful," she replied distractedly, without looking up from her work. "I got my hands on some designs for a device developed by Dr. Robert H. Goddard for the army during the Great War. He called it a Rocket-Powered Recoilless Weapon. It fires little rockets packed with explosives. It's a swell way to cause more destruction for less money."

It was a metal tube about three feet long and as big around as a stovepipe, with what looked like a large pistol stock and trigger assembly attached to the bottom, halfway along its length. There was another grip closer to what Perrone assumed was the front end.

"It's rather wicked-looking," he observed.

"That it is," she agreed. "And its appearance is not deceiving. This little bastard can do some serious damage. I'm gonna trust you to use it wisely, if I ever get it perfected."

Perrone didn't ask how she had come into possession of the designs. Mirabelle Darcy corresponded with scores of people around the world, representing dozens of different scientific disciplines and places of employment. As the possessor of one of the most brilliant minds in the world, Mirabelle had done all manner of mysterious favors for all manner of mysterious people and organizations and most of those reciprocated in one way or another. Perrone regarded all of that as Mirabelle's private business.

She assured him she was breaking no laws, and he pretended to believe her. She had a very strict moral code, which she had developed on her own, without recourse to religious, civic, or familial authorities. Perrone knew she was considerably smarter than he was; whether or not she was more ethical was a question he preferred not to ask. He trusted her innate wisdom to prevent her from straying too far.

"Perhaps I'll never have occasion to use it," he said.

"That's my hope," she replied, "but I'm building it just the same."

That's Mirabelle, Perrone thought. *She hasn't changed a bit.*

Mirabelle Darcy had known the whole Perrone family, years ago, when they all lived in Bayou La Batre, and her mother worked for them as a cook. They had struck her as rather hard people. There was something seedy about the father, Frank, and the mother was something of a shrew, though in a subtle way. The older brother, Anthony, had always given her the creeps. Joe Perrone was the only one who ever paid any attention to little Mirabelle.

Mirabelle already knew that she was too smart for her own good, and she did her best to keep it hidden from everybody. A Negro girl who appeared to be trying to rise too far above her station was regarded with contempt by whites and fearful indignation by other Negroes. She must remain discreet and hide her light under a dull and harmless bushel.

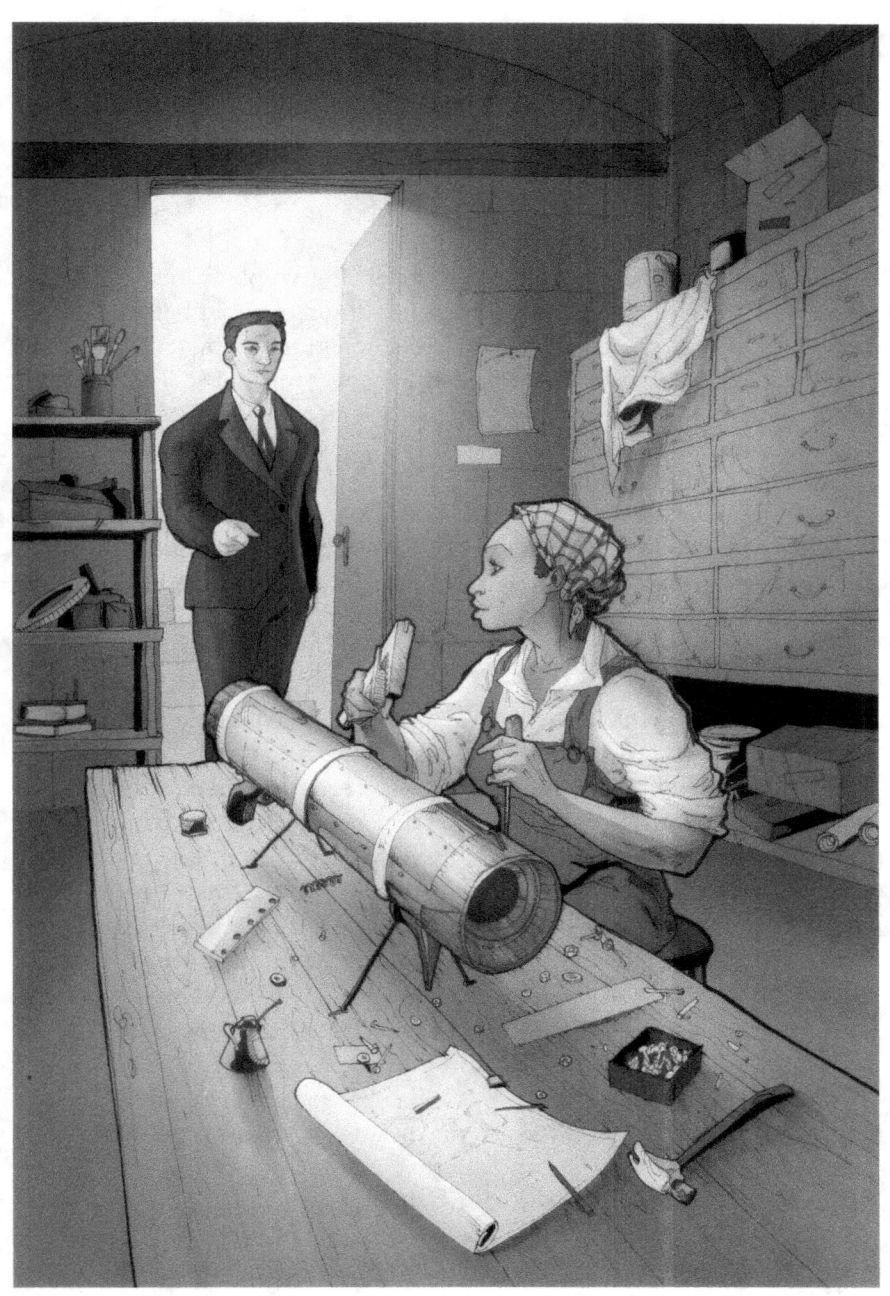

"What are you doing?"

It wasn't too difficult with her own family, because she knew all the right things to say so as not to appear different. Nobody in her family was stupid, but they didn't have to be; she was on an entirely different plane. She played her part, and it made her think of a line from Hamlet: "*That one may smile and smile and be a villain.*" She felt guilty, like she was a spy or an agent of deception.

Or a freak.

No white folks ever paid her any mind at all. Except for Joe Perrone. He seemed to sense that there was something different about her. She'd been wary of that at first, afraid that he was some kind of spy trying to draw her out so somebody could punish her for being too smart. This wariness lasted for almost a year, but she eventually let it slip a bit. Not too much.

Not completely, never that.

Mirabelle's mother had drilled into her head, for as long as she could remember, the dictum that she must avoid any sort of undue familiarity with white people in general and white men in particular. This commandment had sunk deep into her brain, taking up residence in the reptilian core, where all the fearful shadowy phantoms of instinct and racial memory prowled.

Surely, it couldn't apply to Joe Perrone, she thought. But it did. Joe Perrone was different, he truly was but that didn't matter. They could never genuinely be friends. There would always be a gulf between them.

"They're different from us and we're different from them," Eugenia had told her time and time again. "It ain't that one's better or worse than the other." Which was ridiculous, of course. White people were better. They thought so, and most Negroes seemed to think the same thing. Some white folks treated their dogs better than they treated the Negroes that worked for them. The big difference was, a dog might turn around and bite you if you kicked him one time too many, but a Negro would just stand there and smile and wag his tail and all but thank his master for the honor. They all did it; Mirabelle, too. Slavery had ended decades ago, but, in some ways, the new system was more perilous. Slaves, after all, were considered property, and even the meanest white man would think twice before destroying or permanently damaging his belongings.

Joe...*Mister Perrone*, as she called him, even then, gave her books and spent hours with her, discussing a wide variety of subjects. Like her, he seemed to be interested in everything, and wanted to learn as much as he could, just for the sake of knowing it.

Everyone else she knew was only interested in learning about things that were of practical use to them; none of them cared about what the stars in the sky really were and how they worked, or what had happened to the dinosaurs, or whether there were people living on Mars, or why objects fell to the ground instead of floating off into space. Sometimes, when she and Perrone were together, she forgot all about him being white and her being black. That might have been wonderful, but everything she had digested made her suspicious of it.

Joe's brother Anthony seemed to be very intelligent too, more so than Joe, and perhaps even more than Mirabelle herself. But there was a coldness about the older boy, and whatever it was that interested him, he kept it to himself. He was polite but very distant. He seemed to barely notice Mirabelle and her mother. For that matter, he appeared to take no interest in his own family.

"There's something wrong with that Anthony," Mirabelle's mother had once said to her. "I can't figure him out at all, and I don't want to. He's gonna end up in the penitentiary one day, and however soon it happens, it's gonna be too late for some poor soul. It may already be. You remember that friend of his, Gerald What's-his-name? Only friend he ever had? He's disappeared completely. Mister Anthony told Gerald's folks that the boy ran off, but I ain't sure about that at all. I think that Anthony was giving him dope or something. Your father tried to help the boy, but it was just too late. He either ran off, or..."

The "or" was left hanging. The older Perrone brother's dark proclivities and potential for heinous behavior was a frequent topic of speculation on her mother's part.

Eugenia Darcy had been a shrewd judge of character, and her predictions about people were generally accurate. In the case of Anthony Perrone, however, her soothsaying was rendered moot the night the Perrones, with the exception of Joseph, were murdered. The details were vague in Mirabelle's mind, even now. Mister Perrone never talked about it, and she never pressed him. It must have been terribly traumatic for him.

And all of a sudden, just like that, Joe Perrone was gone. She missed him. After he vanished, she felt twice as lonely as she had before she met him. He went wherever he went and she stayed where she was and did what someone like her was expected to do. Nobody knew what kind of a creature she really was. Nobody, black or white, ever bothered to try to find out. It was both comforting and frustrating. Part of her liked the fact that she was an iceberg; that is to say, the largest part of her was hidden under the dark water, unknown to everyone. The tiny bit of her that people could see was a sham, a disguise, a mannequin.

Nobody knew Mirabelle Darcy.

When she was fourteen she discovered the work of Albert Einstein. She wrote him a letter, asking several pointed questions about the true meaning behind the concept of relativity. To her surprise and delight, she received a personal, hand-written reply from Einstein himself. He answered her questions as best he could, and posed a few of his own. Mirabelle gave him her opinions and a lively correspondence was born. Mirabelle knew that she was not in Einstein's class when it came to mathematics, though her overall knowledge base was broader and deeper than his. The questions she had asked him, and the ones he had asked her in return, were of a more philosophical nature; not the mechanics of relativity, but the implications, scientific, social, and psychological, of that and other, even more exotic, theories. Einstein's pursuit of the Unified Field Theory had sprouted from his discussions with Mirabelle and been nurtured by them. He jokingly rebuked her for saddling him with his own Great White Whale.

He had invited her to travel to Germany, at his expense, and attend the Kaiser Wilhelm Institute for Physics, where he served as director. She hadn't dared to accept the offer. She was not destined to be a physicist, she wrote back. While this was quite true, it wasn't the real reason she had declined. She couldn't go to Germany because little Negro girls from Alabama just didn't do things like that. What would her mother think?

Einstein had accepted her refusal with good grace. In fact, he wrote, once he had pondered the matter and gone back over all the letters Mirabelle had sent him, he agreed with her. Her intellect was earthy and fertile, unlike the rather arid mindscape of the typical mathematician. She was comfortable with the abstract and unquantifiable, and had a great talent for finding connections between seemingly unrelated things. He had taken the liberty, he wrote, of mentioning her to an acquaintance of his from Vienna, who had found her ideas so intriguing that he had requested an introduction.

"I did not, of course, presume to answer for you," Einstein wrote. "But if you are interested, I will give him your address. I beg you to accept this offer, Mirabelle. I cannot stand to see you waste your life on fear and mediocrity. You could do anything, and I fear that you will end up doing nothing. Indeed, you are so extraordinarily gifted, I'm not at all sure that you have the right to keep it to yourself.

"At any rate, I believe your unique turn of mind can be a great help to this gentleman, and, further, that *his* unique turn of mind might do the same for you. Tell me yes or no, and I shall abide by your wishes, as always."

Mirabelle was intrigued and she gave her permission. Two weeks later, she received her first letter from Doctor Sigmund Freud. In the years ahead, Freud would become a mentor of sorts, an unofficial collaborator, and a confidante.

"Well," said Perrone, "I'll leave you to your work, then. You know, it's wonderful to have you here. The best is yet to come!"

Mirabelle, apparently engrossed in her work, made no reply.

CHAPTER EIGHT
A LATE ENCOUNTER WITH THE ENEMY

It was time for a foray.

This one had a specific goal from the outset, rather than being a scavenger hunt for random crimes. Louis Rickert had provided the Bay Phantom with a great deal of interesting information. There were many potential starting points, and the Phantom had decided on one.

There was an organized and well-funded bootlegging operation centered in Mobile, and it was rumored to have ties to members of one of the city's most prominent and wealthy families. Actually, it was more of an open secret than a rumor, and it was something to which the police consistently turned a blind eye.

None of the Carters ever took an active hand in the day-to-day workings of their illicit booze trade. If they were involved, they had a small army of underlings, who would be separated from them by several layers of deniability in the form of attorneys, contractors, shady middlemen and dummy corporations.

One such underling was a man known as Shorty Red, and he was to be the Phantom's first target. Shorty was six feet, eight inches tall, with snow-white hair. His skin was pale, and his usually-expressionless face appeared to have been carved out of soapstone. His lips barely moved when he spoke and nobody could recall ever having seen him blink his cold, greenish-gray eyes.

Shorty was an agent and an enforcer. He was in charge of a certain number of restaurants and speakeasies that carried Carter product. When a business owner refused to handle the liquor that was offered to him by the bootleggers, or haggled over the price, Shorty employed his negotiating skills. Five minutes was generally all he needed to persuade even the most recalcitrant entrepreneur. If negotiations went past that point, the business in question would soon be under new management.

"Louis Rickert tells me that Shorty Red makes his rounds in the southern part of Mobile County every Wednesday night," Perrone said to Mirabelle, as he stood in front of a full-length mirror, examining his appearance. The dark suit was an excellent fit, and did not show any telltale bulges in the spots where weapons were concealed. "Rickert said that the proprietor of Max's Restaurant, one Maximillian Santorelli, has been complaining about the quality of the liquor he's been getting and the amount of money he is required to pay for it. Rickert is of the opinion that if Santorelli doesn't end up on a slab this very night, it won't be much longer."

"That's peachy," said Mirabelle. "It just so happens I know about Shorty Red, from the days when he operated up in Prichard. One of my cousins had some dealings with him. I hope you've got something hidden in that costume of yours that can split the Rock of Gibraltar in half. No, into quarters."

"I wouldn't call this a *costume*, as such," Perrone said a bit fussily. "It's an ordinary suit, though it has been adapted to carry my gear. And as for Shorty Red, I hardly think the situation is that dire. He needs a good talking-to for starters. I have no realistic hope of persuading him to change his ways, though I will make the effort. But, if I am to be realistic, the best I can hope for is to frighten or anger him, thus sending a message to his employers."

"Yeah, well."

"Have you no faith in my abilities?"

"Of course I do," Mirabelle said with some heat. "I also have faith in the fact that you are a relatively rational human being, apart from the costume and mask business. Shorty Red is *not* rational. He would truly just as soon kill you as look at you. He is one savage mother..."

"*Mirabelle!*"

"... of pearl. If I were you, I'd just kill him."

"You don't mean that," Perrone said. "You know, if the Carters are indeed involved in this business, I shall have to revise my opinion of them. I'm certain already that they're involved in questionable things. I know their business ethics have always been a bit... malleable, but it's hard to believe that they've become outright gangsters."

"You know what else is hard to believe?" said Mirabelle. "The law of gravity. But try floating up to the ceiling some time."

Perrone pulled the black mask with the built-in dark blue goggles over his head, and placed the wide-brimmed black slouch hat on top of it.

"How do I look?" he asked, turning to Mirabelle.

"Sweet Jesus," she whispered.

After Perrone, the Bay Phantom, was gone, Mirabelle sat and cried for five minutes, without knowing exactly why. Then she went into the kitchen and hunted up a bottle of wine.

The Bay Phantom drove the short distance south to Bayou La Batre in one of his favorite automobiles, a nondescript Ford sedan that would draw no undue attention from anybody. Unless, of course, they tried to break into it or outrun it.

He cruised up and down the main street two or three times, looking at things, places he knew when he was a child but didn't any more. He thought about driving by Gulf Bay Manor, got as far as the nameless little lane that led to the place, but decided against it. Too much darkness out there, and it was almost time for business, anyhow. He headed for Max's Restaurant.

When he pulled into the gravel parking lot, he saw that there was one other car already there. He knew that Max Santorelli lived in a small house behind the restaurant, and did not own an automobile. He jumped from his vehicle and started toward the entrance, hoping he wasn't too late. As he approached the other car, the driver's side door opened and a man stepped out.

"I figured you'd be here," said Louis Rickert. "If you're going to hand Shorty Red his head tonight, I want to see it. I hate that creep. Everybody hates him. Even Jesus hates him."

"This is not a punitive expedition, Louis," said the Phantom. "I want to get his measure, and give him something to convey to his bosses. That may involve physical violence, but I intend to keep it to a minimum. Let's go in and talk with the proprietor."

Maximillian Santorelli, standing behind the bar at the rear of the restaurant, rubbing a beer glass with a rag, did a double take when the masked man walked into his establishment. The strange figure approached the bar, accompanied by Louis Rickert, a small-time hood who was known to Santorelli.

"Louis?" Santorelli said. "Can I, ah... Can I help you gentlemen?"

"Good evening," said the masked man. "I realize my appearance is unconventional, but there's a reason for that, and I assure you I mean you no harm. I am called the Bay Phantom. You've heard of me, perhaps?"

"Uh, yeah, right," Santorelli said cautiously. "You're the one that, ah... The Doctor Piranha thing, right? You're some kind of a cop, aren't you?"

"Not really. And I'm not here because you're selling illegal liquor. Drunkenness is a vice, but I don't think it can or should be legislated out of existence. There are far worse things that men do, and those are the things that interest me. It is my understanding that you've been having difficulties with an individual named Shorty Red."

"I don't know who that is."

"I believe you do. You're expecting him tonight. That's why you have that shotgun under the bar within easy reach. I glimpsed a reflection in that glass you're obsessively polishing. I imagine you're wondering if you'll feel the need to use it on me. You won't. I'm not a threat. Shorty Red is. It seems you've been bucking the system, and may be in some danger."

"I can take care of myself."

"Perhaps. Perhaps not. Shorty Red is a formidable man and he represents an even more formidable organization."

Santorelli didn't know what to say to this odd visitor. He continued polishing the glass.

Rickert had been prowling around the restaurant while the Phantom was speaking. Now he was at the front window, peeping through the venetian blinds. "Oh, jeez!" he exclaimed. "Here comes Shorty."

The Phantom joined him at the window and looked out. It was Shorty Red, all right. Who else could it possibly be? And he wasn't alone. Walking beside him was a young woman. The top of her head was almost level with his solar plexus. Physically slight though she was, the hard look on her face matched or exceeded that of her companion.

If I were to truly fear one of them, the Phantom thought, *it wouldn't be Shorty Red.*

He stepped back to the middle of the room and stood facing the door. "You might want to find a place of safety," he said to Rickert and Santorelli, "in case this goes the wrong way."

Rickert joined Santorelli behind the bar, and both of them crouched down, out of sight.

Shorty Red pushed the door open with a lot more force than was necessary. The Phantom had to admit that the giant cut an extremely menacing figure, lumbering through the doorway. Quite naturally, the masked and caped man standing in the middle of the room caught Shorty's eye.

"What the hell are you supposed to be?" the giant asked, not sure whether to be amused or alarmed.

"I am the Bay Phantom, and I am here to have a word with you."

"Is that a fact? Well, I have *two* words for you." He uttered them; a four-letter Anglo-Saxon verb followed by a common pronoun.

"Really, now," the Phantom said disapprovingly. "Surely we can keep it on a higher level than that."

He studied Shorty Red and his female companion, and was startled to realize that the hard-looking young woman was none other than Penny Carter. He hadn't recognized her at first. She was obviously wearing a wig, but there was more to it than that. Her face was *different* tonight. Not a disguise, not makeup. It was more like something inside her, something even darker than what he had seen at the Bienville Square massacre, had taken possession of her face and form; even her posture and gait were different.

Shorty charged. The Phantom made as though to duck underneath the lunging behemoth. Shorty caught it and compensated, aiming low. The Phantom changed direction, jumped up, and leapfrogged over Shorty, bringing his right fist down like a hammer in the vicinity of the big man's kidney. Shorty grunted and crashed headlong into the bar.

"You see," said the masked man, "violence is a very poor negotiating strategy. You may bully someone into complying with your wishes, but if you fail to win the heart and the mind, you'll always have a dangerous enemy. Your destruction is assured."

Shorty got to his feet and turned around. The Bay Phantom stood in the middle of the floor, empty hands held above his head.

"I'm armed, Shorty," he said, "but I'm not going to draw a gun unless I absolutely have to. I'd much rather be your friend. Surely there is some good in you. I would truly hate to shoot you."

"Okay," said Shorty, reaching into his jacket for the pistol he carried in a shoulder holster. "Just stand still then."

He took hasty aim and fired.

The Phantom had already dodged out of the way, and the bullet went through the front window. The masked man snatched a heavy napkin holder from one of the tables and threw it, striking Shorty's gun hand. The impact broke two of Shorty's fingers and sent the gun flying. It landed on the floor behind the bar, where Rickert and Santorelli were hiding.

Shaking his injured hand and growling, Shorty glanced over at Penny Carter. She hadn't made a move to intervene, and it didn't look as though she intended to. She was just watching the action, a rapt expression on her face.

"This conflict," the Bay Phantom was saying, "is pointless. I only want to learn about the people you work for. Don't you think they might be exploiting you? What do you really gain from all this, in the long run?"

"Don't you ever shut up?" Shorty bellowed, charging toward his caped tormentor. The Bay Phantom pirouetted out of the way at the last possible split-second, giving Shorty a kick in the pants to add momentum to his headlong plunge. The enforcer hurtled into a table, knocking it over, did a flip, and crashed into another table. He righted himself and stood still for a moment, swaying and blinking his eyes. Then he toppled over onto his side and lay still.

"Oh, dear," said the Phantom, moving closer to the fallen behemoth. "Are you injured, Shorty? Can you hear me?" He didn't want to get too close, but he couldn't see Shorty's face, and he feared he might have inadvertently inflicted excessive injuries.

Unseen by the Phantom, Penny Carter reached into her jacket and pulled out a little .22 revolver. She pointed it at the masked man and thumbed back the hammer.

"Watch out, Boss!" Rickert yelled. After the fall of Shorty, he had slowly risen from his place of concealment behind the bar. He had taken possession of Shorty Red's wayward gun, and was aiming it at Penny. "Drop that gat, sister," he barked.

The Phantom crouched down and whirled to face this new threat. Penny quickly adjusted her aim, drawing a bead on the spot between the dark blue lenses of the Phantom's mask.

"Miss Carter," he said, "my associate will not hesitate to shoot you if you do not comply."

"You know who I am," she said. It was a statement, not a question.

The Phantom nodded. "I know a great many things. I know that if you do not drop your weapon, things will happen that we will all be sorry for. I am not here to act as a catalyst for a bloodbath."

She gave him a quizzical look. "Are you for real? You are the cutest thing!" She lowered the gun, then glanced over at Rickert.

"Where the hell did you dig up *that* little dog turd?" she said with a smirk.

"Never mind that," said the Phantom, ignoring Rickert's indignant sputtering. He moved closer to Penny.

"Just give me that pistol, please," he said gently, reaching out a hand. "Then I need to see if your friend is badly injured."

"Okay," she said with a shrug. "What the hell, here you go." She held the weapon out and allowed the Phantom to take it.

"There," said the masked man, turning to Rickert. "You see? No need for lethal..."

That was as far as he got. The moment he turned his head away from her, Penny Carter slipped a large blackjack from some hidden place and walloped him on the side of the head. He went down on the floor and remained there, motionless.

"Oh, Jesus!" Rickert exclaimed. "You've croaked him! You little tramp!"

She stuck her tongue out at him. He responded by firing a shot that deliberately went a foot or so wide. He just wanted to throw a scare into her.

"Could you people please stop shooting holes in my restaurant?" came the voice of Max Santorelli, from the floor where he lay prone. Rickert ignored him and stepped out from behind the bar.

"Okay, sister," he said as he approached the young woman. "Just take it easy and drop that sap." She just stood there smiling at him.

At that moment, Shorty Red stirred and rose like a muscle-bound Phoenix from the wreckage of the two tables.

"Hey," he said. "I know you! You're Louis Rickert! You goddamn little creep!"

"Aw, hell," Rickert whispered.

While Rickert was distracted by the awful sight, Penny lunged forward and brought the blackjack down on his gun hand, forcing him to drop the weapon. Shorty Red was lumbering in his direction, growling and making threats.

It was time, Rickert decided, to exercise the better part of valor, as his old man used to say, and get the hell out of harm's way. He turned and dashed back behind the bar, through the office and storeroom and out the back door.

"Rickert!" bellowed Shorty Red as he gave chase. "I don't know what's going on here, but I am going to break your goddamn neck!"

Oh, God, Rickert thought, *I never should have come out here. That Bay Phantom is as crazy as Shorty Red.*

And now he was going to have to kill Shorty Red. There was no way around it, if he wanted to keep on living; which he did.

He headed for the only possible place of concealment he could see; a small tin shed behind the restaurant. No sooner had he ducked behind it than he heard Shorty Red emerge from the restaurant, calling his name and cursing.

This is it, Rickert thought. *I'm a dead man.*

He looked around and spotted a large crowbar someone had leaned against the wall of the shed. It would have to do. He picked it up gingerly, as though it might be a rattlesnake in disguise. As he stood there, hefting the alarmingly light crowbar and listening to the sound of the behemoth's approach. Rickert silently berated the God he only believed in when he needed somebody to blame something on: *If you were gonna put me into a position like this, you could have at least given me a gun instead of this stupid crowbar. It'll be like trying to kill an elephant with a flyswatter.*

As Shorty Red was about to round the corner, Rickert noticed something else on the ground that might be helpful. He stooped to grab a handful of it. When Red came into view and caught sight of him, Rickert threw the coarse sand into the man's terrible greenish-gray eyes.

Shorty Red cursed and clapped his hand to his face, furiously rubbing at his eyes. Taking a deep breath, Louis Rickert swung the crowbar. It smacked into the right side of Shorty Red's head, making him wobble. Rickert swung again and hit the same spot a second time. This enraged the blinded giant, who stumbled and fell to his knees. Rickert stepped around and whacked Red's hands, breaking three fingers and probably his nose, judging by the blood that was gushing from it. Rickert continued to press his unexpected advantage, delivering a series of blows to the back of Red's head that made his own arm hurt.

When Rickert was done, Shorty Red lay motionless in a pool of blood. Rickert stood there for almost a minute, breathing hard through clenched teeth. His heartbeat gradually slowed down and his respiration approached its normal rate. Suddenly appalled, he flung the crowbar into some bushes and ran a short distance into the copse of trees, where he was swallowed up by the shadows. His legs gave way and he landed on his side in the dirt.

You got him, he told himself, *he can't hurt you. You got him, he can't hurt you. You got him, he can't hurt you…*

"Rickert." It was the voice of the Bay Phantom. "Are you all right?"

Rickert sat up, felt his head, and looked around. "I guess so. What's happening?"

"I'm not entirely certain. Something happened to Shorty Red. I didn't think I'd hit him hard enough to do any serious damage. Perhaps I don't know my own strength. Evidently, he came to and staggered away from the scene of our confrontation, then passed out again behind that wooden shed. I was knocked out momentarily, and by the time I came to and traced his movements, that girl was helping him into their car. All I could do was stand there and watch her drive away."

"He wasn't dead?" Rickert asked nervously.

"Oh, my, no," said the Phantom. "He was in awful shape, but he was walking, thank God. I can't understand how I inflicted so much damage..."

"That dame looked familiar," Rickert said quickly, hoping to divert the Phantom's thoughts from Shorty Red's puzzling downfall.

"Oh, yes," said the Phantom. "I recognized her. That was Penelope Carter." He shook his head. "I knew she was of questionable morality, but I am surprised to find her involved in something like this."

Rickert shrugged. "Some broads like the rough stuff."

"Do you think so? That would indicate some serious anti-social tendencies. But she certainly isn't in it for the money; she's got that already, and has no need to endanger herself to enjoy it."

Rickert shrugged. "She probably enjoys it. There are people like that, you know."

"Well," said the masked man, "I suppose we've learned a little something. Right now, I'm all in, and, if I may say so, you look a little the worse for wear yourself. You might want to go home and get some rest. Have a good meal. And do try to avoid alcohol."

"Uh, yeah, right. You're gonna be okay, then?"

"Of course. I'll be in touch, Louis. You take care."

"Yeah, you too."

Rickert stood and watched his peculiar masked patron start up the Ford and drive away. He still couldn't figure this guy's angle, but it was starting to seem possible that he was on the level and meant exactly what he said. Weird. he glanced at his watch. It was too early to go back to his apartment. He ambled back into Max's Restaurant and sat down at the bar. The proprietor eyed him warily.

"Everything's fine," Rickert said. "You don't have to worry about Shorty Red any more. Me and my partner took care of him."

"Who the hell *was* that guy, anyhow? Was he *really*..?"

"Yep, that was the Bay Phantom," Rickert said flatly. "He's the new big shot in town. Things are changing, Max."

"So, am I supposed to buy my liquor from him now?" Santorelli sounded dubious. "What kinda prices is he charging?"

"We can talk about that later. I'm the guy you'll be dealing with; we'll get the details ironed out. I'm sure I can get you a good discount. Now, how's about you bring me a plate of those fried shrimp of yours? And some cornbread and whatever else you got. Oh, and I wouldn't mind a shot of that rye. In fact, just bring me the bottle."

"Whatever you say, Louis. You're moving up in the world, huh?"

"Looks that way, Max."

CHAPTER NINE
VARIOUS DIFFICULTIES

"We need to have a talk about something," Mirabelle said gravely.

Perrone had only just stripped off the Bay Phantom, and had been hoping for some quiet relaxation. This was not to be.

"Technically, I am your housekeeper," Mirabelle continued. "But I have neither the time nor the inclination to do housework. I've made a few passes at it when I had the time, but I cannot do a thorough job. We need to hire someone else to do the bulk of it, unless you want to live in a pig sty."

Perrone frowned. "I don't like the idea of outsiders poking around in here."

"It won't be a problem. We can lock down everything connected with the Bay Phantom. Nobody will even suspect that there might be a cellar in this house, since we're right at sea level. Everything sensitive goes down there. Anyhow, nobody maintains a house this size without any domestic staff. You want to look normal, don't you?"

Perrone, knowing the folly of opposing Mirabelle when she was in a mood like this, agreed to the plan. And she did in fact have a point. He told her to proceed.

It wasn't until later that he wondered if she might have it in mind to groom a replacement.

In her room, working on her second bottle of wine this evening, Mirabelle wondered the same thing.

The next day, Morton Homes, District Attorney for the City of Mobile, was in a quandary. On his desk were two envelopes, both stuffed with money. Each envelope had come with a "request."

The first envelope had come, through the usual intermediaries, from Caleb Carter. Homes owed his job to the Carters, and their "requests" normally took priority. In this case, Caleb Carter wanted Homes to convene a grand jury to look into allegations that Hector Sams and the Bay Phantom had been behind the massacre at Bienville Square. Homes had been assured that plenty of evidence would be made available to him. Ordinarily, this would have been done quickly and without question.

But things were not ordinary. The other envelope had the potential to change the rules forever. This envelope contained a great deal of money; six times the amount in the one from Caleb Carter. The party who had sent this cash wanted Homes to ignore the massacre and concentrate on an unspectacular attempted burglary at a warehouse owned by Hector Sams.

And there was the source of the quandary. Hector Sams was running for mayor this year, against the Carters' usual candidate, Simon Brickell. Homes knew that Sams wouldn't bother unless he thought he had a real chance. And, in this town, nobody had a chance against the Carters... *unless*...

Unless they had some very powerful backing indeed. Powerful enough to casually toss around six times as much cash as Caleb Carter did. It was plain that a war for control was brewing. Homes had always been loyal to the Carters, but that loyalty was based on the size and frequency of the "cash considerations" that came to him from the Carter machine. It was obvious now that Hector Sams had backers who were prepared to up the ante. Anybody with such resources and such sheer nerve might just have it in them to *win* a war against the Carter machine.

This placed Morton Homes in a very tricky position. Which of these requests should he honor? He had given it a great deal of thought, and had consulted with his most trusted advisors. But not even the best bartenders and the highest-class whores had been able to guide him out of this wilderness. In the end, he knew there was only one answer...

He opened the beloved leather briefcase that his father had given him the day he graduated from law school. Into it, he placed the contents of both envelopes. Then he picked up the telephone on his desk and rang his secretary.

"Yes, Mrs. Wiggins, I need you to do something for me. Please call the airport and reserve a seat on the next flight to Rio De Janiero, Brazil. Yes, that's right. No, I'll pick up the ticket myself, just before boarding time. No, Mrs. Homes won't be coming on this trip. Oh, and reserve the ticket under the name 'John Smith,' if you would, please. Yes, thank you. Oh, I'll be returning in... a few days. It's a... conference. I'll phone you when I get there. Thank you, Mrs. Wiggins."

CHAPTER TEN
THE BIG UNEASY

Mirabelle finished filling out the classified ad form she had obtained from the Mobile *Press*, folded it up, and placed it in an envelope. Then she filled out a check and took it to Perrone for his signature.

He signed it without a word and handed it back to her. She knew he didn't like the idea, but he was going along with it because... why? He trusted her? He was afraid of what she might do? She realized she had a sort of power over him, but she didn't understand it and didn't want to think about it. She put the check in the envelope and sealed it, then took it out to the mailbox by the road.

She stood there for a while, looking out across the Bay. All that water, constantly moving. Coming down the rivers, then into the Bay, then into the Gulf of Mexico, and so on. So many people depended on it without ever thinking about it.

The population of the world was somewhere in the neighborhood of two billion, one hundred million people, depending on dark mysteries to sustain them. Mirabelle Darcy was smarter than approximately two billion, ninety-nine million, nine hundred and ninety-nine thousand, nine hundred and ninety-one of them. There were only eight people out there in the world more intelligent than she was, according to Doctor Sigmund Freud. He had never explained to her how he arrived at these figures, and she had never asked.

If I'm so goddamned smart, why am I such a goddamned mess?

She put her classified ad into the mailbox, along with a few letters to various correspondents of hers, including Doctor Freud. She wished she could share the details of her current dilemma with him and ask for his advice, but she couldn't. The secrets weren't hers to give away. She slammed the box shut and raised the little metal flag. The postman would see this, and he would take her letters and carry them on their way, because that was what he did. He had no idea what passed through his hands every single day, from this mailbox and all the others. How much smarter was Mirabelle than the postman, and how much better off did that make her, exactly? Did the postman have to drink himself to sleep every night because he knew things he didn't want to know?

Being one of the smartest people in the world, she decided, was worth just about as much as being the smartest fish or bird or bug.

She walked back to the house, acutely aware of everything around her and how little power she had over any of it.

Mister Perrone was sitting in the front room, going through his daily stack of newspapers. Mirabelle sat down in a chair across the room from him.

"So you didn't learn anything of value from Shorty Red last night?" she said.

"I wouldn't say that. I think I learned a great deal, though not necessarily from Shorty."

"You beat the living shit out of him," she said, smiling at the pained expression her profanity evoked from her employer. "That's an accomplishment."

"Hardly. It's funny, Mirabelle, but I didn't think I hit him that hard. He's still unconscious. Someone took him to the hospital last night, probably his companion. It was the identity of that companion that I found most intriguing."

"Who was it?"

He put down his newspaper, looked Mirabelle in the eye, and said, "Caleb Carter's sister, Penny."

"She was out doing the rounds with one of the Carters' enforcers?" Mirabelle said, frowning. "How come?"

"That's exactly what I'd like to know. I wonder if Shorty Red has some kind of a hold on her."

Mirabelle laughed harshly. "More likely, *she's* got a hold on *him*. I bet you she has a firm grip on his..."

"*Mirabelle...*"

"... short hairs. Mister Perrone, that woman is a bad news. I've heard stories about her that you wouldn't believe."

"So have I, and I don't know if I should believe them or not. But I think she bears looking into."

"I'm not even gonna touch that one. I wish Doctor Freud could hear what you just said. What are you going to do?"

"There's nothing I *can* do right now," he said. "I need to clear my head for a while. And, since tonight is the full moon, I think it's time to look into the matter of Charles Fort's werewolf."

"I was hoping you'd forgotten about that," Mirabelle said.

"Not likely."

"It seems to me that you have more than enough to occupy you right here."

"I know that. I just told you I needed a break from it. A brief one, a single night. Besides, I promised Charles I'd look into it."

"If you want to look into things for Charles Fort," Mirabelle said sourly, "why don't you start with frogs falling out of the sky or something?"

"Because frogs are not known to fall out of the sky in New Orleans every time there's a full moon."

"Oh, for God's sake!" Mirabelle exclaimed, throwing up her hands. "That isn't even remotely logical. I guess I better go along with you. If it starts raining goddamn werewolves, you'll need someone to hold your umbrella."

"Mirabelle, please, language. Anyway, it will do *you* good to get out of town for a while, too."

"If you say so," Mirabelle said without conviction.

"Why the French Quarter?" Mirabelle asked several hours later. They were sitting in Perrone's roadster, parked on a side street close to the French Market in New Orleans. He was wearing his Bay Phantom getup, everything but the mask.

"Because the fiend hasn't struck here yet," Perrone replied. "He has killed in the Garden District, the Lower Ninth Ward, the area once known as Storyville, the Irish Channel, and City Park. He is not limited geographically, but there is no pattern that I can discern. Therefore, the Quarter is as likely a place as any."

"Okay. There's not enough logic there for me to argue against. Now, I'm just gonna assume from the outset that this is not an actual werewolf. Ghosts I can swallow, but not werewolves or vampires or zombies."

"The killer only strikes on nights when there's a full moon," Perrone reminded her. "Folkloric werewolves do the same."

"Sure," said Mirabelle. "I have no doubt, based on what you've told me about these killings, that we're looking at a deeply psychotic individual.

The full moon thing is certainly a part of it. If he thinks he's a werewolf, or wants to be a werewolf, then he's gonna act like a werewolf. It's possible that he leads a very ordinary life most of the time, and only cuts loose when it's that time of the month.

"Furthermore, it is probable that at least some of the cops in New Orleans don't believe in werewolves either, and have arrived at the same conclusion I have. Which means there will be officers crawling around everywhere. You'll want to be careful to avoid the kind of attention you're likely to attract if you parade around town in that getup of yours."

"I'm not wearing the mask, and nobody will pay me any mind. Let's go."

There weren't nearly as many people roaming the streets as Perrone was accustomed to seeing when he came to New Orleans. The few that he saw were either furtive or purposeful. Many of the latter, he felt safe in assuming were undercover police officers. There was tension in the air, no doubt about it, a feeling of hidden menace just beyond the reach of one's five senses. The public had been told that a mad killer might be at large, but the bulk of the details had been withheld from the press.

As the Bay Phantom made his meandering way through the French Quarter, the full moon hung in the sky, somewhat arrogantly it seemed to him, like a taunt or a dare. Somewhere behind him, keeping to the shadows, dressed in black from neck to toe, with a small pair of dark-lensed goggles to hide the whites of her eyes, was Mirabelle. She had offered to act as the "bait," but Perrone had vetoed that. The bait might end up dead before the stalker could spring the trap. Perrone was fitted out with a number of interesting devices and unusual items of clothing that would minimize the physical danger to him should the werewolf strike. He also had the advantage conferred by his extensive training in physical combat.

For her part, Mirabelle was carrying two guns, one in each hand. The first was an ordinary .38 revolver loaded with silver bullets, just in case. The other was a powerful air pistol that fired tranquilizer darts. There were three of them, and each one carried enough fast-acting soporific compound to put a very large man to sleep almost instantly. She moved quietly, keeping half a block between herself and her employer.

They covered the Quarter in a rough spiral, skirting first around the edges, then working their way in toward the center.

They were on Dumaine Street, roughly two blocks north of Jackson Square when, as Mirabelle put it later, "the big, hairy pile of shit hit the fan."

Perrone had just passed the darkened front widow of a little restaurant and was about to cross the street when something erupted from behind a line of metal garbage cans at the side of the building.

Whatever this thing was, it was almost seven feet tall, and covered from head to foot with matted, dark brown fur. The head was oversized, with a thick neck to support it. Perrone could not see its eyes. It hopped over the cans and landed right in front of him, dropping into a menacing crouch.

"I don't want to harm you," said Perrone in a voice meant to be both soothing and firm at the same time. *Show compassion while establishing authority.* That often worked on habitual criminals, but he didn't know about homicidal madmen dressed as werewolves.

"Let's just slow down a little," he continued, "and see if we can't agree on one or two things. You have to stop all this killing, you must see that."

The werewolf rocked back and forth on the balls of its feet, then leaped. The claws on the beast's right paw raked across Perrone's chest, slicing through fabric and flesh.

Perrone stepped back a few paces, looking down at the damage he had just sustained, and said, "Now, really, this isn't necessa..." His remark was cut off by a fierce blow to the head, which knocked him to the ground. *Oh my*, he thought, *I suppose I've at least got a concussion, if not a cracked skull...* That was as far as he got before darkness claimed him. His head rolled back and he lay there on the street, unconscious, bleeding, and helpless...

The werewolf moved in for the kill...

CHAPTER ELEVEN
MIRABELLE MEETS THE WEREWOLF

But Perrone had a defender, and she wasted no time. Mirabelle Darcy recovered quickly from the sudden shock of what she had just witnessed and went into action. She had never been called upon to fend off a werewolf, but she had done a great many other dangerous things in her life. She was no stranger to combat, physical and otherwise, and she knew how to take care of herself and anyone else who needed it. Not allowing people she cared about to come to harm was almost a religion with her; the only sacred thing of which she was capable. She acknowledged her fear, then thrust it as far into the back of her mind as she could.

"Hey, Rin Tin Tin!" she shouted. "Over here! I got something for you!"

"I'm not wearing my mask..."

The beast whipped its head around in her direction. Its eyes were invisible in the shadows under its furry brow, but Mirabelle felt the look it was giving her. It was a disconcerting sensation. She took a deep breath and started moving forward.

"Look at you," she said, drawing both of her firearms from their holsters. "Standing there in the middle of the damn street like a big, hairy gooney bird. You look stupid!"

The werewolf crouched down slightly and swiveled on its feet, positioning itself to spring at this new threat.

Before that could happen, Mirabelle aimed the .38 and fired three shots in quick succession. She hit the monster square in the chest each time. The impacts produced sparks and the sounds of metal-on-metal ricochets, and seemed not to faze the werewolf at all.

The beast started moving in her direction.

"Hold it right there!" she shouted. "I'm gonna kill your stupid ass!"

She adjusted her aim and fired a single shot at the werewolf's forehead. The result of that maneuver was a lot more gratifying. The monster stopped in its tracks and howled, clutching its face with both of its clawed hands. She fired another shot, which connected audibly with the back of the furry head. The werewolf staggered around in the middle of the street, but didn't fall.

Mirabelle moved forward, holstering both the .38 and the air gun. She didn't say a word. Her only aim now was to drag Perrone out of the way before the werewolf could regain its bearings. She was sure she had hit her marks, but it didn't look like either bullet had penetrated the monster's skull. Whatever it was wearing over its head and face had likely absorbed most of the impact.

When the werewolf paused in its caterwauling to take a breath, Mirabelle heard the sound of police whistles, several of them, coming from all directions.

She slid her hands under Perrone's arms, got a good grip, and started walking backward as fast as she could, dragging her unconscious employer roughly over the cobblestones. The werewolf had stopped spinning, but it was still howling and pawing at its face. Mirabelle kept scuttling backwards, up onto the sidewalk and into the mouth of a dark passage between two buildings. When she was sure they couldn't be seen from the street, she dropped Perrone, made sure he was still breathing and in one piece, and slumped against a wall. Her whole body was quivering and she doubted she would be able to stand up again for a few minutes. Out on the street, the werewolf's godawful howling tapered off to a low growling whine, over which the sound of more police whistles and shouts could be heard.

As she fought to control her breathing, Mirabelle heard the police arrive on the scene.

"What the hell?" exclaimed one.

"Jesus, look, it's real!" shouted another.

"Hey!" bellowed a third. "Stand still! You're under arrest!"

Good luck with that, thought Mirabelle. She pushed herself forward, and crawled the foot and a half to where Perrone lay. Using her tiny flashlight, she determined that his color was good. She pulled back an eyelid and everything looked okay in there, too.

"You're alive, Mister Perrone," she whispered. "We both are. If you'll just wake up and say something to me, I swear to God I won't say I told you so. Even though I did."

And then, out on the street, the shooting started. The cops were yelling and the werewolf had started up his damn howling again.

Perrone's shirt and coat had been slashed to ribbons diagonally across his chest, and there was blood. Tearing away the strips of fabric, Mirabelle saw three narrow wounds, parallel to one another, each one about six inches long. It didn't look *too* bad. She hoped his skull wasn't fractured.

"Holy shit!" one of the cops yelled, "look at that!"

More gunfire.

"Goddamn!" came the voice of another officer, "Did you see that? He jumped fifteen feet straight up!"

"Where the hell did he go?"

"Over that roof! Somewhere! Hell, I don't know! Thompson, Beck, you follow me! The rest of you get over to the next street! *Go!*"

"Mister Perrone, get up," Mirabelle breathed as she attempted to haul her employer to his feet. After she had dragged him out through the opposite end of the alley, and half a block in the direction of the French Market, Perrone regained consciousness, more or less. He was dizzy and confused, and still required Mirabelle's support to walk.

"That was no werewolf," Perrone said, once they had reached the car and were safely inside. "It was a disguised human being."

"Uh-huh," Mirabelle said. "Take off your jacket and shirt, Mister Perrone, so I can see if you need the last rites."

He complied, and Mirabelle examined the damage. "These slashes are pretty clean," she said. "More like razor cuts than anything."

"Those claws were metal," he said, "not keratin. Of that I am certain."

"Uh-huh. But I'm still worried about infection. You're gonna take some penicillin when we get home. I've been experimenting with a new strain, and this is a good chance to try it out. Alexander Fleming has decided penicillin can't last long enough in the human body to kill pathogenic bacteria, but I say he's full of beans. I've just about proven it already."

"I'm sure you're right," he said, and it was true. He had no doubts about anything Mirabelle said or thought. She was, for all intents and purposes, infallible when it came to things like that.

She got the first-aid kit out from under the back seat and went to work. Perrone winced as she daubed raw alcohol on the long, thin wounds. He clenched his teeth as she scrubbed them briskly with cotton. He sighed with relief as she wrapped his torso in gauze and secured it with surgical tape.

"There," Mirabelle said brightly. "That should hold you together. It wasn't as bad as it looked before. You really ought to get some stitches, and I'm all thumbs when it comes to sewing. You need to get a doctor on the payroll, I guess. Do you want me to drive?"

"I can manage," said Perrone. "Just help me get my shirt and jacket back on."

"Do you wanna put your mask and goggles on, too, so if we get pulled over, you can explain to the police how you're a masked hero on a case? You can tell them I'm a vicious Negro criminal that cut you up with a razor, and you're taking me out in the woods to face some rough justice."

"Mirabelle, please! Why are you so cantankerous this evening?"

"It happens every time I see somebody nearly get killed by a fake werewolf."

On the way out of town, Perrone stopped at a pay phone and called the private detective he had hired several days earlier. The man had excellent contacts inside the New Orleans PD. Perrone learned that the police had failed to apprehend the werewolf. However, there had been no killings so far tonight. Perrone thanked the man, asked him to pursue his investigations, and promised to remain in touch.

The remainder of the journey passed in relative silence. By the time they got back to the old house on Mobile Bay, Mirabelle was asleep and Perrone was well on his way. He woke her up after the car was secure in the attached garage. She cleaned his wounds again, administered a dose of penicillin and discarded the ruined garments.

Perrone dragged himself up to his bedroom, got between the covers, and fell rapidly into a dreamless sleep.

Mirabelle sat at the kitchen table and drank half a bottle of wine. Then she punched the icebox, kicked a small wastebasket hard enough to dent it, and went on up to bed. Her slumber was fitful and riddled with brief but intense nightmares.

CHAPTER TWELVE
UNDER THE WIRES

Several miles to the north, in his comfortable old house, Hector Sams was aroused from his slumber by the ringing of his bedside telephone.

"Hullo," he mumbled into the receiver. "D'you have any idea what time it is?"

Sams was well into middle age, but had a remarkably unlined face, a powerful physique, and black hair that had not yet begun to turn grey.

"Not really," said the caller.

"Who is this?" Sams asked.

"Somebody who has your best interests at heart. That is to say, someone who truly has it in for the Carters. I want to see them crushed just like you do. Does it matter who actually does it, or who uses who for his own ends, so long as those ends are achieved?"

"Okay," Sams said. "Keep talking."

"I know you're out to destroy the Carter family's power. I applaud you, but you have bitten off more than you can chew. I'm calling to offer you another set of teeth; very sharp ones. I've been receiving reports from a source I consider reliable. The Carters have hired someone insane and lethal. The only way to counter that is with someone even *more* insane and lethal. Your opening gambit was clumsy, and probably would have failed even if it had succeeded. You can't deal with these people in that fashion. I'm something of a social Darwinist, but I believe in fair play. If your opponents have artificially augmented their own innate fitness, they should expect to be dealt with in kind."

"I don't know who the hell you are," Sams said sternly, "but I..."

He was interrupted by what sounded like a scream, coming from outdoors. "Hang on a moment," he said, laying the receiver down and getting out of bed. He went to the window, pulled the drapes aside, and peered out.

There, on his front lawn, under his bedroom window was a scene from a nightmare. Septimus Jones, a bodyguard Sams had recently hired lay supine on the grass in a rigid, unnatural pose. Standing over him was a man wearing a white smock and some sort of peculiar headgear. This individual was twisting a long metal rod which he had apparently inserted into Jones' stomach. Blood trickled out around the insertion point. The bodyguard's shirt had been removed and it lay on the ground next to him.

The man in the smock reached behind him and flipped a switch on a queer-looking apparatus he had strapped to his back. It consisted of two cylindrical tanks and what appeared to be a small motor. The switch activated the motor, which began chugging away; Sams could hear it from where he was. It was then that he noticed a length of hose running from the tanks to the metal rod embedded in Jones' body.

That would have been horror enough, but there was more to come. The man in the smock knelt down, pulled a long, flat-bladed knife from his belt, and made two long incisions, one on each side of Jones' chest. Blood bubbled and spurted from the cuts, as though it had been under intense pressure and was now finding release.

Sams forced himself to close his eyes. Panic was mounting in him, and he struggled to maintain control.

He picked up the receiver and said, "I have a... ah, situation going on here, and I need to..."

"What's going on?" the caller asked. "Tell me."

Sams went back to the window, carrying the phone with him. Steeling himself, he looked down. The man in the smock was still there, still kneeling beside Jones' body. He wasn't doing anything now; just watching Jones bleed.

"There's someone outside my house," he said into the phone. "He has killed my bodyguard, I think."

"Be calm, Sams. Tell me what you're seeing."

Sams described the scene as best he could. While he was talking, the man in the smock stood up and removed the metal rod from Jones' body. Then he turned his head and looked up. The man's face was covered by a white mask that looked like a poorly-sculpted and unpainted Mardi Gras false face.

"Well," said the caller, "it seems I have uncanny timing, doesn't it?"

"Oh, God," said Sams. "He's looking right at me. He's going to kill me."

"Be calm," the caller repeated. "I don't think this is an attempt on your life. Not this time. Someone is giving you a message. I think we both know who that is. You've made yourself some powerful enemies."

The masked man on the lawn nodded his head, then turned and began walking toward the street. Soon, he vanished into the gloom.

"Shit..." Sams said. "They're... they're going to kill me."

"Yes, they are, eventually. What did you expect?"

"What should I do?"

"Right now, call the police," said the mysterious advisor. "Don't try to hide anything. If it came out that you had, you'd be up a creek. Tell them everything that happened, with the exception of this conversation. Then call the telephone number I'm about to give you. The individual who answers may not strike you as the most rational person you've ever spoken to. Don't worry about that; it will work to your advantage. Just say, 'Alpha is omega,' and that you know everything. Tell this party to come to Mobile and meet you. You will have at your disposal a force that can counter the one your enemies are bringing to bear against you. Get a pen, and I'll give you the number."

Sams got pen and paper from his night table jotted down a New Orleans number.

"Very good," said the caller. "I have just given you a valuable means of defense and offense. I hope you will use it wisely. Goodbye, Hector Sams, and good luck."

The caller hung up. Sams did the same, then lifted the receiver again and called the police. When the dispatcher answered, he identified himself and said that he had just witnessed a murder in front of his house. He gave his address, and offered no further details.

As he waited for the police, Sams sat in his chair and contemplated recent developments. This mystery caller was an enigma, but he might just be a godsend. Sams wasn't just being quixotic, going up against the Carter man in the election; he had some powerful forces at his disposal. But he didn't want to squander them. If things were going to get ugly, and if this mystery man could help him bring down the Carters, he could conserve his other resources for what was to come. And if things got really dire, he always had his ace in the hole, the one who had first emboldened him to take the steps he had taken. But he didn't want to use that resource too freely, either.

He picked up the phone and dialed the operator.

"Yes, I'd like to place a long-distance call to New Orleans..."

Mirabelle did not come out of her room the next morning, and Perrone thought it best to leave her alone.

His wounds weren't as bad as he had feared. When he removed the old dressings, he saw that the cuts had already started to knit back together. He decided they must have seemed worse than they actually were, in the confusion and alarm.

He called the private detective again, and was gratified to learn that the werewolf had not claimed any victims in New Orleans last night. And he had until the next full moon to make preparations.

"Something's going on," said Louis Rickert. "I'm hearing crazy stories. It seems like the Carters are gearing up for a war, but nobody knows who with. It's been brewing for a while, I gather.

The Phantom and his new agent were meeting in Rickert's apartment for one of their regularly-scheduled information exchanges.

"I'd like to talk to Shorty Red," said the masked man.

"Well, you can't," Rickert said, too quickly. "He's in the hospital under intensive care, and it looks like he'll be there for a while. Gosh, you really beat the hell out of him! Anyhow, he probably doesn't even remember what happened. I bet he got anesthesia."

"I hope he did, but I think you mean *amnesia*. At any rate, I'm not interested in that at the moment. I'd like to know about his association with the Carters."

"He's not gonna tell you about it, even if he remembers it. Which he probably won't. Someone gets beaten that bad, they forget everything that ever happened to them, don't they? Isn't that what happens?"

"I really couldn't say," the Bay Phantom replied. "Do you have anything else for me?"

"Oh, yeah! Damn, I almost forgot," said Rickert. "There was a weird killing last night. The kind you told me to keep an eye out for. It happened on Hector Sams' property."

Mirabelle finally emerged from her bedroom late in the afternoon. She still looked tired, but she was cheerful. Perrone wondered how hard she was forcing herself.

He relayed to her the information Louis Rickert had given him.

"Well," she said after he finished, "if it ain't one goddamn thing it's another."

"Yes. While we were chasing the werewolf in New Orleans, it seems my friend the Black Embalmer was at work here. I should have put more effort into tracking him down."

"How do you know it was the Embalmer?" Mirabelle asked. "You said Rickert didn't have any details."

"He said it was a 'weird death.' The Embalmer was present at the attempted murder of one mayoral candidate, but the nature of his involvement was unclear. I saw him kill a man, and what he did was unequivocally *weird*. And now someone in the employ of the other candidate has been killed in an unconventional way. There *must* be a connection."

"Maybe," said Mirabelle, "but you're still *assuming*. You know better than that, you've been reading Conan Doyle your whole life. As Sherlock Holmes said, 'When you *assume*, you make an *ass* of *u* and *me*.' And if you're gonna..."

"Sherlock Holmes never said any such..."

"... *and if you're gonna* do this kind of stuff, you have to be thorough and logical. This is not some Saturday afternoon ladies' garden club mystery hour or something, and it isn't a rain of frogs. This is life and death!"

Perrone sighed. "You're right, of course," he said. "I really need a contact on the police force."

"Maybe some cop in trouble will come to you, like Gandhi said."

"Perhaps," he said. "But, in the meantime, I shall have to get my information the old fashioned way."

"And what is that?"

"Breaking and entering, Mirabelle. What else?"

CHAPTER THIRTEEN
THE PHANTOM WHO CAME INTO THE COLD ROOM

This has got to be the low point of my career, thought Detective Tom Dart. I'm about to snap. Something has to give.

He snatched a perfectly good fountain pen from the desk in front of him and broke it in half, throwing the pieces savagely onto the floor.

"Sorry old man," he said. "But it was you or me."

Dart was a solidly-built six-footer with sandy hair and brown eyes. At twenty-three, he was one of the youngest detectives on the force.

He looked angrily at the clock on the wall. *One oh-goddamn-clock in the morning.* He'd been here for two hours that had seemed like a week, and he still had six more hours to go on this lousy goddamn shift in this lousy goddamn morgue.

He was being punished, and he knew why. *When in the history of the world has a police detective been punished by his superiors for* not *taking a bribe?* It was a hell of a thing. Most of Dart's comrades on the force, and all of his superiors, received a steady stream of graft from various shady persons or organizations; the ones who preferred buying the law to obeying it.

One simply did not, under any circumstances, refuse anything from or to anybody named Carter.

Everybody on the force knew the Carters were dirty, and all of them, to a man, turned a collective blind eye to anything the family did.

To be perfectly honest, Dart didn't care. Organized crime was a fact of life everywhere, and he certainly didn't mind if someone was defending his right to get blotto when he felt like it. Prohibition was for the birds, more damn trouble than it was worth. He accepted his monthly stipend from one of the family's lawyers and concentrated on arresting such scum as did not live behind an impenetrable wall of graft. He had no beef with the Carters, and they had never had reason to take the slightest notice of him.

That's how it had been, at any rate, for several years. But then one of them decided to make it personal.

Penelope "Penny" Carter was the one whose ire Dart had aroused. The bribe she had offered was business as usual, a rather tidy sum for "losing" a certain fingerprint card at headquarters and "finding" another one to replace it. But there was also a strong implication that something else was being offered, and Dart didn't want any part of that. So he had just turned down the deal, bribe and all. He was sure she could find someone else to switch the card for her, and as far as the other thing was concerned, she was hardly desperate for contenders.

Even if Dart didn't take his marriage vows seriously, which he did, and even if he didn't love his wife, which he also did, he wouldn't give that harpy a tumble. That would be a good way to get into every kind of trouble known to man.

Undaunted, Penny had made another pitch, a much stronger and more direct one, at the Brickell rally in Bienville Square. He had been forced to tell her point-blank that he wasn't interested and never would be. She had not taken it well.

On top of all that, the Carters seemed to be getting bolder and more reckless in general. Dart was sure they were becoming involved in things he just couldn't stomach, but there wasn't anything he could do about it. It was a nasty business. Times were changing, and not for the better. Tom Dart was just one man; he had no power and no capacity for foolhardy heroics.

And now he had been "loaned" to the sheriff's department to guard the county morgue from 11 p.m. until 7 a.m. every night, until further notice.

Though nobody would own up to it, of course, this ridiculous assignment was the result of his unwillingness to dance to Penny's tune. She had sent him a nasty note to make sure he understood the power she could exercise over him. He was sure there was worse to come, unless he could find a way out.

So far, he had come up with exactly nothing. He stood up, stretched, and looked at the clock again. The lousy goddamn thing was mocking him, he was sure. It hadn't moved five minutes in the past hour. He decided to go ahead and make his rounds early.

He secured the little office and walked down the short hallway to the stairs. He would descend to the bottom story and check out the cold room first.

It was dark down there, and chilly. There was a subtle but unsettling chemical smell that Dart didn't care for at all; it seemed to work itself into his sinuses and stay there, long after he had left the place. One wall was taken up with refrigerated drawers, and the cold air leaked out through small gaps between the drawers and the wall. Everyone who worked here had gone home hours ago.

One of the drawers close to the rear wall had been pulled all the way out, and the sheet covering the corpse had been removed. A dark figure crouched over the chalk-white cadaver. Dart couldn't tell what the hell was going on here, but he didn't care for it. The individual fiddling with the dead man was wearing a dark suit and hat and, of all things, a long, black cape!

"What the hell is this?" Dart demanded, drawing his revolver.

"Oh, my," said the black-clad stranger, turning to face Dart. The guy was wearing a black mask, too. Terrific.

"I'm really eager to hear you explain this," Dart said.

"You're off your schedule," the masked man said sharply. "I should have had at least forty uninterrupted minutes in here."

"Well, I sure do beg your goddamn pardon," Dart replied. "Do I need to shoot you or what? How come you're screwing around in the morgue in the middle of the night? You're not one of those birds that have romantic feelings toward stiffs, are you?"

"If you wouldn't mind asking a question and then waiting for an answer," said the apparition, "this would go a lot more smoothly."

"Okay. Start with the first one, then. Who the hell are you?"

"I'm the Bay Phantom," said the masked man with a goofy little bow. "Feel free to introduce yourself, if you like."

"Oh yeah," Dart said. "You're the guy that knocked down Doctor Piranha three years ago! I was just a beat cop then. Where have you been? Everybody figured you were dead."

"I don't know why. That's quite a conclusion to jump to. I've been traveling and working to prepare myself to continue my career as a crime fighter."

"We've got police for that," Dart said. "There's this whole thing called the law, you know. Society is basically set up around it. It really doesn't allow for independent contractors, especially not ones that wear masks, and *most* especially not ones that break into places they aren't supposed to be in the middle of the night. Are you with me so far?"

"If the police could be relied on to do their jobs in the manner prescribed by the law," said the masked man, somewhat archly, "I wouldn't feel compelled to do it this way."

Tom Dart did not reply. He leaned back against the metal desk, chewing his gum and thinking, his pistol still pointed at the Bay Phantom's chest. The silence continued for almost two minutes. Then Dart's face relaxed, he nodded once, stood up straight, and holstered his weapon.

"Okay," he said. "I'm gonna take one hell of a chance here that you're on the level. Some people are saying you were behind that massacre in Bienville Square, but I haven't seen anything at all that ties you to it. I have my own ideas about that. And it just so happens that I agree with you about most of the cops in this town. People are getting away with murder, and I mean that literally. I'm not brave enough to make waves myself, because I know what'll happen if I do, and I got a wife and kid at home. *But...* If I can help you a little without getting any mud on my own britches... *maybe* we can do business, Mister Phantom. But if you're screwing with me, I promise I will track you down and blow your head off."

"That's fine," said the masked man. "Actually, I'm a bit surprised you're willing to go that far."

"Well, you may not remember it, but three years ago, down on Royal Street, when all those bombs started going off, you shoved me out from under a falling chunk of masonry. I was still wearing the blue uniform then. You yelled at me to get my stupid ass out of the way, and I'm sure that was the same voice I'm hearing making smart remarks at me now."

The Phantom chuckled. "As a matter of fact, I do remember you, and I'm quite certain I didn't say *that*. Most people clean up the language when they paraphrase; you have an interesting slant on it. You struck me as something of a lackwit, for which I apologize. It was something about the expression on your face, but now that I reflect on the events of that day, it's quite understandable. You were witnessing a disaster of unprecedented proportions in your experience."

"That's true, and I've been through four hurricanes," said Dart. "They say that day would have been a whole lot worse if not for you."

"That may be true."

"You saved my life. I don't forget things like that. Thank you."

"You're quite welcome," said the Bay Phantom.

"So, what are you doing here?"

"I wanted to have a look at this body. There was no information about this killing in the newspaper. I learned of it, and, considering who this man was employed by, I wanted to see if certain suspicions of mine were correct. They are."

"How do you mean?"

"This body has been embalmed, after a fashion," said the Phantom, which did not answer Dart's question. "And I believe it was done, or at least commenced, while the poor man was still alive."

"What?"

"This man was still alive when a large metal tube was inserted into his heart, and he was pumped full of formaldehyde," the Phantom said softly. "The embalming fluid forced the blood out of his system through these cuts on his sides."

Dart, looking a little green, sat down on the desk and unwrapped a stick of gum.

"Jesus, man," he said when he felt able to speak. He shoved the gum into his mouth and started chewing furiously. "That is really, really disturbing."

"This isn't the first time this has happened," the Phantom remarked. "Right here in Mobile."

"My God! What kind of a monster have we got running loose in this city?"

"An incredibly dangerous one, who will stop at nothing," said the Phantom. "This poor man here, Septimus Jones, works... *worked*, I mean... for Hector Sams, correct?"

"Yes," said Dart. "The mayoral candidate."

The Phantom nodded. "This murder *could* be unrelated to the upcoming election, but I doubt it, and I can tell by the look on your face that you do too. But we must consider carefully. The Carters are a lot dirtier than I used to think they were, but are they *this* dirty?"

Dart smiled ruefully. "You may not be aware that I'm on the outs with the Carters," he said. "One of them anyhow; maybe the most dangerous one of all. And so, of course, I'm on the outs with the force as well. That's why I'm here tonight and every night for the foreseeable future."

"You're referring to Penny Carter, I take it?"

Dart nodded.

"We need to get you off that hook somehow," said the Phantom, "before things get any worse. I believe I can help with that."

"How?" Dart asked incredulously. "What are you going to do? Kill her?"

"Certainly not!" the Phantom snapped indignantly. "I do not employ murder as a problem-solving tool. I have an idea, but it must remain my secret, I'm afraid. Give me a few days and let's see what develops. But for right now, let me tell you about an interesting fellow I met the other day. He called himself the Black Embalmer..."

CHAPTER FOURTEEN
STRIFE

"Well, it's finally happened," Mirabelle said, shaking her head sadly. "I ought to have seen it coming. You have slipped completely beyond the bounds of sanity. A date with Penny Carter? I could get a peace bond against you, and have you taken in for psychiatric observation, you know."

"Mirabelle, please," said Joe Perrone. "This isn't a whim. I'm doing it for a very good reason. It is, in fact, quite urgent."

"I'm sure it is. Look, if you're that lonely, there are other avenues you could explore. There are plenty of nice girls out there, Mister Perrone. Messing with that Penny Carter is like sticking your..."

"*Mirabelle!*"

"... head into a bear trap. No, make that a meat grinder."

Perrone made a face.

"I have no intention of sticking anything anywhere," he said. "This matter relates to the murder of a man named Septimus Jones, in a roundabout way. I'm doing it as a favor to a new ally of mine, so that he can be free to give me the kind of help I need. I have already called her and made the date."

"Holy shit," Mirabelle said.

"It can serve more than one purpose," Perrone continued. "Penny is a Carter, and it looks as though the Carters are involved in all manner of questionable activities. What better way to gather information than to keep company with one of them?"

"I guess," Mirabelle said sourly. "Seems to me there's a third purpose, too. When was the last time you got your ashes hauled, anyhow? Have you *ever*?"

"Mirabelle, please don't be disgusting."

"I'm not the one proposing to go out with that harridan. I'll make sure I have plenty of penicillin on hand, in case your 'inquiries' run a little too deep."

Perrone shook his head. "That kind of talk isn't very ladylike," he said primly.

"Good thing I'm not a lady, then. I'm just a glorified house nigger."

"Mirabelle, for the love of God!"

She glared at him for a few seconds, then her expression softened. "I'm sorry," she said. "That wasn't fair."

Perrone was silent for a few moments, then he said, "This line of conversation brings up something that's been on my mind. I think we might as well get it out in the open right now. I'm going to ask you a straight question, and I want a straight answer."

"You know how I am," she said.

Perrone nodded. "Does it bother you that I wear a mask when I do these things I do?"

Mirabelle didn't hesitate. "As a matter of fact, it does. The only time I've ever seen anybody wearing masks around here, outside of the Mardi Gras, they were white ones. With those pointy hoods. You know the kind I mean."

He nodded again. "You must know I'm not like them."

"Intellectually, I do. But the viscera is a different matter. Part of me just cannot fathom why a good man has to put on a mask and a funny outfit to do good things."

"Would you prefer I didn't?"

"I'm not gonna say that, because you're so damn contrary, you might just stop doing it to prove some kind of a point, and *that* might not be good. I know you believe in it."

"You're not going to leave?" He said it in a timid way, as though he were afraid she might.

"No," she said unconvincingly. "Where the hell am I gonna go? Princeton? Harvard? Those Ivy League schools are falling all over themselves trying to sign up little pickaninnies from Alabama."

The fact of the matter was, she had been giving serious thought to leaving. She had no idea where she would go, but she didn't think she could take much more of this business. She hated to leave Perrone on his own, but she might have to. For the sake of her own sanity, she might have to go far, far away from here.

"Mirabelle, I wish you wouldn't say things like that," said Perrone. To Mirabelle, at this moment, it sounded condescending.

"Why do you keep telling me what I ought to do and say and think?" she snapped.

"I don't! I'm just offering you advice. As your friend..."

"You're *not* my friend!" she exclaimed, cutting him off. "Don't you get it? I *work* for you! We're not goddamn friends!" Her eyes were wild and tears ran down her cheeks. "We don't live in the same world! Quit trying to pretend we do!"

With that, she whirled around and dashed out of the room, leaving a stunned Joe Perrone sitting in his chair, wondering if he should run after her. He decided it would only make things worse. He had to help Mirabelle, but she was struggling with things he could not understand.

He thought for a long time. Then he picked up the telephone and dialed "0."

"Yes," he said, when the operator answered, "I need to place an international call..."

CHAPTER FIFTEEN
WHAT'S INSIDE A GIRL?

Mirabelle kept mostly to herself for the next few days, while Perrone busied himself working on his crime chart, talking with Louis Rickert, and prowling around at night, stopping random petty crimes.

One afternoon, he received a call from Lee Rosenberg, the New Orleans private detective he had hired to investigate the werewolf.

The detective gave him a most interesting report. Rosenberg had plotted all of the Werewolf sightings on a map of New Orleans, and concentrated his inquiries on a neighborhood that lay at the center of the activity. He had learned of a peculiar young man who had lived in a small house there for at least ten years. None of his neighbors knew his name. Many of them had gone for more than a year without seeing him, but there was always a light on in a room at the rear of the house. That is to say, there *had* been, for many years, until quite recently.

"How recently?" Perrone asked.

"Two days after your incident in the French Quarter."

"Interesting. Continue."

Rosenberg had gained entry to the house and found almost nothing there. The living room contained a sofa and a chair. The kitchen looked as though it had never been used. Of the two bedrooms upstairs, one was completely devoid of furniture, while the other contained nothing but an old mattress. A check with the power company revealed that the account had been opened by a "John Smith," who had always paid his bills, eleven years' worth of them, on time. Until quite recently. The current bill had been overdue for almost a week.

"There is nothing to indicate that this 'Smith' has been dressing up like a werewolf and killing people," Rosenberg admitted, "but he is a queer duck. Queer enough to stand out in a city full of queer ducks. He lived in the middle of the killings, and seems to have disappeared after the last one."

"I agree that it is suspicious. Keep at it, Lee. And be careful. I don't want you getting yourself killed over this."

"Neither do I. Don't worry, there isn't much you could throw at me that I couldn't handle."

Perrone wished he had the same kind of self-confidence Rosenberg had. He did not fear criminals, Black Embalmers, or werewolves. But he had a mission tonight that filled him with dread, and he was not sure of himself at all.

Tonight, he had a date with Penny Carter.

Joe Perrone had never been what you would call a ladies' man. During his adolescence, he had been too preoccupied with his mission to take much notice of girls. In fact, this preoccupation had continued until the present day. When hormonal demands became too insistent, they were addressed in an efficient, businesslike manner, and not permitted to interfere with the work. Three or four very awkward dates when he was in college constituted the entirety of Perrone's personal experience with human females.

He checked his appearance in the rear-view mirror. After dealing with a stray wisp of hair that had fallen untidily over his forehead, he judged himself presentable. Steeling himself, he picked up a bouquet of flowers from the passenger seat, got out of the car, and strode boldly toward the unknown.

He rapped on the door. Cold dread blossomed in his stomach and chest as he listened to the clicking of a pair of high-heeled shoes on a hardwood floor, coming closer and closer. He thought of Poe's *The Telltale Heart*. The door opened, and there she was.

"Well," she said. "Here you really are, in the flesh! Come on in and have a seat."

He followed her down a short hallway to a lavishly-appointed living room. She told him to sit on the sofa. To his relief, she sat down in a chair.

"I must say, I was a bit surprised when you called," she said. "You didn't seem all that interested when I gave you my card."

"I was just, you know, distracted. By everything that had happened. I suppose I was in a state of mild shock. How else could I have failed to notice that you... I mean, it's quite obvious that you're a... Well, you have quite a pleasing personality, and..."

"I've got a swell pair of tits," she said in a frightfully offhand manner. "A pretty sweet ass, too, so I'm told."

Perrone started coughing. Penny moved to the sofa, sitting down perilously close to him and slapping him on the back.

"You okay, Joey?"

"Oh, yes, just fine. I must have... You know, I've got this thing where I..." He coughed a few more times, then took his handkerchief out of his pocket and wiped his lips.

"Oh, by the way, Miss Carter," he said, desperate to change the subject, and seeing an opportunity to kill two birds with one stone, "do you happen to know that young detective, Tom Dart? I thought I saw you speaking with him in Bienville Square that day."

"Kind of," she said, a chill creeping into her voice. "Are you jealous?"

He started to deny it, but saw how such a perception on Penny's part might work to his advantage.

"Oh, of course not," he said as unconvincingly as he could manage. "Why should I be? He's a fine fellow. I knew him slightly in college, you see. Hard working, but not very ambitious. I spoke with him the other day and he told me he's been reassigned to the county morgue as a sort of night watchman."

"And how does he like that?" Penny asked in a neutral tone. Her eyes were hard, but the corners of her mouth turned up slightly in a rather reptilian approximation of a smile.

"Oh, he's overjoyed! He said it's like being on vacation. As I say, he's a hard worker, but only when someone is putting work in front of him. In this new position, he has very few duties to speak of. He seems to be having the time of his life."

"Really? That's interesting." Penny's little smile had turned into a straight line.

"Dear me, yes. He used to get fearfully exhausted, he said, but now he feels well-rested. He's able to spend a lot more time with his wife and child. He told me he's been praying they don't move him back to the detective bureau."

"Is that a fact?" The straight line started curling downward at the ends.

"It is."

"Well, well," said Penny. "Y'know what, Joe? I don't want to talk about this Tom Fart. He's a bit of a wet rag, it sounds like. I'd rather talk about *you*."

"Oh, there's hardly anything to talk about, I'm afraid."

"Bullshit, Joey. There's more to you than you're willing to own up to. I assure you, I *will* get to the bottom of it. But not right now. Right now, since you can't think of anything you'd like to do this evening, let me tell you what I'd like to do."

"Certainly! I'm up for anything. Dinner, or a movie, or a ride in the park, or..."

Penny shook her head. "I don't want to do any of those things."

"What do you want to do?"

She told him.

He started coughing again. A feeling of panic rose from deep within him. Something else was rising, too. When he realized this, he was appalled.

Penny, giggling and shaking her head, jumped up and disappeared into the kitchen, returning with a glass of water. She handed it to Perrone and encouraged him to take a swallow.

The cough was almost under control, and he accepted the glass gratefully, his mouth had gone quite dry, swiftly gulping down half of its contents.

"Well, y-you see," he stammered, "I have a... It's sort of... That is, I injured myself when I was in college, you see, playing... Ah, football, I think. Something very rough and tumble, anyhow. I'm afraid I pulled a... That is to say, I sustained an, uh..."

Penny laughed. "Your words say eunuch, but I spy a telltale bulge that says different. It's very impressive, I must say and I'm something of a connoisseur."

He looked at his watch. "Oh my goodness," he said, "I just remembered, there's a matter that I simply must take care of! I'm so sorry, but I..."

"No," Penny said, in a voice that contained both fire and ice. "There's no way you're getting out of this, Joey."

He swallowed hard and resigned himself to the inevitable.

Just close your eyes, he told himself, *and think of Mobile.*

Six hours later, Perrone, looking a bit dazed, drifted out to his car and drove away. Ten minutes after that, there was a knock on Penny Carter's

"Are you jealous?"

back door. She opened it and invited her caller into the kitchen. They sat down together at the small table.

"I hope you had your fun," said the Black Embalmer. "Because we have things to discuss. As far as the situation in Chicago is concerned, you can forget about Eliot Ness and his boys. They'll never nab Alphonse on any Volstead Act crap. But I know of a fellow in the Bureau of Internal Revenue who just needs a word or two in his ear..."

CHAPTER SIXTEEN
A DISTINGUISHED VISITOR

The following day, as Perrone and Mirabelle went over the Bay Phantom's chart of the criminal underworld; she pressed him for the details of his date with Penny Carter. He refused to divulge any. Mirabelle pressed harder and Perrone became more intractable. He was pleased, though, that she seemed to be in better spirits.

"Something happened," she said, sounding more amused than anything. "You have kind of a glow about you."

"Nothing happened, Mirabelle."

The standoff continued for the better part of an hour, until it was interrupted by the front doorbell.

"I'll get it," Mirabelle said. "You sit right there and work on your memory."

Mirabelle went to the door and opened it. Standing there was a man she was sure she had never seen before, though he looked very familiar.

"Can I help you?" she asked politely.

"You already have," replied the man, in English, with a thick accent. German or Austrian, Mirabelle thought. "Time and time again. I am here to return the favor."

He looked to be in his seventies, pale and somewhat stooped, dressed in a neat tweed suit that must have been uncomfortable in the near-tropical heat. He was mostly bald, with a neatly-trimmed beard and moustache that contained more white than grey, and he peered at her through the circular lenses of a pair of tortoiseshell spectacles. When Mirabelle processed all of this, the man started to look quite familiar.

Oh my God, she thought, *this can't possibly be...*

"And now," he continued, "I am here to see if I can help you. Your last few letters were… shall we say a little *troubling*. I apologize for materializing here without any warning, but I know you would rather suffer in silence than ask for help, so I have taken the choice out of your hands. I am here, and you shall have my help. Do you plan on inviting me in?"

"Of course," Mirabelle said, embarrassed. "I'm sorry, it's just that I'm a little stunned. Come right in."

Mirabelle closed the door and stood in the foyer with her visitor. Both of them were smiling broadly.

"It is very nice to see you in person at last," he said.

She stepped forward and embraced him. He put his arms around her shoulders and gave her an avuncular squeeze.

Perrone had stepped from his study into the hallway. "Is everything all right, Mirabelle?" he asked.

"Indeed it is," she replied. "I have a very special visitor here I'd like you to meet. One of my dearest epistolary friends."

Perrone, looking a little bemused, walked to the foyer and shook hands with the man.

"Joseph Perrone," Mirabelle said with humorous formality, "allow me to present Doctor Sigmund Freud!"

Twenty minutes later, the three were seated in the large parlor, sipping tea. Freud mentioned, in response to a question from Mirabelle, that he was staying at a hotel in Mobile and had come to Tull House in a taxi.

"Mister Perrone," said Freud, "I apologize for invading your home, but I was most concerned about Miss Darcy, and felt that it was the proper course to take."

"I understand perfectly, sir," Perrone said wryly. "Sometimes Mirabelle has to be coerced or tricked into looking after herself properly."

"I know that. She is as stubborn as she is brilliant. I imagine the two go hand-in-hand."

"I'm sitting right here," she reminded them.

"I'm sorry, my dear," said Freud. "Would you prefer to discuss these matters privately?"

She shook her head. "No, not right now. You can say anything in front of Mister Perrone that you can say to me."

"Very well. I have been concerned because, while everything I know about you precludes the notion that you are paranoid or delusional, your most recent letters to me have contained some disturbing elements. You have hinted at strange mysteries taking place around you, and you have also made reference to masked men, ghosts and other things.

"Aside from that, you have simply not been yourself. Your letters to me have been less informative, but more frequent. I get the impression that you are withholding things from me that you would like to discuss, but dare not. You also seem preoccupied with thoughts of violence and death. All of these things are so unlike the Mirabelle Darcy I have come to know that I grew alarmed. I knew you would not ask for help, and would likely refuse it if it were offered. Therefore, I decided to present you with a *fait accompli* in the form of myself at your doorstep."

"You came all the way here for me?" Mirabelle asked.

Freud nodded sharply. "Of course. I owe you a great deal for your contributions to my work. You have refused numerous times to share the credit publicly, and I have always reluctantly agreed to that. Coming here was the very least I could do, Mirabelle."

"I appreciate it," she said, "and it's wonderful to see you, but… I think you may have misinterpreted some things. I just meant…"

"Mirabelle," Perrone interrupted. "I know you've been having difficulties lately, though they are not the ones Doctor Freud fears. I'm afraid I'm to blame for much of it, and I have no idea how to help you. Perhaps the doctor can."

Mirabelle said nothing. She just looked at Perrone. He met her gaze silently for half a minute. A question hung between them.

Perrone took a deep breath.

"We have now arrived at a certain point," he said gravely. "If Doctor Freud is to help you, you must have no secrets from him. The choice is yours, Mirabelle. I know Doctor Freud by reputation, and I know that you respect and admire him. I have no qualms about revealing everything."

"Are you sure?" she asked.

"Absolutely. Your well-being is more important than my little intrigues. If you believe the doctor can be trusted, then so do I."

"Okay." She turned to Freud. "We have a story to tell you, Doctor. Once you've heard it, you may be tempted to have the both of us committed, whether you believe any of it or not."

CHAPTER SEVENTEEN
NIGHT OF THE BEAST

"**M**ayor Brickell is really coming down on you, Mister Perrone" Mirabelle said, shaking a newspaper in her employer's direction.

Several days had passed since Freud's arrival. The doctor had been very intrigued by the story of the Bay Phantom, and did not seem to disapprove. He and Mirabelle had spent quite a bit of time together while Perrone pursued his investigations.

Perrone had also pursued his relationship with Penny Carter. He had learned nothing of the Carter family's unseen activities, but he had learned other things. *Lots* of other things. He was a little alarmed at how much he had begun to enjoy the duties he was required to perform. It seemed he had an unexpected knack for it.

"Not *you* you, but Bay Phantom you," Mirabelle continued. "He says he's certain you were behind the Hot Dog Massacre and that he may soon be in a position to offer proof. That lying little shit!"

Perrone was too pleased to see Mirabelle in good spirits to admonish her for her language. Her mood had improved markedly since the doctor had shown up. The three of them were sitting together in the living room, listening to the radio and chatting.

"I find it interesting," Freud said, "that whoever engineered this crime used the hot dog as his symbol."

"You would," said Mirabelle.

"It probably had to do with the fact that the hot dog wagons were just the right size and shape to conceal the machine guns," Perrone offered. "I don't think it's necessary to look for a lot of symbolism there."

"I was joking," Freud said. "I can't make a wisecrack now and then?"

Mirabelle laughed, but Perrone remained grim and thoughtful.

"I'd like to know where Brickell's getting all this," he said. "If he has any proof, it's fabricated. If he doesn't, I'd like to know why he is so vehement on the subject. I'm going to have a talk with him; a private talk."

"Uh-huh," said Mirabelle. "You mean the kind of private where you're wearing a mask and it's the middle of the night and you've broken into someplace where you aren't supposed to be. Like Simon Brickell's house."

"Exactly," Perrone said, nodding. "You're getting the hang of this, Mirabelle!"

"*Hang* is right. That's what they're gonna do to you one day, and maybe me, too, for helping you."

"You're going to do a crime?" Freud asked, intrigued.

"Well, yes," said Perrone, "I suppose I am. And I may as well do it tonight."

The old Church Street Graveyard could be a creepy place after midnight. Rickey Harvard didn't like to admit that the place scared him a little, and always had, even during the day. He had avoided it ever since he was a child. Tonight, however, things were different.

Rickey had discovered a cache of bootleg bourbon in his father's workshop, and had helped himself to a generous quantity of it. He'd been tipsy before, on several occasions, but never as flat-out pickled as he was tonight. The alcohol had emboldened him. Tonight, he would have revenge on the old cemetery.

Rickey went to the wrought-iron gate and found it locked. A small sign told him the graveyard was off-limits after dark. Laughing, he moved away from the gate and found a spot on the low wall that had a couple of handholds to help him climb over.

And here he was, on a dark, moonless night, standing in the middle of his persistent nightmare. He was much too drunk to feel fearful, and he wondered why this place had ever bothered him at all. This was just a bunch of old stones, stained and weathered, leaning to one side or the other, like drunks who couldn't stand up straight.

He walked over to one of the stones. It was square and flat, a foot or so across and no more than an inch thick. He kicked it and saw that it gave a little bit. Placing his hands flat against it, he pushed as hard as he could, until the moldy old monument cracked near the bottom and toppled over.

Take that, you asshole, Rickey thought. *I ain't a bit scared of you!* He looked around for his next victim. Emboldened by his easy victory, he figured he ought to pick on someone more his own size this time. He selected a seven-foot obelisk he spotted near the back wall. It had an insolent look about it, like it was daring him to try something. *Here I come, wise guy!*

As he moved toward his quarry he heard a sound, a steady humming, overlaid with irregularly-spaced clicks. He stopped to listen. It seemed to be getting louder. He looked around for its source and saw nothing. He took another couple of steps, then stopped again. The noise *was* getting louder, and what's more, he was sure it was coming from underneath the ground. He stood quietly, holding his breath.

The noise stopped.

Rickey felt a bit of relief. *It wasn't anything*, he told himself. *Probably a truck going by on the street.* He was pretty well convinced of this, when he heard a different noise, much louder and closer. This was a sort of grinding, accompanied by a faint creaking. He turned his head in the direction from which it seemed to be coming.

A large, flat grave marker seven feet from where he stood was moving. One side of it was slowly rising; *it was opening up like a trapdoor*! Rickey stood and stared at it, unable to move or look away. The marble slab stopped when it had reached an angle of ninety degrees relative to the ground. A thin, white mist rose from the rectangular opening in the ground. In the midst of this Rickey saw a dark figure. It, too, was rising from the aperture. The mist blew away in the slight breeze, but the figure remained. It looked like a man wearing a long, black cloak and a black, wide-brimmed hat. Its face was completely black, but for a pair of large round eyes that were solid blue, with no whites or pupils to be seen.

He lit out for the wall and scrambled over it, then took off at a dead run for home.

The Bay Phantom pushed the slab back into place. The lock clicked and his secret tunnel was safely concealed. The phony grave marker hid a shaft that dropped down into the earth and met one of the tunnels the Phantom had taken over. From underneath Tull House, he had excavated for a distance of two city blocks until he hit one of the main tunnels used by Doctor Piranha. This was in very good repair, and Perrone had spent some time shoring it up. Running the length of this stretch was a set of light railroad-type tracks. Using these, he traveled to and from the cemetery on one of two small motorized handcars he kept on hand.

Keeping to the shadows, the Phantom traversed the six blocks from the cemetery to Brickell's house, a three-story whitewashed cube with a sizeable extension built out from the rear. The original structure dated back to well before the Civil War. There would surely be ghosts in a place like this, thought the Phantom. The only light in the place came from a window on the third floor, at the rear of the house. This, the Phantom knew, was Simon Brickell's study.

The Phantom tossed a heavy grappling hook up toward the eaves. It lodged itself at the top the brick wall, just below the roof. Tugging at the attached rope to make certain it was secure, he began his ascent. When he reached the window, he peeped through the blinds and saw Brickell seated at his desk, no more than three feet away, poring over what looked like a bank book.

The Phantom dislodged his grappling hook, and, wrapping the rope around it, stowed it in his jacket. In less than a minute, he opened the window and climbed through. Brickell turned around. When he saw the Bay Phantom, his face registered anger first, then astonishment, then terror, all in the space of two seconds.

"You and I should talk," said the weird apparition. "I think you may have some misconceptions about me."

"I have a guard on duty downstairs," Brickell said, his voice quavering. "All I have to do is press a button and he'll be up here on the double."

"If I were here to harm or kill you," said the Phantom, "you would already be harmed or dead. That you are not speaks well of my intentions, I think. I only want to talk."

"About?"

"I have a theory, if you'd care to hear it. I believe the Carters themselves were responsible for the assassination attempt at Bienville Square."

"That's absurd!" Brickell exclaimed. "The Carter family and I... We have a... Well, that is to say, they have always... uh, lent their support to me."

"Oh, I know that. They have purchased for you every election you've run in. You owe them, and you pay that debt on a daily basis. Please, don't bother trying to deny it. I have no power to arrest or indict you, anyhow."

"Well," said Brickell, "I'm not admitting anything, but just suppose you're right. If you believe that, how can you believe they would try to have me killed?"

"There are all sorts of possibilities. Perhaps the Carters have tired of you and want to clear the way for new blood. You may be too Old South to keep pace with a rapidly changing era."

"That's foolish," Brickell scoffed. But he sounded less sure of himself.

"Is it? How about this, then: Since you weren't killed, maybe the Carters intended for you to survive. Maybe the attack was a sham, to make it look as though someone were targeting you and, indirectly, the Carters themselves."

"Why would they do that?" said Brickell. He was sounding a little worried.

"I really don't know. Ponder it and see what you can come up with. I'm sure you know more about them than I do, though you probably don't examine it too closely. You know, even if those gunmen had been instructed not to hit you, it could easily have happened in that melee, with all those bullets flying around."

"Jesus," said Brickell, sounding utterly forlorn. "You may be right. To be honest with you, I have had some serious misgivings of my own. There was a time when they would never have considered such a thing. But now… Ever since the Doctor Piranha fiasco, they've gotten… worse. Coupled with what you've said to me tonight…"

The mayor closed his eyes for a moment and took a deep breath.

"I have received information that I find disturbing," he said, "with regard to the machine guns used in that ghastly attack. I intercepted this information as it was on its way to Chief Peller. Those guns were part of a cache of military weapons that were stolen in 1928. Ten guns were missing. And only seven were accounted for after the atrocity in Bienville Square. The message to Peller indicated that the three remaining guns might be found in a certain warehouse near the docks."

"Let me guess," said the masked man. "The warehouse belongs to Hector Sams."

Brickell nodded. "It was fortuitous that I got my hands on that message before Peller could see it. I do not know exactly where it originated, but I have reason to believe that Caleb Carter himself sent it."

"How did you happen to intercept it?"

The mayor shook his head. "I won't tell you that. I don't want to implicate a party that may be innocent of any wrongdoing. I've been trying to decide what I ought to do with the information. The whole thing goes a lot further than I'm comfortable with. It seems clear that they're trying to implicate Sams in something."

"It is suggestive, indeed," the Phantom said. "I must say it does not come as a surprise. In fact, I was rather expecting something like that to come to light. I imagine someone has planted those guns in that warehouse. And I don't…"

The Phantom was interrupted by a large, dark shape that smashed through the window he had just used, as though it had been hurled by someone outside. Shattered glass and splintered wood cascaded across the room as the dark shape rolled to a stop and rose up on two powerful-looking legs. The invader was covered in fur and had three long, curved claws on each hand.

"Good heavens," said the Bay Phantom. "Whatever are *you* doing *here*?"

"You know this thing?" Brickell said as he backed toward a far corner of the room.

"We've met before, in New Orleans. Stay back, Mister Brickell. This might get ugly."

"I think it already is."

The Phantom studied the creature. Mirabelle thought the werewolf had some kind of armor under the fur suit. So gunplay was likely to do more harm than good. Judo would probably be a good option; use this maniac's weight and strength against him. *Perhaps, in the process, I can divest him of some of his gear.*

"Who are you?" the Bay Phantom demanded. "I know there's a human being in there. Don't you have a name?"

The werewolf lunged at the Phantom, who dropped to a crouch and let the beast sail over his head. He grabbed a furry leg as it passed over him and added thrust to the monster's momentum, propelling it into one of the large bookcases. The bookcase rocked violently, and looked for a moment as though it might come crashing down on the werewolf. But the monster noticed this and steadied it with one hand, giving it a hard shove. It slid to the side and toppled over, blocking the door to the hallway.

So, there is intelligence, thought the Phantom, *and the ability to be pragmatic.*

Speaking of pragmatism, Simon Brickell was obviously waiting for a chance to get across the war zone to press his panic button. The werewolf swiveled in his direction.

"If you won't give me your name," the masked man said, drawing the creature's attention away from Brickell, "you can be *the* Werewolf from now on; with a capital W."

The Phantom thought he detected a faint seam on the Werewolf's arm where the fur-covered gauntlet overlapped the sleeve of the upper-body garment. Slipping a long, thin-bladed knife from his own sleeve, he moved in.

The Werewolf snarled and took a swipe at him with one clawed gauntlet. The Phantom ducked under it and jabbed the blade of his knife up under the other gauntlet and applied pressure, slicing through fabric and fur all the way up to the wrist.

"Who sent you here?" the Phantom shouted.

He felt certain the beast was not acting alone. How could it possibly be? Two salient facts stood out in the Phantom's mind:

This was obviously not a random attack.

And there was no full moon tonight.

That meant that the monster could adapt to changed conditions and step outside the boundaries of his psychosis, but it was doubtful that he could do so unaided.

The Werewolf slammed the Phantom against the wall, hard enough to make him see stars. He bounced off onto the floor and rolled over a couple of times. Getting back to his feet was more difficult than he had anticipated. He had taken quite a lick to the head, which hadn't been softened very much by the thin padding in his mask.

He got his bearings just in time to watch the Werewolf open up Brickell's throat with the claws he still had, almost severing the head from the body.

"You fiend!" the Phantom bellowed. With tears in his eyes, he unholstered his gun and emptied it at the monster, knowing full well it would do no good. The Werewolf whirled on him and charged. With his last breath, Brickell finally brought his hand down on the panic button. Alarms shrieked through the hallways of the old house.

The Phantom tried once again to duck under the Werewolf's lunge, but the beast was ready for that. The monster feinted high, then dropped to all fours even as the Phantom did the same, and barreled into the masked man, pushing him along the hardwood floor on his back until his head slammed into the wall a second time.

The Phantom barely noticed it. A sort of madness had descended upon him, the same kind that had almost led him to end the life of Doctor Piranha three years before. He rose to his feet, lifting the Werewolf off the floor and flinging him backward, sending the murderous monster crashing onto the top of Brickell's desk. Before the beast could get upright again, the Bay Phantom was on top of him, pounding the armored snout with his fists, oblivious to the pain he was causing himself.

"You're just a man under all that," the Phantom snarled, pounding the headpiece again and again, "and I will by God have your head for this! Who is holding your leash?"

Pinning the monster to the desk with one hand, the Phantom reached into one of the voluminous inside pockets of his jacket and brought out the most foolproof weapon he had: an army-issue hand grenade.

"I will blow the both of us to Kingdom Come," he said through tightly-clenched teeth, "if you don't give me some answers!"

He meant it, too. The rage in him was too pure and too powerful to knuckle under to reason or pity or self-preservation. At that moment, the Bay Phantom would gladly destroy himself if he could take this abomination with him. He was barely aware of his surroundings; his mind was filled with flashes and impressions from other places and other times. *Fire. Screams. A dead man being thrown into a blazing room. A pair of eyes that he knew and did not know.*

The Werewolf writhed and growled, trying to push the Phantom away, to rally in the face of this oncoming doom. The Bay Phantom had him pinned, his knees pressing down on the monster's elbows.

"You've got five seconds, you piece of filth!" he shouted. "Talk!" Darkness had gripped his spirit, just as it had the day he apprehended Doctor Piranha. He gave no thought to the consequences of his actions. All that was important was his lust to destroy this murderous creature. He put his index finger through the pin and started to tug.

Before he could get it out, the Werewolf freed one arm and took a swipe at him. The metal claws didn't connect with anything, but the grenade was swatted out of the Phantom's hand. It bounced off the wall and rolled away into the shadows. The Werewolf sat up and threw off the masked man, propelling him halfway across the room. He smashed into the fish tank and it shattered, dousing the Phantom with water.

The shock snapped him back from the dark place into which he had fallen. He shook his head and got to his feet, lunging at his opponent once again, but without the earlier murderous rage.

Get a grip, Joe, he admonished himself. *That is not the way to get things done. The madness is your servant, not your master.*

This time he fought the Werewolf scientifically, dodging some blows, allowing others to connect. His own strikes seemed to have little effect, but he wasn't trying to disable the monster; he was endeavoring to "map" the costume and the armor beneath it. He didn't find any weak spots, so he concentrated on the glove he had damaged earlier. Gripping the monster's other wrist with his free hand; he worked the glove loose and tore it off of the very human hand beneath.

Unfortunately, this left him open to a savage blow to the head from the ungloved hand. As he staggered backward, the Werewolf made for the window and dove out. By the time the Bay Phantom regained his bearings, it was too late too pursue the monster.

The Bay Phantom stooped to pick up the furry glove with the three wicked metal claws. He turned to the bloodied corpse on the floor. "It's cold comfort, sir, but I promise you I shall find out who it was that did this to you, and at whose behest he acted. You will be avenged, though I'll admit it seems ludicrously inadequate."

The hammering at the door increased in volume, and the wood began to crack and splinter.

The Phantom was moving toward the shattered window, grappling hook in his hand, ready to descend to the ground, when a voice from the doorway stopped him short.

The guard had finally succeeded in breaking through the door and shoving the remains of the bookcase out of the way.

"Hold it right there!" he shouted. "You just freeze, mister, and I mean it! The cops are on the way!" The pistol he had pointed at the Phantom's head gave his words a certain undeniable authority.

CHAPTER EIGHTEEN
UNDERCOVER

The Bay Phantom sighed wearily and turned to face the newcomer. He dropped the grappling hook to the floor.

"I know how this looks," he said.

"Shut the hell up," said the guard. He cut his eyes to the right and caught sight of Simon Brickell's decidedly ghastly remains. "Oh, my God! What did you do to him?"

"Nothing," said the Phantom. "I tried to save him. The Werewolf did it."

He held up the gruesome clawed glove. Brickell's blood still dripped from the curved blades.

"Shit!" the guard exclaimed. "You're nuts!"

"I didn't do this," said the Bay Phantom. "Unfortunately, I can't possibly prove that. So I think it's in my best interest to escape from you now, and try to catch the killer."

"I think we can do that," came a new voice. "Looks like we already have."

Six uniformed officers piled through the door, each one pointing a gun at the Bay Phantom. One of them turned to the security guard and said, "Go downstairs and call headquarters. We need the homicide boys out here."

"I didn't kill that man," said the Phantom as the guard left on his errand. "And I cannot allow you to arrest me."

"Really?" said one of the cops. He seemed amused. "And just how are you going to prevent it? I mean, there's just one of you, and there are six of us. The odds aren't good."

"Agreed," said the masked man. "If there were fifty of you, it's possible that you could stop me. I'm not bragging."

"A wise guy! I'm gonna have fun breaking your legs."

"That's an unhealthy attitude. Revenge never solves anything, especially not when it's misplaced. I understand your feelings, but I didn't do this, and I can't allow you to break my legs or anything else."

"And how are you gonna stop me, smart guy?"

As the Phantom prepared to demonstrate, events took a different turn. The Werewolf came back.

The monster had evidently been hiding on the roof. He swung back through the window frame, knocked the Phantom to the floor, and waded into the cops. Shots were fired, but none of them had the desired effect. The Phantom's head had struck the floor with terrific force, and he was having difficulty getting upright. The thing that happened next happened very quickly. The Werewolf cut all six of the officers down in very short order, one right after another. Six lives were ended in less than three seconds. Two seconds after that, the monster was gone again.

As the Phantom got to his feet, head throbbing, he could hear shouts and footfalls downstairs. More police, no doubt. It wouldn't do for him to be caught up here with *this*.

"I hate to leave with all of this unresolved," he said, pocketing the bloody glove and retrieving his grappling hook and rope from the floor, "but I think it's for the best."

Gladys Turnbull had been prowling the dark downtown streets when she heard the alarm bell. The Bay Phantom had been sighted here and there by people who might or might not have been credible witnesses. Since many of the reported sightings had taken place downtown, Gladys decided a little foot patrol might produce some results.

Well, *something* was sure going on. The alarm sounded like it was coming from the next street over, so she cut through a narrow passage between two dark houses, emerging directly across from the Sams residence. She circled around the house. The action seemed to be centered in a room on the top floor, at the rear. She stood behind a large bush and watched.

Something huge dropped down from the roof and swung through the window frame, into the house.

She heard shouts and crashes, a terrible din. This went on for a while. When it finally stopped, a shaggy beast emerged through the window and climbed rapidly down the wall, using the little chinks between the bricks as handholds.

Then came the Bay Phantom! There he was, in person. He swung down from the window on a rope, then made his way through the backyard to the street behind. Looking around to make sure she wasn't being observed, Gladys took off after the Phantom. *Oh my God,* she thought, *is this really happening?*

She didn't notice another figure in the shadows beneath the oak trees, a specter in white that emerged from its place of concealment to follow her.

Police cars were zooming around all over the place, but none of them spotted the Bay Phantom as he crept along toward whatever mysterious destination he had in mind. *That guy,* Gladys thought, *is the luckiest man in the world.*

Keeping in the shadows as best he could, Perrone made his way to the Church Street Graveyard. He slipped around to the rear and quickly climbed over the wall. He sat down for a moment to rest and get his bearings. He didn't see Gladys Turnbull climb over the wall a dozen yards to his left and slip behind a large tree.

Neither he nor Gladys saw the man in the white smock do the same thing from the opposite side of the cemetery.

The Phantom stirred after a few minutes and found the slab that was really a trap door. Taking a key from his pocket, he unlocked it, pulled it up, and disappeared inside. The slab swung back down and clicked shut.

Half a minute later, the figure in the stained white smock stepped out from behind a concealing tree and moved to the flat grave marker, examining it minutely and locating the keyhole beneath the marble lip. He stood up straight, nodding and rubbing his gloved hands together. Then he reached into a pocket and dug out something that looked like a small, slender chisel.

The Black Embalmer crouched down and worked the little lock-picking tool into the keyhole. He manipulated it for a few seconds until he was rewarded with a series of faint clicks. He pushed on the slab and it moved upward. He raised it two or three feet and poked his head into the aperture that was revealed.

And then his examination was interrupted by loud sirens, squealing tires, bright lights, and voices raised in anger and alarm.

Six police cars had converged on the Church Street Graveyard, and the uniformed occupants were swarming over the low wall.

"There he is!"

"Freeze, you sonofabitch!"

"My, my," said the Embalmer to himself. He quickly removed his mask and lab coat and tossed them into the brick-lined shaft, and gently pushed the grave marker back into place. Underneath the smock, he wore a black sweater and black trousers. He stood up, hands held high over his head.

He offered no resistance as he was thrown to the ground and seven uniformed officers piled on him, delivering a series of unnecessary punches, kicks and curses. He took three large fists and two or three boots to the face and did not retaliate.

When the police had gone, with their strange prisoner in tow, another figure crept out of the shadows. Gladys Turnbull had been lying on the ground underneath a bush and had seen everything that had transpired.

She moved carefully, quietly and slowly toward the large, flat grave marker the two masked men had shown such interest in, her eyes darting here and there, straining her ears for any sound that might mean danger.

She squatted down and examined the grave marker that also seemed to serve as a gateway to the underworld. Under the lip of the slab, she found a short vertical slot that must have been a keyhole of some sort. She gripped the slab under the lip and tried to pull it up. It moved a little bit. It was heavy, but didn't seem to be caught on anything. The weirdo in the lab coat must have picked the lock; then, when he lowered the slab, it had failed to catch. She spread her feet apart and heaved. The slab swung upward on a pair of hinges and some kind of spring/hydraulic assembly.

She peered down and saw a metal ladder bolted to the brick wall of a shaft.

What now? She asked herself.

What do you think? She answered. *Quit standing here trembling and climb down there, see what you can find. This is incredibly stupid, and you're scared to death, but if you don't do it, you'll never be able to live with yourself. On top of that, this is the best chance you'll ever have to save your job.*

Right, then. Rolling up her metaphorical sleeves, she climbed down onto the ladder and pulled the slab down on top of her. Switching on her little flashlight and clamping it between her teeth, she began her descent. At the bottom of the ladder, she found what looked like a set of miniature railroad tracks.

She followed them.

The tunnel made a subterranean bee-line from the cemetery to Tull House, a distance of just under six miles, but Gladys was not aware of this. After an hour spent following the rails, she was beginning to worry. *What if this tunnel goes all the way to the center of the earth, and I get captured by a band of Morlocks with their three-legged war machines?* She briefly considered turning back, but then she imagined the look on Mark Marvel's face when she delivered the goods on the Bay Phantom, and this gave her the courage to forge ahead.

When an exhausted Bay Phantom finally made it back to the cellar of his home, ascended the stairs, and entered the kitchen, he found a note from Mirabelle taped to the icebox. She had taken Freud downtown to the Saenger Theater to attend a performance of the New Orleans Opera.

That was good. He was too wrung out to talk with anybody right now.

He got himself a glass of milk and sat down at the table. He removed his hat and mask, tossed them onto the floor, drank his milk, and put his head down on the table. Within seconds, he was asleep.

Some time later, he was awakened by the sound of Mirabelle's voice:

"Well, now you've done it! Wanted for murder! And not just one murder, oh no, *seven* of them! Six cops and the mayor of Mobile! It's all over the radio! Manhunt! *Get the Bay Phantom!* Sweet Jesus, Mister Perrone! What the hell happened, anyhow?"

She sat down in the chair to Perrone's right, while a bemused Freud took the one to his left.

"You know I didn't do it," said Perrone. "It was the Werewolf."

"I *knew* something like this was going to happen," Mirabelle went on. "I told you so! I said to you, very plainly..."

"Yes, you *told* me," he interrupted sharply. "Time and again. You don't need to reiterate. That won't help anything."

"I know that, and I won't mention it any more. But I told you. I *told* you."

"Mirabelle..."

"Okay, okay. Are you hurt?"

"I'm not injured. And I did manage to get away with one piece of physical evidence; the Werewolf's glove."

She sighed and said, "Give it here. I'll run some tests on it, once I figure out what kind of tests need to be run. Maybe I can find something that'll help us find the Werewolf. Because that's what we have to do now."

Perrone reached into his overcoat and produced the furry, bloodstained glove with the metal claws attached to the fingertips and handed it to her. She looked at it from various angles. The pinkie, ring and middle fingers were tipped with very sharp steel claws, each one nearly seven inches in length.

"My God," she said, "this thing is the work of a madman. A brilliant, obsessive madman. Very nicely built, actually. The stitching is excellent. A *lot* of work went into it. But there's no innocent use this thing could be put to. It's for killing people. What do you think, Doctor?" She handed the glove to Freud.

"Yes," he said after a minute examination. "Certainly obsessive. Very compulsive when it comes to details. He is convincing himself of something. His personality is... *damaged*, I would say, but not fragmented. It could be that he feels himself descending into chaos, and is trying to impose some order, however bizarre."

Mirabelle nodded. Freud handed the glove back to her.

"What do you want me to do with this thing?" she asked.

"Hang onto it," said Perrone. "Run some kind of tests on it, whatever it is you scientists do. And try not to damage it; I've a feeling it might come in handy later."

Gladys Turnbull stood at the top of the cellar stairs, her ear pressed to the door. She had heard everything that Perrone, the woman, and the older man with the accent had said. So, Brickell had been killed, eh? And the Bay Phantom was being blamed for it. He claimed it had been done by a werewolf.

And she had seen something that looked like a werewolf go into that window and come back out again. She was probably the only one who had, with the possible exception of the weirdo in the lab coat.

Gladys crept back down the stairs and waited for almost an hour in the shadows before daring to leave her hiding place. When the house was dark and quiet, she slipped out and made for a wooded area behind the property. She had no idea where she was, but believed that she had traveled south all the way through the underground tunnel. There had been no curves at all. Just a straight line from the cemetery to here. The house was right across the road from the Bay. That would be east, so she headed west, through the trees, emerging a few minutes later on Dauphin Island Parkway.

She used a payphone outside a filling station to call a taxi.

She had memorized the house number, and now she knew the place had to be on Bay Front Road. A look at the city directory would tell her who lived there.

All that remained was to secure some proof.

On her face was grin she couldn't have suppressed if she'd wanted to. It seemed determined to permanently deform her facial muscles. *This has got to be the high point of my career,* she thought, as the taxi took her downtown.

In the intensive care ward at Saint Germain Hospital, Shorty Red was making progress. He had regained consciousness and stirred a bit, though he wasn't quite ready to get up. It would be a few days at least before he could think about moving around. As soon as he was able, he tried telephoning his contacts in the Carter family hierarchy. Nobody wanted to talk to him. Penny Carter hadn't visited or sent word. He had been humiliated, and now he had been abandoned. The encounter at Max's restaurant had cost him everything, it seemed.

The only thing he truly cared about now was recuperating and getting out of the hospital so he could go looking for the Bay Phantom and Louis Rickert.

CHAPTER NINETEEN
OPPORTUNITY

This has got to be the low point of my career, thought Gladys Turnbull as she savagely slit open an envelope. Want ads, for the love of God! News staff is not supposed to have anything to do with want ads, but here she was. Some idiot named Violet who was supposed to be doing this crap had come down with the flu. The advertising staff was already stretched to the limit, they said, so someone from news would have to step in. There was already an enormous backlog of unprocessed ads, and customers were starting to complain.

She knew what it was about. Mark Marvel was giving her a ham-fisted warning that he probably thought was brilliantly subtle. She'd been ducking him, and evading his pointed questions about her Bay Phantom assignment. She had given him countless reassurances that she was on the verge of a major breakthrough, but that kind of thing only went so far.

Late last night, early this morning, actually, shortly before sunrise, she had filed a fantastic story on the deadly melee at Simon Brickell's house. She had obtained further details from a contact at the police department. She thought it wise not to reveal the fact that she had witnessed some of the action herself. The story was sensational, but it did nothing to connect the Phantom with Hector Sams.

It could not, however, be denied that the Bay Phantom seemed to be responsible for seven murders, which should have been enough for her editor. But, incredibly, he was still harping on the Hector Sams angle, which, as far as Gladys knew, was entirely bogus. Marvel had been on her about her lack of results so far, and she knew this want ads thing was a warning. But she wasn't going to reveal anything until she had the whole story, ready to publish and with plenty of proof to back it up. She knew who the Bay Phantom was, and she knew that there was more to the murder of Simon Brickell than was publicly known. What a scoop! Once she established her facts and went public with them, she could write her own ticket.

And there's the goddamn rub.

She didn't know how she was going to go about finding this proof. She needed to think of something. She knew it wouldn't be easy. It might be incredibly dangerous. She wasn't going to give Marvel a hint of what she knew before she had the proof. It had to be done, and she knew the answer wasn't going to just fall into her lap.

As she removed the want ad forms from the envelopes, sorted them by category, and entered the numbers and amounts of the accompanying checks in a ledger, she formulated and discarded one plan after another.

It was after some 45 minutes of this fruitless cogitation that the answer just fell into her lap.

Literally.

She tore open an envelope and shook it to dump its contents onto her desk blotter. The form and the check fluttered out, missed the desk, and landed in her lap. She was already in an ill mood, and this effrontery on the part of the enclosures incensed her. She snatched them up and slammed them down on the blotter. She shoved the ad form into the pigeonhole

"Want ads, for the love of God!"

representing the category marked at the top: DOMESTIC HELP. Then she started to enter the check information into her ledger. When she saw the name on the account, her eyes went wide. She read it four more times to be sure she had read it right:

JOSEPH PERRONE

Yes, that was him. The address on the check was the same as the house she had been in last night.

With a trembling hand, she reached into the pigeonhole and retrieved the ad form she had just filed. As she read the text of the ad, her excitement grew:

"WANTED: Reliable lady, non-drinker with good references, for general daily housekeeping, duties to include cleaning, some cooking, some laundry. Full-time position, NOT live-in. Must have own transportation. Salary negotiable, employer will offer generous compensation and benefits to the right party. Reply by mail to this newspaper."

Gladys smiled. Then she grinned. Then she laughed out loud. *I have you,* she thought jubilantly. *I have you now, Mister Joseph Bay Phantom Perrone.*

She wrote a note instructing the clerks in the mailroom to forward any replies to the ad directly to Gladys Turnbull, *personally,* and stapled it to the ad form before depositing it back in the pigeonhole.

After a day or two, Gladys Turnbull would succumb to the flu whose symptoms she would immediately begin faking. Then she would begin a new career as a domestic servant.

Watch yourself, Markie Marvel. I might be sitting behind your desk before this is finished.

Things were looking up for Detective Tom Dart. He had been reinstated in the detective division, without so much as a word of explanation from the chief. He hadn't heard anything further from Penny Carter, either. No more notes, no more phone calls, no more threats. The Bay Phantom must have worked some kind of magic on his behalf.

He was back in his old office going over some disturbing police reports when the phone on his desk rang.

"This is the Bay Phantom, Tom," said the caller after Dart answered. "I thought I ought to tell you..."

"I don't believe you did it," Dart interrupted. "But a witness placed you there. Was he mistaken?"

"No, I was there. But someone else was, too."

"I believe you. There was other evidence at the scene that suggested as much, but it's being ignored. Deliberately. Somebody doesn't like you, and they want to hang this thing around your neck."

"It's a fine mess, all right."

"Wait, there's more," said Dart, "They picked a guy up last night, and they think he may be the Bay Phantom. I happen to know he ain't, of course, but I didn't think it was wise to correct them. I got a look at him before they locked him away, and he wasn't the man I met in the morgue. He didn't have any papers or anything on him, didn't even have a wallet. He won't say anything. Just sits there and smiles."

"I hadn't heard about that," Perrone said.

"You wouldn't have. They're keeping it out of the papers until they can determine something one way or the other."

"Where was this man arrested?" the Phantom asked.

"In the Church Street Graveyard. A patrolman spotted him going over the wall."

"Why do they think he might be me?"

"An old lady called in and said she spotted someone of your description heading toward the cemetery. Of course, she didn't know what had happened at Brickell's house. She's one of those kind that sit by the window half the night and call in reports on just about everybody they see. The desk sergeant would have ignored it, but he'd heard about the Brickell thing, and it seemed like it might be connected. Then the patrolman saw you, or *somebody*, go over the fence. He called for backup and when they got there, they moved in.

"Look, I'll help you as much as I can to get to the bottom of this. Do you have any suggestions as to how I can proceed?"

Phantom related the previous night's events to Dart, and suggested that he take a look at the series of "werewolf" killings in New Orleans.

"The Werewolf is real," the Phantom concluded, "and he's still out there. You know, I would dearly love to have a talk with this prisoner they think is me."

"That is impossible. Even if it wasn't, I doubt he'd give you anything. If he didn't eat the meals they bring him, I'd think his jaw was wired shut. He literally has not said a single word. He takes his right to remain silent more seriously than anyone I've ever seen. He's in maximum security right now, and access to him is strictly limited."

"Well," said the Phantom, "he isn't me, but he *may* be the real killer. What

I saw in Sams' study was a man dressed as a wolf. Perhaps he discarded his costume before he was picked up. I can't help you there, but I have two bits of information you might find interesting." He told Dart about the machine guns that were supposedly in one of Hector Sams' warehouses. "Brickell didn't know which warehouse, but it might be the one that the Volker gang broke into."

"You're thinking it's an attempt at a frame."

"I am."

"Okay, I'll keep it to myself for right now. What's the other bit?"

"If nobody has discovered it, there is an unexploded hand grenade somewhere in Simon Brickell's study. I was going to use it on the Werewolf, but he had other ideas."

"I see. I'll check it out."

"Good. Now, I have an idea, Tom, if you're willing to help me with it. It could be risky."

"Hell, you've saved my ass twice now. I owe you some risk."

"Mirabelle," said Perrone, "I want you to create a human being for me."

She gave him a sharp look.

"I appreciate your faith in me," she said, "but I'm only a super-genius, not a goddess. I'm not Victor Frankenstein, either. I wouldn't know where to start. Give me twenty years and an unlimited budget, and I might be able to..."

"No, no," he interrupted, laughing. "That's not what I mean. I want you to create someone on paper. I need a very unsavory individual, one with an extensive criminal background. I'll need some identification papers. Driver's license and all that. You can use the printing equipment I bought."

"*Forgery* equipment, you mean. That's fine, but may I ask what kind of shit you're up to now?"

"Mirabelle, please, language."

She rolled her eyes. "Never mind my language. You're probably planning on doing something incredibly dangerous, and I want to know what it is. Why do you need this identification?"

"I'm going to pose as this fictional criminal and get myself arrested."

"Of course! I guessed the first part, but why the hell do you want to be arrested?"

"I need you to do a good job on this fictional man," Perrone said, ignoring her question. "I want him to be a thoroughly lethal character.

The kind of vicious criminal that would be sent directly to a maximum security cell upon arrest."

"Yes, I get it, but I... *Oh*. Okay, I see what you're saying. Do you think that's a good idea?"

"Not necessarily, but I don't have any others. I must speak with that prisoner. Now, please be a dear and whip me up a dangerous lawbreaker."

CHAPTER TWENTY
A MEAN SONOFABITCH

Roy Markham was wanted for any number of serious crimes all over the Southeast. Mirabelle prepared a couple of flyers and a "Wanted" poster, and sent them by private messenger to police headquarters. The following morning, she called Chief Peller on the phone, posing as a representative of a sheriff's office in Florida. She warned him that the notorious Roy Markham might be on his way to Mobile, and that his men should keep a sharp eye out for him if they didn't want to end up with a bloodbath on their hands.

"I thought about making him a psychopathic mass murderer," Mirabelle remarked, "but that would be gilding the lily. He's only killed five people during armed robberies, but he was unnecessarily brutal."

"Delightful," Perrone said. "Yes, he's an extremely rough customer. He ought to be sufficient for my purposes. I'll put him into action in a day or two, after I've done some groundwork."

"Oh, yes, I have a great deal of experience," said Gladys Turnbull.

"I see that," said Mirabelle Darcy as she thumbed through the stack of documents Gladys had given her. "Your references are very impressive, Miss Page."

"Thank you, Miss Darcy," said Gladys. "I have always endeavored to give satisfaction."

Perrone had gone out to do his "groundwork," whatever that meant. Mirabelle was just glad to have him out of the house, since she had made an appointment to interview one of the candidates for the housekeeping position.

In spite of a few productive sessions with Doctor Freud, Mirabelle's emotional condition was not improving. If anything, it had deteriorated slightly, though she had done her best to act more cheerful than usual around Mister Perrone. It seemed certain that she would have to leave his employment, and she wanted to be sure things were in good shape at Tull House.

Mirabelle Darcy had interviewed "Beth Page" for the better part of an hour, and she seemed like the perfect girl for the job. She had a few flaws and idiosyncrasies that kept her from being too good to be true, which short-circuited any suspicions Mirabelle might have developed. Gladys, who understood a thing or two about psychology, had been very careful to include those things in Beth Page's makeup.

"Well," said Mirabelle, "I feel satisfied that you can handle the duties that will be expected of you. And, as time goes by, perhaps we can add other duties…with a corresponding increase in salary, of course."

"Oh, thank you, Miss Darcy."

"Call me Mirabelle, please. I think you'll do just fine. We can start you out tomorrow if that works for you. If you'd like, I can show you around the house now."

They had a little tour, and Gladys took in every detail, committing the layout to memory. Of course, Mirabelle didn't show her the cellar. But, as they passed the door on their way to the kitchen, she noticed that it sported a brand-new lock.

Damn…

"I need your help with this, Louis," said the Bay Phantom. "I want you to vouch for Roy Markham."

They were sitting at a table in the speakeasy where Rickert had met the strange little blonde. Rickert couldn't get her out of his head, and he had become a regular here, in hopes of encountering her again. The Phantom was unmasked, but had disguised his features with theatrical makeup.

"Okay," Rickert said. "I don't know who the hell that is, but okay."

"He is *me*. Or, rather, he is a fabrication whose mantle I have assumed."

"Oh, sure. Incognito. I get it."

"Talk about him to your criminal associates. Drop hints that he may be on his way to Mobile. Really play him up, you know, as an exceptionally ruthless ruffian."

"Ruffian?"

"Yes," said the Phantom. "You know, a hooligan. A moral cripple capable of the most atrocious outrages."

"Oh, a mean sonofabitch."

The Phantom winced. "Ah... Yes. Talk about him to anyone you know to be a police informant. I want to pave the way for him."

"Yeah, I can do that. Say, listen... I been having a little trouble lately and I could use a few bucks, you know?"

"Certainly," said the Phantom. He took out a wallet and extracted four twenty-dollar bills. "Will this be sufficient?"

Rickert swallowed hard. "Uh, yeah, absolutely. You're mighty generous, Boss."

"I do hope you won't drink it up. It's none of my business what you do with your money, of course, but you might want to start putting some of it back for a rainy day."

"That is excellent advice," Rickert said. "For a rainy day."

"Good man," said the Phantom. He got out of his chair and patted Rickert on the shoulder. "I must be off, but I'll see you soon."

Rickert went up to the bar and got the bartender's attention. It wasn't the regular guy. This was some joker he'd never seen before.

"Have you heard a weather report lately, my good man?" Rickert asked.

"No," said the bartender, eyeing him skeptically. "Can't say I have. How come?"

"Well, the forecast calls for heavy rain storms all night long, starting right now." He tossed one of the twenties onto the bar. "A shot of whiskey and a bottle of beer, if you please, and keep 'em coming!"

The following evening found the suddenly-notorious Roy Markham raising pure hell in downtown Mobile. While a memorial service was being held across town for the late Simon Brickell, the disguised Joe Perrone was in a speakeasy, making a dangerous nuisance of himself. So extreme was his behavior that the bartender actually summoned the police.

He cut up rough with the officers, though he stopped short of inflicting serious bodily harm. He targeted parts of their bodies that would produce a great deal of pain and blood in the immediate short term, without causing any real damage. Thus, the struggle appeared a lot more fearsome than it actually was. Perrone took quite a few lumps from the officers, but minimized the damage by expertly rolling with the blows.

This went on for a further fifteen minutes before he allowed himself to be subdued, handcuffed, and bundled into the back of a squad car. The ride downtown was uneventful, but for the steady stream of verbal abuse and flamboyant threats against the whole police force coming from Markham. He was cuffed on the ear twice and told to keep his big trap shut, but this only inspired him to pick up the pace and volume of his ranting.

Perrone had altered his appearance in ways that would not be recognized as elements of a disguise. A false beard and moustache had been attached with an adhesive that could only be dissolved by a chemical compound Mirabelle had created. Small glass lenses had been placed directly onto his eyeballs, changing their color from blue to brown.

"He's going right into maximum security," said the desk sergeant, after the cops had dragged him into the building and established his identity, based on the contents of his wallet. "We've had a bulletin about him."

Perrone smiled. He knew there were only two small cells on the top floor that were so designated. That would put him right next to the man he was so eager to talk to.

The cells were more like free-standing cages, built into the cinder block wall of a featureless room at the end of a bare corridor. Each cell was equipped with a bunk and a toilet. The bunk in the cell on the right was occupied by a bulky form underneath a thin blanket.

"Not so tough now, are yah, Markham?" said one of the cops who had escorted Perrone to his cell and locked him in. "A lot of people are looking for you. We'll get it all sorted out in the morning."

They left him there. He took in his surroundings. The dim light came from an overhead fixture that was never switched off. He knew the guard stationed at the end of the hall was supposed to walk down and check on the prisoners every ten minutes. He'd have to work around that. The man in the other cell had not stirred or made any sound.

When he was sure he was unobserved, Perrone felt around in the gap between the cell door and the floor, running his fingers along the bottom edge of the iron. He found a short piece of very stiff wire, held in place with a small wad of chewing gum. Tom Dart had come through!

"Hey, fella," he whispered to the man in the next cell. "I'm gonna get out of here. You up for a break? Two have a better chance than one." He didn't expect the man to answer right away. He figured it would take some work, but he was in for a surprise.

"What's your name?" asked the mystery prisoner, his voice muffled by the blanket he had pulled over his face. He lay unmoving, his back to Perrone.

"Markham," Perrone said gruffly. "Roy Markham."

"Hm. Seems like I've heard that name recently."

"What's *your* name?" Perrone asked.

"Ha! That's a damn good question. The police have asked me that one about a hundred times. You know what they got from me? The sound of one hand clapping."

The man on the cot sat up and looked at Perrone. He was a very average-looking fellow, with brown hair and bland, regular features. There was nothing remarkable about him that would stick in anyone's mind.

He had evidently been subjected to some rough treatment, judging by the bruises and swelling on his face.

"As it happens," he said, studying Perrone, "I could use somebody like you. Would you like a bit of paying work?"

"Sure," said Perrone.

"I have a job that needs doing. I could use some bloodthirsty, psychotic help. I was toying with the idea of breaking out of here in the near future, but I don't have any good ideas yet. You sound like you do."

"I might," he said, holding up the lockpick for the other prisoner to see.

"I'll be damned, it looks like you do. How did you get that in here? Never mind, I don't want to know. Let's get the hell out of here."

CHAPTER TWENTY-ONE
JAILBREAK

The guard wandered down the corridor to check on the prisoners. Both of them lay on their bunks, apparently asleep. When he was gone again, Perrone rolled off of his bunk and went to work. It took him less than two minutes to open the door of his cell, and no more than 30 seconds to unlock the other one.

The mystery man rose from his bunk and joined Perrone in front of the cells.

"The guard is at the end of this hallway," Perrone told his new acquaintance, pointing down the corridor. "I'd like to kill the sonofabitch for smarting off to me when they brung me in here. But that would raise one hell of a stink, and I want to draw as little attention to myself as I can manage. Still... Maybe I'll croak him anyhow."

"No, no," said the other man. "I understand the impulse. I was thinking along the same lines myself. But you're right. We need to get out of here without any undue fuss. There are plenty of other people we can kill later."

They made their way stealthily down the corridor until they could see the guard, seated behind a small metal desk just around the corner.

Perrone held up the little lockpick he had used and made a gesture. His companion nodded.

Perrone tossed the implement over the guard's head. It landed in the far corner of the room, making a small pinging sound. When the guard turned his head to look, Perrone sprang from the corridor and got him in a headlock. A few moments of pressure on a certain nerve, and the guard was out cold.

"That was very good work," said the nameless man, clearly impressed. "I think I can find a place for you in my organization, if you're interested."

"I'm in," said Perrone enthusiastically. He helped himself to the unconscious guard's key ring. Three unlocked doors later, he and his new acquaintance slipped out of police headquarters without being seen. It had been a lot easier than Perrone had expected, for which he was grateful. The alarm would soon be raised, but for now, they were safe.

"Okay, Markham," said the prisoner, "I guess you can be trusted. Follow me to my place, it isn't far from here and we'll get this ball rolling."

The pair crept through alleyways and darkened side streets until they reached Cathedral Plaza. The man led the way around to the back of the Cathedral Basilica of the Immaculate Conception, to a small, very nondescript door. He reached up and removed a key from its hiding place on top of the doorframe.

"I'm constantly losing keys," he said as he unlocked the door and pushed it open. "It always pays to have a spare."

They stepped into a dark, narrow hallway. Perrone had been through the Cathedral many times. He loved the old building. But he had never seen this corridor and could not place it in the mental blueprint he had of the place. At the end of the corridor they came to another door and descended a short flight of stairs.

The air was cool down here, and it had what Perrone always thought of as the "church smell." It had once been a comfort to him; now it was vaguely disturbing, like a voice nagging at him in a language he didn't understand. They passed through a third door, into what appeared to be an ordinary foyer, furnished with a hat and coat rack, a little bench, and... something else.

Propped up against the wall was the corpse of the man Perrone had seen the Black Embalmer murder after the carnage in Bienville Square.

"Don't mind him," said the other man. "He's just a cheap decoration. I plan on replacing him soon. I have my eye on a certain fellow who wears a black mask. I want to take my time with him, though, you know? Sort of cultivate him, get to know him. I like my tchotchkes to have sentimental value. Now, I have more to show you, but I need to get out of these filthy clothes. Give me a moment, please, while I slip into something more comfortable."

There were two other doors leading from the foyer, one opposite the entrance they had used, and a smaller one to the left. The man opened the latter and passed through, pulling it shut behind him. Perrone stood and contemplated the corpse of the machine-gunner.

The little door opened again. Perrone looked around and saw exactly what he was expecting to see.

The Black Embalmer.

"These are my work clothes," said the man, "but I like to relax in them, too. Come along, let us penetrate further into my sanctum."

He opened the larger door and Perrone found himself looking at a most disturbing tableau.

Seated around a large dining table were what appeared to be corpses, and not very fresh ones. They were dressed in the sort of finery Perrone associated with Catholic Bishops. They were reasonably well-preserved, some more so than others. Small patches of decay were visible on the cheeks and foreheads of a couple of them. The flesh he could see was waxy, with a strangely vegetable appearance, an impression created more by texture than color.

"You may not know this if you're from out of town," said the Embalmer, "but a lot of the Bishops from this region are interred in a crypt under this cathedral. I was feeling whimsical one night and I went and fetched a few of them, just to pass the time, you know. Bishops make poor domestic companions, unless they have been dead for some time. Rigor mortis goes away early on, you know, and, depending on how they have been embalmed, they can be quite pliable. A bit of strong, heavy wire threaded through the limbs and torsos, and one can pose them in a variety of attitudes. I spray them with a sort of lacquer I invented."

Perrone swallowed hard. This was a bit difficult to take. But he couldn't give himself away after coming this far. He centered himself, then removed Joe Perrone from the mental stage, yielding the footlights to Roy Markham.

He understood that Markham wasn't a stranger, and Markham's evil was not complete artifice. There was a vileness inside him, he knew, the same monstrosity that lived in every human being, the wellspring of Original Sin. He wasn't sure about its nature, whether each person had his own version of it, or if the same swamp served everyone; a communal well, as it were. Whatever it was, it was there, and it could not be extinguished. It could only be fought *or utilized*.

"Now that's a hoot," he said. "I never did like priests, even when I was a kid. So high and mighty. They don't look like much of anything now, do they?" He laughed.

"No, they don't," the Embalmer agreed. "You understand, don't you? I thought you would. That's why I wanted to show you. So few people get it. It makes me sad. You *do* know what I mean, don't you? I'm preaching to a choir here, right?"

"Yes," said Perrone. "But listen: They *do* understand. They all do. They're just afraid of it."

"Do you think so? I've often wondered. I like to think I'm unique, but I suspect that I'm really very common. It's just a matter of perspective. Under the right conditions, *everyone* is a Black Embalmer."

"I think you're right," said Perrone. And he was telling the truth. He knew it. The Bay Phantom existed because of it; he was designed to rise above it. He knew he would never make it, but perhaps, because of his efforts, the next generation would. Such was the process of evolution. When he was much younger, he might have dismissed Darwin's theories as heathen doctrine, but he had come to understand that gradual change was the essence of divinity. Were it not so, saints would not require patience.

"Are you hungry?" the Embalmer asked. "Can I offer you a snack?"

Perrone shook his head. He had no desire to learn any of the Embalmer's culinary secrets. The mere prospect of dining in this macabre setting twisted his stomach into a knot.

The Embalmer went into a small room at the rear of his lair that was fitted out as a workshop, where he busied himself with some arcane task. Perrone joined him and asked what he was up to.

"I have my own unique ways of doing things," he told Perrone as he worked. "I have this gas I use, a nerve agent of sorts. It causes temporary paralysis. It is normally just a precursor to my preferred method of dealing death, but it can be an effective tool in its own right. I'm going to fill up a few of these ampoules with it and bring them along when we go to conduct our business. I think I'll leave the embalming rig behind. I'll be at this for a while, Markham. You might want to get some rest."

Perrone left the Embalmer to his work and stretched out on a sofa in another room for a much-needed nap.

"Wake up," said the Embalmer some hours later. "I'm ready to get started now."

Perrone sat up and rubbed his eyes. "What's up?"

"I'll give you details later on. We will be looking for some men who work for someone who is a threat to the people I'm working for. Something odd is going on, and I want to find out what it is. We can make the rounds of the speakeasies and see what turns up."

They visited three of the most notorious dives in the downtown area, but didn't find any of the men the Embalmer was looking for. Perrone attempted to subtly question him about their "mission" and his activities in general, but got nowhere.

"That's very curious," said the madman as they trudged up Royal Street. "We should have found one or two of them. This defies the laws of probability."

As they passed Louis Rickert's favorite speakeasy, the Embalmer glanced through the front window, did a double take, and stopped dead.

"Well, looks like we're in luck after all," he said. "I can't believe they'd come in *here*." He pushed the door open, and poked his head inside.

"I'll be damned," he said. "Come on, I have a couple of people I need to kill before we go any further. Those boys are the real thing, not just imported hired hands."

Perrone followed him inside, wondering what the Embalmer meant, but thinking it best not to ask just yet.

Louis Rickert was not there, nor was the regular bartender. Sitting at a pair of tables in the back was a group of four men who were unfamiliar to Perrone. But the Black Embalmer certainly seemed to know who they were.

"Hello, boys," he said jauntily, giving them a mock salute. "You're out of your territory, aren't you?"

"Oh, Christ," said one of the men. "It's this goddamn lunatic again."

"It's a free country," said another.

"Indeed it is," chirped the Embalmer. "And I'm on a mission. I know who you birds work for, and I have a proposition for you. If you would like to go on living, and to make a great deal of money, you can join me. Or, if you prefer to remain where you are, you can be murdered. By me. Right now. I believe that covers it."

One of the men uttered a filthy epithet then said, "You must be crazy, coming here like this! You know how many mugs are out there looking for you? The boss wants you pretty bad. Looks like he's gonna get what he wants tonight."

The Embalmer turned to "Markham" and said, "I knew it was going to go this way, but it's all part of the script. Are you ready to do some killing?"

Perrone just nodded. Things had gone too far here, and his original plan would have to be discarded. He wouldn't be able to remain in the Embalmer's company until the madman made contact with his employers. He'd have to get out as cleanly as he could.

But not without something he could take home.

The men stood up, pushing back their chairs and moving closer to the doorway. The Embalmer nodded at Perrone and said, "Two for you and two for me. Last one to finish both of his off buys the beer."

Perrone nodded back and charged at the two thugs to his left. He needed to take them out quickly and non-lethally, then somehow prevent the Embalmer from killing the others. The first part would be comparatively easy, given his skill at unarmed combat. He made it look good, letting the two land a couple of blows, and making a lot of noise. During the first ten seconds of combat, he relieved both of them of the knives they'd been brandishing. Then he punched each of them in the nose, measuring his blows so they caused a great deal of bleeding without inflicting any permanent damage.

Glancing over, he saw that the Embalmer had not yet traded any blows with his opponents. He was jumping around and taunting the men, obviously trying to anger them and cause them to act without thinking. Perrone delivered a series of sharp jabs to certain points on his opponents' bodies, and they became increasingly weak and disoriented. He knocked one of them to the floor, then maneuvered the other one into position for what he had in mind.

By now, the Embalmer had engaged both of his foes, trading blows, then jumping back out of reach. It was plain that he had them outclassed and was having fun with them. But Perrone knew the fun would soon turn deadly unless he did something. He drew back his fist and delivered a blow to his opponent's jaw, sending the man backwards. He plowed right into the Embalmer, and his momentum put both of them on the floor.

As the Embalmer struggled to throw off the semi-conscious man on top of him, Perrone turned to the two remaining thugs and put both of them on the ground in just under three seconds.

The four men had regained enough composure to realize they needed to be someplace else. One of them turned to the others and said, "We gotta scram and get word to the Grand Wizard. He'll know what to do."

As the quartet hastily took their leave, Perrone dashed over to the Embalmer, who was attempting to rise. Perrone slipped an arm around his waist to help him. His other hand dug into the pocket full of poison ampoules and extracted a few of them, which he slipped into his own trouser pocket.

"You okay?" Perrone asked.

"Oh, yes, certainly," the Embalmer replied. "I have a question, though. Why did you pick my pocket?"

The game was up.

"Never mind," said Perrone. "This charade is over. I'm going to subdue you and turn you over to the police."

"I trusted you," the Embalmer said, sounding genuinely hurt. "I *liked* you!"

"This isn't personal," said Perrone as he moved toward his erstwhile comrade. "I'd like to get it done without any bloodshed, but that's up to you."

The Embalmer reached into his pocket and extracted one of the remaining ampoules. Before Perrone could react, the Embalmer thumbed the little valve, spraying him with the invisible gas. Perrone found that he could not move.

"Don't worry," said the Embalmer. "I only gave you a small dose. I'm not ready to kill you right now. By the way, I know who you are! I knew it the moment you spoke to me in the cell. I thought you might be coming around to my way of thinking. You can keep those ampoules. Maybe they'll show you what you're really dealing with. Have fun!"

He gave Perrone a nod, and made a quick exit.

The paralysis lasted for less than a minute. When he could move again, Perrone dashed out into the street. There was no sign of the Embalmer.

Weary and disgusted, Perrone headed up the street toward a supposedly abandoned building that housed one of the entrances to his network of secret tunnels. From there, he went straight home.

What now? thought Gladys Turnbull.

She was walking up Royal Street when she saw four large and dangerous-looking men come piling out of the speakeasy she had visited a few days ago. They had blood on their faces and clothes, and as soon as they hit the sidewalk, they took off running. A few seconds later, a strange-looking masked man in a white lab coat emerged. He was much calmer than the four who had preceded him, and strolled nonchalantly up the street for half a block before disappearing into an alley.

Then came a rather ordinary-looking fellow who stepped out of the place, looked up and down the street, shrugged, and headed north.

Gladys felt a little stirring of excitement and quickened her pace. She had been on her way to the speakeasy, anyhow. *Maybe there's a story here,* she thought. *A good enough one to help me keep my job until I can expose the Bay Phantom!*

There wasn't. The bartender wouldn't talk about it. *Oh, well.* Gladys ordered a gin and sat down at a table.

The door to the men's room slowly opened and Louis Rickert stuck his head out.

"Jesus Christ," he said, "is it safe? What the hell happened out here? I go to the can for five minutes and World War Two breaks out!"

The bartender shrugged. Gladys Turnbull smiled.

"Ah!" she exclaimed. "I was hoping I'd find you here."

"Really?" said Rickert.

"Yeah. Now, don't be offended, but I figure you for a petty crook of some kind. I've been around, and I know the signs."

"Naw, lady, you got me wrong."

"Oh? That's too bad. I was hoping you were because I need some help that only a crook can give me. Well, I'll just be on my way and see if I can..."

"Wait!" Rickert said in near panic. "Don't go. I can... I mean... Aw hell, lady, yeah, I'm a crook. Honest, I am. I got a rap sheet as long as your legs. I can help you. You still want me to, don't you?"

"Maybe," she said. "Tell me, do you know how to pick a lock?"

"Hell, yeah. Just lead me to it."

"No, I don't want you to do it; I want you to teach *me* how."

Rickert smiled. As it happened, he had a set of lockpicks on his person. They were practically brand new; he had purchased them with some of the Bay Phantom's money, since his previous set had been swiped by a lousy detective the last time he'd been picked up for something he didn't do.

He selected his second favorite lockpick from the set and presented it to the blonde. He explained the principle behind it, and gave her detailed instructions.

"Come on," he said at one point, "let's go out back for a minute. There are some doors with locks on them out in the alley. I can give you a practical demonstration, then you can practice."

She was a bit dubious, but he swore to behave himself, so she went. He proved to be as good as his word, and twenty minutes later, Gladys was able to open three of the locks by herself.

When they returned to the bar, there was a minor disturbance in progress.

"What do you mean you can't serve me? I got money."

"Kid, you're too young," the bartender said. "What are you? Fifteen?"

"What the hell difference does that make? It's illegal to sell it to me because of my age? It's illegal to sell booze to *anybody*, not just kids. Who the hell's gonna report you?"

"I don't care. That ain't the point. I got a moral code, and I ain't selling you anything. Hell, it looks to me like you're already drunk, anyhow."

"I run out of what I had, and I need some more," the boy whined.

"Beat it, kid. You're too young to be a stinking drunk. Leave that to your elders."

"You're a fairy, that's what you are," the boy declared, his voice cracking. "A goddamn lily livered fairy!"

The bartender scowled. "Kid, if you don't get the hell out of here in five seconds..."

"Yeah, yeah," said the kid as he made for the door. "What're you gonna do, get your boyfriend to beat me up? I don't want your lousy rotgut anyhow. I was just kidding."

"Well," Gladys said to Rickert, "thanks for the lessons. I have to go now, but I really appreciate it."

"Can I see you again?" Rickert asked.

"Nope."

"Will you tell me your name?"

"Nope. I gotta go. I really am grateful to you, but... I just have to go."

Rickert sat back in his chair and watched the little blonde walk out the door. A fine thing! Who the hell did she think she was, anyhow? She wasn't really all that good looking, was she? Her eyes were too close together and her nose looked like a goddamn potato.

A goddamn *cute* little potato...

Rickert hung around for a few more minutes, then decided to go home and forget the whole damn business. That dame was crazy. He didn't need to fool around with somebody like that.

The moment he stepped out onto the sidewalk, he was approached by the smart-alecky kid the bartender had shooed away earlier.

"Hey, mister," said the kid. "How's about you help a fella out, huh?"

"Get lost," Rickert said coldly.

"That ain't nice. I just wanna do some business. I know who you are, I seen you around here. You could get your hands on some good hooch!"

Rickert thought for a moment. He had spent most of his cash buying drinks for himself and the blonde. He could use a few bucks, and he did happen to know where he could obtain a case of perfectly good bourbon, with very little risk to himself. He was all primed to pick a lock anyhow.

"Aw, what the hell. Okay, kid, you've got yourself a deal. Follow me."

Rickey Harvard grinned and rubbed his hands together. "Now you're talking." He'd be able to drink himself to sleep tonight after all!

Tom Dart was on his own tonight.

Now that he was free to help the Bay Phantom get to the bottom of the recent disturbing events in Mobile, he wanted to make up for lost time. Not knowing who was involved in what, Dart thought it best to pursue certain lines of inquiry off the clock and on the sly.

After his shift was over, he went home for supper and some time with his wife and child. After the rest of his little family had gone to sleep, Dart set out for the house where Simon Brickell had been killed. Though it was still, technically, an active crime scene, Chief Peller had not seen fit to post guards there. The front of the house was secured by a brand-new padlock, one of several owned by the department for situations like this. All the locks could be opened with the same key and Dart had a copy of it. He let himself in and ascended the stairs.

A search of the "death chamber," as the press was calling it, turned up the hand grenade the Phantom had told him about. The thing had rolled under a heavy oak cabinet, all the way to the wall. No wonder it had been missed. Whoever had gone over the room probably hadn't seen a need to be thorough. He pocketed the grenade and let himself out of the house.

Next stop was the warehouse where the Phantom believed the machine guns might be stored.

Sams did not employ a guard here, even after the abortive burglary. He had a passkey of another kind in his pocket: a set of lockpicks he had lifted from some petty crook a few months earlier. He had the rear door open in no time.

The first thing he saw when he stepped through the doorway and turned on his flashlight was the pair of corpses.

Evidently, Sams had employed some guards here after all, but they hadn't done much good. He quickly examined the bodies, inspecting them closely enough to assure himself that he was looking at the Black Embalmer's work. He popped a stick of gum into his mouth and searched the rest of the premises.

He prowled around for forty-five minutes before discovering three light spots on the floor. The floor around them was dusty and grimy, but the spots were clean. Three rectangular objects that had rested there for some time had been moved very recently. If they had been crates, they were the right size and shape to hold the kind of machine guns that had been used in Bienville Square. Evidently, whoever had been trying to frame Sams had changed their game plan.

He made an anonymous call from a pay phone, alerting the dispatcher to the presence of the bodies at the warehouse.

He said nothing about machine guns. That information was going to the Bay Phantom.

"They have some kind of sorcerer working for them," Perrone said. "Someone they believe has special powers. I know nothing of witchcraft."

He and Mirabelle were sitting at the kitchen table, eating sandwiches and drinking tea. Perrone had returned home half an hour earlier, divested himself of the false whiskers and colored lenses, and taken a quick shower.

"A sorcerer, huh?" Mirabelle said.

"I believe so. Actually, they referred to him as a *wizard.* 'The great wizard,' they said."

Mirabelle narrowed her eyes and said, "Are you sure they used the word 'great?' Or did they maybe say '*grand* wizard?' Think about it."

"I believe they did, now that you mention it. Is that significant?"

Mirabelle sighed and shook her head. "You don't know a whole lot about the Ku Klux Klan, do you?"

"Well, no, not really. I never knew anyone personally who was a member."

Mirabelle gave a harsh and mirthless laugh. "I'll bet you *do* know a few members. They don't exactly advertise their affiliation, you know. There's

"...he was looking at the Black Embalmer's work..."

a reason why they wear those masks."

"Granted. Is the term 'grand wizard' significant in that context, then?"

"Very. They don't use it any longer, but in the original incarnation of the Klan, the one that started up during the Reconstruction, that was the title they gave to their head honcho, 'Grand Wizard.' Nathan Bedford Forrest was the first one. These days, in the 'new' Klan, the leader is called the *Imperial* Wizard, or something equally dignified. A Grand Dragon is the head of the organization in a particular state."

"Seems a bit juvenile," Perrone observed. "Dragons and wizards. Have they any elves or goblins or krakens?"

"No, but I think there's an Exalted Cyclops."

"You're joking."

"I'm not that funny."

Perrone sighed. "So, this business wasn't complicated enough already," he said darkly. "Now we have the Ku Klux Klan involved."

"Maybe, maybe not," said Mirabelle. "Like I said, the term Grand Wizard is no longer officially used. The original Klan petered out around 1871. If whoever they were referring to was a legitimate Grand Wizard, he'd have to be eighty years old or more."

"It's too strange a reference to have any other meaning, I think. How might one go about approaching the current Klan leadership in Alabama?"

"You're asking *me*? Do I look like I'm on their mailing list?"

"Hmm, I wonder if Penny would know anything."

"It wouldn't surprise me."

The arrest and subsequent escape of the anonymous prisoner who might or might not have been the Bay Phantom was never made public. Likewise the brief incarceration of the notorious Roy Markham...who, very curiously, seemed not to exist at all, as the Mobile police found out when they made inquiries.

The memorial service held for Simon Brickell was well-attended. Mark Marvel was among the pallbearers, as was Chief of Police Peller. The Chief swore that his department would bring the Bay Phantom to justice. Deputy Mayor Felix Birdsong, who was temporarily in charge, more or less, made a few vaguely coherent remarks at the graveside service in Magnolia Cemetery. The eulogy was delivered by Caleb Carter. This was, he said, the end of an era in the Port City.

He had no idea just how right he was...

CHAPTER TWENTY-TWO
THE KKK TOOK MY BABY AWAY

The following evening, Perrone was in the living room reading the newspaper when the telephone rang. Miss Page answered, then handed the phone to Perrone.

"Hey, baby," chirped Penny Carter. "I looked into that stuff you asked me about. If you're still interested, we can go to a thing. A get-together. Ten o'clock tonight."

Joe Perrone found Penny Carter's casually intimate mode of speaking to him both disturbing and intriguing. Perhaps even a little exciting. Darkly delightful sensations and terrifying promises had begun to worry at him.

"Where?"

"I can't tell you," she said coyly. "I'll show you. I'm going with you."

He had mentioned to her that he was interested in finding out about the inner workings of the local KKK. Penny had expressed surprise, but promised to see what she could find out. It looked as though she had come through.

"I hardly think such a function is a proper place for a young woman," he said.

"Ha! It's not a proper place for anybody. I may lay down with the occasional dog, but I'm not going to come away with fleas. In fact, it's going to end up getting rid of some troublesome bugs that have been annoying me."

"What on earth are you talking about?"

"Maybe I'll explain one of these days. Keep up the good work, Joe, and maybe I'll let you in on a whole lot of things. I don't make commitments lightly, so just possess your soul in patience, dear boy."

Perrone swallowed hard. He hoped he wasn't getting himself into something he'd never be able to get out of. In some ways, Penny wasn't as bad as he had believed her to be; in other ways, she was worse. What if, at some point, he felt obligated to marry her?

"I don't know why you're interested in these dimwits," she continued. "You say you're just curious, but I'm not buying that, not entirely. If I thought for one minute that you genuinely sympathized with those cocksu..."

"*No*, Penny! I don't sympathize with them, of course. I assure you, it is pure curiosity on my part."

"Yeah," she said. "Okay. We'll leave it at that for now. I wish I knew what was going on in your head, Joey."

"No you don't, Penny."

Gladys Turnbull couldn't help wishing that Joe Perrone and Mirabelle Darcy weren't so goddamn nice. It was going to make doing what she had to do a great deal more difficult. They were genuinely good people, and must have had good reason for doing what they did. And then there was their remarkable houseguest, Doctor Sigmund Freud. Gladys was a longtime admirer of the psychiatrist. If Mirabelle and Mr. Perrone numbered him among their close friends, they must be remarkable people indeed.

She had too much conscience to be a reporter in this town, she decided, and she didn't know how to go about killing it. She hated Mark Marvel more and more every day, but she knew that was just a substitute for hating herself. It would eventually wear out, and then what would she do? Because she was going to proceed with her plan. She was going to expose Perrone and assure her own future. Not *that* much conscience, then. Just enough to make her miserable.

She finished washing the dishes and went to dust in the front room. There she found Doctor Freud, standing by the big window, gazing out at the Bay, smoking a cigar.

"I thought you had given up smoking, Doctor," she said.

"I gave up smoking in Vienna," he said. "This is not Vienna, my dear."

"Such sophistry!"

Freud raised his eyebrows and looked her in the eye. "Tell me about yourself, Miss Page," he said. "If I may be frank, you seem to be a bit below your station at present. You are obviously an educated woman. You know a great deal about me, and you use words like 'sophistry.' Is this typical of parlor maids in America? I mean no offense, Miss."

"I know you don't. You're a public figure, sir. It's not unusual that I would know things about you. As for the rest of it... Well, there is a Depression on, and sometimes a girl has to take whatever work she can get."

"According to the references you supplied to Miss Darcy, you've been doing this sort of work since well before the Depression began."

"Maybe I've been depressed longer than the country has."

Freud clapped his hands. "Now *that* is sophistry! Well, your life is your own business, Miss, and it is not for me to pry into it. I don't really know you at all, but I like you. There is something about you that tells me you are a fundamentally good person. This is not scientific, it is just a feeling I have. I sense that you are very uneasy about something. Perhaps you are contemplating a course of action about which you are uncertain."

Gladys was a little taken aback. "What you said is... not without some personal meaning for me," she said. "But it isn't that big a deal. I mean, every one of us finds himself in a dilemma now and again."

Freud smiled. "You used the correct pronoun, I noticed. *Himself*, in reference to an unidentified theoretical person. Most people in this country would say *themselves*, or even *herself*, if she were female, which you clearly are. You take language seriously, don't you? For the most part, your grammar is impeccable."

"The word you want is *diction*, not *grammar*."

"You have just proven my thesis!" He was silent for a moment, then he said, "They are very fine people, Miss Mirabelle and Mister Perrone, don't you think?"

She stopped what she was doing and remained silent for almost a minute.

"Yeah," she finally said. "Yeah, they really are."

"You took a very long time to answer. Do you have doubts?"

"Yes, I guess I do. But not about them."

"Beth Page" waited, but Freud said nothing more.

Perrone picked Penny Carter up in front of her house. She gave him directions to a spot some forty miles north of the city, parceling them out a little at a time until they reached their destination.

They were out in the country somewhere when Penny instructed him to leave the main road and take a rutted dirt path to the left.

"We're almost there," she said. She took a swallow of wine and offered the bottle to Perrone.

"Penny, I'm driving," he said.

"I know. I don't see how you can stand to do it sober."

They came to a gate. An armed guard stepped up to the car. Perrone rolled down the window.

"I guess you're supposed to be here," said the man, "since you wouldn't know where it was if you weren't. You're Joe Perrone, aren't you? I had no idea you were one of us. I still need to see your pass, though."

As Perrone started composing a plausible yet vague excuse in his head,

Penny reached across and handed the guard a slip of paper. He looked at it, nodded, and unlocked the gate.

"What was that?" Perrone asked.

"Something I stole," Penny said. She didn't elaborate and he didn't press her.

It was a large building that looked like a cross between a barn and an airplane hangar. It appeared to be relatively new, and there was a gravel lot next to the building where twenty or thirty automobiles had been parked.

"These cars look rather expensive," Perrone said.

"They are," said Penny. "This isn't a bunch of rednecks from out in the sticks, Joey. I told you some pretty prominent people were involved in this thing. I gather there's been something of a renaissance within the Klan in recent years. They're more secretive than ever, and they have some sort of sinister agenda. You'd be surprised by how much these rich types resent the few freedoms the Negroes are allowed to have. They long for the days of the old plantation economy. You're not going to find a bunch of farmers here, because their families never had any real stake in all that shit."

"It sounds a bit pathetic," Perrone observed.

"And how," said Penny. "They're a bunch of douchebags, honey. I sincerely hope you don't sympathize with them. I still don't understand why you wanted to come."

Perrone parked the car and they got out. Penny finished the bottle of wine and tossed it across the parking area. It shattered on the fender of a Mercedes-Benz roadster.

They entered the building. A hard-faced man sat on a folding chair just inside the door. He looked as though he were about to challenge them, but Penny bent over and whispered something into his ear. He nodded and motioned for them to proceed.

The cavernous interior had been set up like an auditorium, with a wooden speakers' platform and podium at the rear, faced by several rows of folding chairs. The concrete floor was covered with sawdust. Red, white and black bunting had been hung around the walls. As he and Penny made their way to a couple of vacant seats, Perrone saw several faces he knew, all of them members of the so-called upper crust. He recognized a judge, a prominent physician, two state senators, a banker, even a priest. He hoped none of them would recognize him. Several men in white robes with white, pointed hoods stood behind and to the sides of the platform.

"I don't think this is any ordinary Klan rally," Penny whispered as they took their seats. "It's some kind of special conclave, according to my informant. Even more bullshit than usual, I suppose."

"Penny, is it necessary for you to use that kind of language?"

"Yes."

Perrone scowled and looked around the room again. "I'm surprised by some of the people I've seen here. I wouldn't have expected them to be involved in a thing like this."

"These are the men you never think about," she said. "They don't draw attention to themselves. They accumulate money and information and they sit quietly and wait."

"How do you know so much about this?"

"I know so much about *everything*," she whispered back. "I'm a girl that keeps her eyes and ears open. You haven't noticed that? You've paid plenty of attention to that *other* thing I've been keeping open for you."

Perrone's cheeks reddened. "Ah, yes, well..."

"I just called some people I know," Penny continued, "and then I called some people I don't know, and I learned a lot. The KKK has been reorganized several times since the original organization fizzled out after the Civil War. This new Klan operates differently from any of its predecessors. No public demonstrations or anything like that. They seem to be more interested in money and resources than they are in recruitment. They aren't interested in anyone who doesn't have the juice to fund whatever it is they think they're trying to do."

"Which is what?" Perrone asked.

Penny shrugged. "That, I do not know. Maybe we'll find out. I think the show's about to start."

A man stepped onto the speakers' platform and moved to stand behind the podium. He was elderly, stooped and sour-looking. He made Perrone think of some of Dickens' seedier villains.

"Good evening," he said when the buzz had died down. "Most of you know who I am. We won't be using any names tonight, of course."

In fact, Perrone *did* recognize this man. He was Harley St. Crippen, a former United States Supreme Court Justice. He had resigned in 1896, in protest of the majority verdict handed down by the Court in the case of *Plessy vs. Ferguson*, which established the doctrine of "separate but equal" public facilities for white citizens and Negroes. While the decision was a victory for proponents of segregation, St. Crippen just couldn't swallow the "but equal" part. His family had owned slaves, and it was his opinion that Negroes were little more than livestock who didn't deserve public accommodations *at all*.

"I could stand here all night," he said in his grating, high-pitched voice, "and tell you about what has been done to our way of life, and why this horror cannot stand. My opinions are well known. I remember what it was like before the curse of the damnable Lincoln descended upon us. I gave up my position on the highest court in this blighted land in order to protest the encroaching darkness."

"That scummy old gasbag," Penny whispered. "Ask him about that twelve-year-old girl in Georgetown if you want to know why he *really* gave up his position."

"We all do our humble best to express our indignation," the gasbag gassed. "But we have here tonight a gentleman who has a great deal more for us than opinions and lamentations. He has a plan. And he has the will to implement it...*with your help.*

"Here, now, please welcome our brother and our leader, the Grand Wizard!"

There was applause. Perrone joined in, just to keep up appearances. Penny let out a loud Bronx cheer. Fortunately, it went unnoticed.

A bizarre figure mounted the steps to the stage and moved to the podium. He was dressed in a similar style to the other Klansmen, but his vestments were deep purple, rather than white.

He stood at the podium, arms raised, and waited for the cheering and clapping to die down.

"Good evening, my friends," he said. "I am encouraged by the support you have shown and I appreciate your coming here tonight. And this is a very special night, my friends, as you will soon see.

"Dark days have arrived. Our moves to assume our rightful place of power are being blocked. Most of you know who I am referring to. They are white people, like us, but they care nothing for their heritage. They are followers of Mammon, seeking only money and the power it brings. To these people, the Jew and the nigger are no different from people like you and I. They glad-hand the Elders of Zion and they sit down at the table with the NAACP, shamelessly, as long as it fills their pockets!"

Angry rumblings rose from the crowd.

The Wizard raised his hands. "I feel your anger," he boomed, "and your righteous indignation. And, I assure you, my friends, I am not a man who is content to sit and watch as my world crumbles into black, filthy, foreign, impure dust!"

The audience cheered.

"Oh, brother," Penny whispered to Perrone.

"You know who he's talking about," he whispered back. "Your family."

She nodded. "Yeah, I get it. You and I have never discussed it, but you know what the Carters do. Everybody does. Most of them aren't aware of the extent to which we do it, but everyone knows we're a power. And they resent it. Rich as goddamn Croesus, every one of them, but they resent the fact that we're just carpetbaggers and we have more power and money than they do."

"Our time is at hand," the Grand Wizard was ranting. "We have money and we have people in power. We have awaited the right moment to activate our resources and throw off the yoke of tyranny! We are everywhere! We shall take political and economic control of Mobile first, then the state of Alabama. After that... Well, there is a gentleman in Germany whose goals are not unlike our own. Working together, we will establish the full dominion of the white race over every corner of the globe!"

"Globes don't have corners, jackass," Penny said in an undertone.

"And tonight we clear the way in the ethereal world," the Wizard continued. "The stars and the planets are in conjunction to release to us the power of the Upper Spheres. This is the night of the Great Sacrifice. Bring in the Son of Cain!"

A side door near the platform opened and two large Klansmen entered. Between them was a stooped and elderly Negro man. He was festooned with iron shackles from his neck to his ankles. He shuffled along between his two "escorts," as they approached the platform.

"Look upon the face of the beast!" said the Grand Wizard, pointing at the shackled man. "This animal used his dark magic to destroy my brother! A fine white boy was brought to grief by this nigger's voodoo! We knew it. We knew he did it! We went to him to bring him justice! He was hanged in the proper manner, but what do you think happened? He did not die! Hanged, his neck broken, his breath cut off, and he did not die!

"Tonight, he will finally be destroyed, and his destruction will mark the beginning of the end of the Yankee carpetbaggers' nigger-loving world! We will send him to his wretched hell and open the door to the return of our way of life and truth! We will rise again, and none may stop us! Bring out the altar!"

Two of the Klansman stationed at the rear wall ducked behind a set of dark red curtains, to emerge moments later carrying a flat, stainless steel table. As they brought it onto the platform, Perrone saw that the surface was covered with odd runes and symbols that he did not recognize. The Klansmen placed the table near the front of the platform, then returned to their stations.

"The sacrifice!" crowed the Grand Wizard.

The shackled man was led onto the stage by his minders. They walked him to the table, then lifted him up onto it. He lay prone, perfectly still and silent. The Grand Wizard reached into his robes and produced a long-bladed knife.

"They're going to kill that man," Perrone said in a horrified whisper. "I can't let that happen." He drew a gun from a special holster inside his jacket. "Stay back, Penny."

He eyes gleamed. "See, I knew there was something about you!"

"Release that man," Perrone said in a commanding tone, moving toward the platform. "This is the Twentieth Century, and that kind of thing is extremely unscientific. And this man looks as though he has been abused."

A white-robed goon charged at him. Perrone brandished his gun and ordered the man to stop. The Klansman slowed down, but continued his advance.

"I warned you," Perrone said sadly, squeezing the trigger. The shot caught the man in the knee and put him on the ground.

"Oh, hell yeah!" Penny whooped, drawing her little .22 from her purse.

She fired four shots in quick succession. Every one of them found its mark, and four Klansmen went down, never to rise under their own power again. The auditorium erupted into absolute screaming chaos.

People were running to and fro, most of the "civilians" making for the exit and trampling all over one another in their cowardly eagerness to get there. Penny was jumping up and down and running from one side of the room to the other, shooting anything in a white sheet.

Perrone headed straight for the stage, as swiftly as he could run, dodging and ducking all who tried to stop him. He had a gun in each hand, now, and he fired a couple of shots toward the ceiling. The Grand Wizard had raised the knife above the prisoner's chest.

Perrone stuffed his guns into his jacket pockets. When he got to the platform, he threw himself on top of the poor wretch on the table. The Grand Wizard's knife came down and struck his shoulder, but he rolled to the side before it could penetrate his flesh. He took hold of the shackled man and rolled all the way off the table, dumping both of them onto the platform, then off the edge and onto the sawdust-covered floor.

Perrone got to his feet and stood protectively over the old man, guns drawn and ready, alert for any threat that might head his way.

Penny also had two guns by this time, and neither of them were the one she had brought with her. She had appropriated them from the bodies of two of the Klansmen she had ushered out of this mortal coil, and seemed to be having a grand time. When she ran out of white-sheeted targets, she started taking potshots at the fleeing mob of Mobile's elite. Perrone wanted to intervene, but he was too busy with the Grand Wizard.

"You," hissed the hooded man, stalking to the edge of the platform to glare down at Perrone. "Why are you protecting that beast?"

"I see only one beast here," Perrone said coldly. "And it isn't this man at my feet."

"If I'm a beast," said the Wizard, "then shoot me. All I have is a knife. Kill me. My cause will continue after I'm gone. Pull the trigger."

"I don't have time for games," said Perrone. "I'm sure you've got bullet-proof garments under those robes. Why didn't you give any to your men? Several of them are dead now."

"They don't matter. Neither do you. But that nigger does. He has witchery in him and I need it. I pried his secrets out of him, but he still has power. This is bigger than you. Put those guns away and leave now, or else you'll be..."

That was as far as he got before Penny Carter jumped on his back and knocked him flat on his face. She brought the butt of a pistol down on the back of his head, hard. He grunted, then lay motionless. Penny stood up and smiled at Perrone, making a little bow.

"Penny, step away from him. That hood is probably padded. He might not be..."

He wasn't. The Wizard rolled over onto his back, grabbing Penny by the leg and pulling her off-balance. There was a very brief scuffle, and the Wizard dropped his knife and wrested Penny's weapon from her grasp. It happened too quickly for Perrone to even think of intervening. The Wizard grabbed a handful of Penny's red hair and pressed the barrel of the gun to her temple. He stood up, hauling Penny with him, holding her in front of him as a shield.

"Now," said the Wizard, "drop your weapons and back away from my property, or I will put a hole in this tramp's head."

Perrone's eyes met Penny's. She shook her head almost imperceptibly and she gave him a look that said, unequivocally, *Don't worry about it, I'll be fine. Do what you need to do.*

He nodded back and said, "Forget it. I won't be bullied into accepting your terms. If you kill her, you die one second later."

"Fine," said the Wizard. He started backing toward the rear of the platform, keeping Penny between himself and Perrone. "But you don't want her to die. You'd rather she didn't. So take the beast. I'll get him back. And until I do, I'm keeping her."

Penny wasn't much of a damsel in distress, Perrone thought. She didn't seem the least bit frightened. If anything, she looked a little bored. She actually gave Perrone a wink before the Wizard dragged her behind the drapes.

Perrone helped the shackled man to his feet and made for the exit, whispering reassurances. Once they were through the door, he made a dash for his automobile, pulling the poor man with him.

"Come on," said Perrone. "I'll take you somewhere safe."

"Hell, no you won't!" came a voice from behind them.

Five masked and robed Klansmen, each holding a shotgun, came sprinting around the corner of the building, heading straight for Perrone and his charge.

"Let go of him and walk away," one of them said.

"And what if I don't?" Perrone replied.

"Let go of him and walk away," the Klansman repeated emphatically.

Why on earth don't they just gun us down? Perrone wondered. *It seems they don't want to harm this man. Why?*

Then it dawned on him. *Of course!* They wanted him to live until he could be properly sacrificed.

"I'm sorry again, sir," he whispered as he pressed the barrel of his pistol to the chained man's temple.

"*You* walk away!" Perrone barked. "Or I'll kill him right now!"

The hooded men stepped back, exchanging glances. They seemed stunned. A couple of them looked back at the building, as though for orders from on high. But they didn't find any; their Grand Wizard wasn't there.

They stood and watched as Perrone got to his car, hustled the man onto the passenger seat, then got in and started the engine. He turned the vehicle around and gave it the gas, spraying gravel everywhere as he roared out of the lot and onto the dirt road.

The car bounced down the rutted path toward the main road. Two guards, armed with rifles, stood by the locked gate. They must have secured it again after some of the guests had fled. A few cars had been abandoned. Perrone zig-zagged around the other vehicles and aimed the car directly at the sentries. They stood their ground for a few seconds, one of them taking aim with his rifle, but when it became clear that Perrone did not intend to stop, they dove out of the way.

Perrone pressed the accelerator all the way to the floor. The speedometer read seventy-five when the front end hit the gates, tearing them loose from the wooden posts.

The road was only a few yards away. He couldn't see anything on account of the huge clouds of dust he had raised. Going by memory rather than observation, he hit the brakes and put the car into a hard, some might say suicidal, left turn. He avoided going across the road and into the ditch, but the car slewed wildly, spinning around twice before he could get it back under control. Once he was sure he was headed in the right direction, he hit the gas.

"I'm going to find you some help."

Easier said than done. He could not take this man to any ordinary doctor or hospital. Based on what he had seen that night, he was sure there were "invisible" Klan members all over the city. Wherever he took the man, there was a danger that he would be recognized.

What on earth do I do?
He thought for a moment, then smiled.

CHAPTER TWENTY-THREE
LIFE AND/OR DEATH AND/OR NONE OF THE ABOVE

Perrone drove up to Prichard and found the street he wanted. He drove slowly, trying to read the house numbers; what few there were. He found the house he was seeking. A simple clapboard affair, two stories, painted a very light green. A rectangular sign on the wall next to the front door said:

AMBROSE V. ATTICUS, M.D.

Perrone parked on the street in front of the house and went to the door. He knocked several times, increasing the volume as the seconds ticked by. He knew the doctor was probably asleep, but if this didn't qualify as an emergency, he didn't know what would.

Peering through the front window, he saw a light come on in the rear of the house. He heard footsteps coming his way. The door was opened by a dark-skinned man in middle age, with graying hair. He eyed Perrone skeptically. He didn't look like the sort who was apt to put up with a lot of foolishness.

"Something I can do for you?" he said warily. He was not accustomed to finding strange white men at his door in the middle of the night.

"We've never met," Perrone said, "but my friend Mirabelle Darcy speaks highly of you."

"And you're who, exactly?"

"Joe Perrone. Let me explain the situation."

Atticus had looked cranky and put upon at first, but after Perrone explained the situation, his expression turned to one of concern. "I brought him here," Perrone concluded, "because I dare not take him to any hospital in the area. He has been held captive for some time by members of the Ku Klux Klan. Years, perhaps."

"Come on," Atticus said, "let's get him into the house."

They helped the shambling wreck of a man walk into the house and down the hall to the examination room.

"You know Mirabelle, eh?" said Atticus as he and Perrone got the man situated on the examining table. "How's she keeping these days?"

"She's doing well," Perrone said, wondering if it was the truth.

Atticus performed a routine battery of tests on his new patient. All of his vital signs were much too low. His respiratory rate, for example, as about half of what it should have been. And his reflexes were virtually nonexistent. His heart rate was slow but strong. Atticus could find nothing the matter with the man's eyes. They seemed to be in perfect condition. So the glassy stare had its origins inside the unfortunate fellow's skull.

"He's in good shape and he's in bad shape," Doctor Atticus said. "His vital signs are odd but acceptable, and he is obviously impaired. He looks like he's been drugged. Can't tell you what with. Definitely a soporific of some kind. Maybe morphine, laudanum... I don't know. Could be something else, something you don't see much of in these parts."

"You've got an idea?"

"Maybe. I don't know. I don't want to say anything until I check into it more. A *lot* more."

Perrone nodded. "I'll leave him in your hands, then. If it becomes complicated, we can move him to a private sanitarium in Baldwin County. I'm on the board of directors, and I can arrange it."

Perrone spent much of the following day in an attempt to track down the Grand Wizard and Penny Carter. He had taken a few minutes to relate the events of the previous night to Mirabelle, but had omitted any mention of the chained man. He wasn't sure why, but something made him hold his tongue on that subject.

His efforts came to nothing. He visited the site of the rally, only to find that the building had been burned to the ground. There was nothing left in the way of clues. A feeling of grim oppression overcame him, as though he were dealing with forces that were beyond his ken. Late that afternoon, he disguised his features and met with Louis Rickert at the little speakeasy on Royal Street. The Bay Phantom's agent had nothing helpful on Penny or the Wizard, but he did have other news.

"Something's going on," Rickert said. "Lots of guys have gone missing. Thugs, you know, hard cases, enforcer types. Muscle. None of them have turned up dead, though. So where are they? And on top of that, I've heard that a lot of talent from out of town has been arriving here, but nobody knows where any of them are, either."

"A recruitment drive, do you think?"

"That's how I see it," Rickert said, shaking his head. "Someone is planning something big. In fact, I think there are *two* someones; two different factions. They're gearing up for God knows what."

Shorty Red had made excellent progress. He was able to get out of bed unaided and walk around as much as he wanted to. He did little isometric exercises, increasing his regimen as his mobility and stamina improved.

Every night, before he went to sleep, he repeated two sentences, as though they were prayers:

"I'll see you soon, Bay Phantom. And I *will* pay you back."

Caleb Carter was in his office in downtown Mobile, doing some creative bookkeeping for one of the real estate companies he owned, when the phone rang. He sighed, rubbed his eyes, put down his pen and lifted the receiver. Before he could get a hello out of his mouth, the caller began talking.

"Caleb? It's me, Penny."

She sounded out of breath and on the verge of hysteria. Caleb wondered what could have had such an effect on her.

"I don't have time to go into a lot of detail," she said, "but I was kidnapped by the KKK of all things. They held me for a while, but I got loose. Trouble is, it wasn't a clean getaway, and they're on my heels. You won't believe what they're planning. I have some things to tell you, so just listen. I know what's going on and who's behind it. And they're getting ready to hit us hard."

"Okay," Caleb said, reaching for pen and paper. "Shoot."

The information she gave him was indeed startling. By the time she finished, he knew just who it was that had been causing his family such grief. The person's identity wasn't a surprise at all, but the resources that had been mustered were.

"Shit!" said Penny, "I have to go. They're here. Jesus, Caleb, I think I finally bit off more than I can chew. Take care, and use that information I gave you before it's too late."

"Penny..?"

She hung up.

It was shortly after midnight when the security guard outside Caleb Carter's manor house on the Eastern Shore, across the bay from Mobile, made a gruesome discovery.

A body had been affixed to the front door with large nails. It appeared to be female. It had been badly burned, either before or after death. The face was almost completely gone, but the red hair remained.

The nails had been driven through the feet and forearms. The corpse's hands were intact. The fingerprints matched the ones the Mobile Police Department had on file for Penny Carter.

Perrone had spent most of the night in a fruitless search for the missing bully boys and the mysterious "recruiters." Even with the help of Louis Rickert, he had come up empty. He had also passed the information to Tom Dart, who had met with a similar lack of success. Someone was covering their tracks with admirable efficiency.

He returned to Tull House an hour after sunrise. Too exhausted for further effort, mental or physical, he went to bed for a few hours' sleep.

When he awoke and went downstairs, he found Mirabelle sitting in the living room with a copy of the afternoon edition of the *Press* in her lap. She stood up, handed him the newspaper, and said, "I'm sorry, Mister Perrone. I didn't think much of her, but I'm sorry." She touched his cheek and left him alone in the room with the news of Penny Carter's gruesome death. She knew him well enough to know he wouldn't want her to see him. She also knew he'd want to talk later; probably *much* later. That was good, because she had some things of her own she needed to work out first.

"I thought that whole Cathedral thing was blown," said Hillyard Parnell.

"So did I," said Caleb Carter. The two men were sitting in Caleb's downtown office, holding what amounted to a council of war. "Someone tipped off the cops, and they raided the place very delicately; it's a church, after all; but it looked like he had moved out. They didn't find anything. But the Embalmer told me he still has some 'major assets' squirreled away there."

"So, how do these Klan jokers know about the Cathedral?"

"I imagine they got the location out of Penny. She didn't say so, but what else could it have been? She was telling the truth about this planned assault, I believe, and we need to be ready. If they're going to hit the Cathedral, we're going to hit *them*…hard."

"Are you sure you're not getting carried away? That's pretty public. Why not just tip off the cops?"

"Because, goddammit, they have made this personal by killing my sister. Maybe I didn't like her very much, but she was family. If we let them get away with it, we look like punks, Hillyard. We're finished. The boys from Chicago will drop us like a hot potato, then what will we do? We've been gearing up, doing some hiring, and now is the time to use what we've got."

"I wish we could count on more help from Chicago," said Parnell. "But they've got problems of their own. Capone is going on trial for income tax evasion. Nitti and a couple of the others, too."

"They'll beat the rap," Carter said dismissively, "just like they always do. Who the hell cares about income tax? At the moment, I'm more concerned about us. We've got to jump right on this."

"Okay," said Parnell, "how do we handle it?"

Caleb Carter told him. When he was done, Parnell wondered if Caleb might not be crazier than his sister.

CHAPTER TWENTY-FOUR
UNLOCKED

"You want me to try hypnosis?" Freud asked.

He and Mirabelle were at the kitchen table, drinking tea and eating scones. In spite of several marathon sessions with the doctor, Mirabelle seemed no closer to resolving her difficulties than she had been before Freud arrived.

And now she was worried about Perrone. She didn't know how he had taken the news about Penny Carter. He would blame himself, of course. He had gone down into the secret rooms in the cellar shortly after she'd given him the newspaper, and she hadn't seen him since. She had gone down there less than an hour ago and found one of the two electric handcars gone.

"Yes," said Mirabelle. "Do you still think it's a valid clinical tool?"

Freud nodded. "As you know, I have all but abandoned it in favor of psychotherapy, which I believe is much more effective. However, therapy takes a very long time. I do occasionally use hypnosis as a 'shortcut' in some cases, and I believe it would be appropriate here. There is something in your past that you have buried."

"I believe so."

Freud nodded. "I think this is a good time to bring up something I have noticed over the last few days. And, indeed, for the last few years, through your letters. Tell me, are you aware that you go to almost any lengths to avoid speaking of your father?"

"Do I?"

"Yes. I am convinced there is something there that should be uncovered. You have told me that your father disappeared when you were ten years of age. There was gossip to the effect that he had left you and your mother for another woman."

"That's correct."

"And you have also told me that you did not believe he was the sort of man who would do such a thing."

"Well... my memories of him are hazy."

"Hazier than they should be? Mirabelle, the mind does not go to all the trouble of concealing information from itself unless it has good reason. You know all of this yourself. You are as conversant with this school of thought as I am. You helped me shape it! And now that you have come to this realization, I know you will not be able to let go of it."

He leaned forward and took her hands in his. "Mirabelle, you are terrified of *yourself*. You live in fear of your own mind, your own potential. Where did this come from? Not just the society in which you were raised. There is something deeper. Uncovering this information *could* have unfortunate consequences. I give you this warning with no hope that it will be heeded. I assume, Mirabelle, that you will take the same attitude Admiral Farragut took during a naval battle in that Bay out there: '*Damn the torpedoes, full speed ahead!*' Am I correct?"

"Yeah," said Mirabelle, with no enthusiasm. "I dread it, but I have to know what it is."

"Just so," said the doctor with a crisp nod. "When would you like to begin?"

"Well, if it were done when 'tis done, then 'twere well it were done quickly, sir. How about right now? I'd just as soon get it out of the way before Mister Perrone comes back. He might need me."

"I thought as much. We may proceed immediately."

It's now or never, Gladys decided. Mister Perrone was out and Mirabelle and Freud were doing something behind the locked door of the parlor. She got out the little implement Louis Rickert had given her and tried to remember everything he had taught her. Working quickly, spurred by her fear of being caught, she got the door open and descended the stairs to the Bay Phantom's secret lair.

Having placed Mirabelle in a trance state, Freud sat next to her with his fingertips pressed against her forehead, a technique he had developed well before the turn of the century, as a means of helping the subject maintain concentration. He went through the standard preliminary questions and instructions, then got down to business.

"Let us just go back a bit," he said. "Let's go back and have a look at your father. His name was Paul, you said. Paul Darcy. When was the last time you saw him, Mirabelle?"

"I was young," she said. "We lived in our own little house, a few hundred yards from Gulf Bay Manor. That's where I am, it's late at night, and I'm reading a book, and... And my mama is asleep, and my... And my... my..."

"Yes?" Freud gently prompted. "Your..?"

"My *Daddy*. My Daddy is there. I don't... I don't remember this at all, but here it is... I was there, I experienced it, but..."

"Don't worry about that. Just tell me what you see."

"Yes. Daddy is... He's out behind the house, in that little shed of his that he uses to... He goes back there. What does he do? I know he has a... Well, he's out there. He's out there, working, and... And the men come. They're not... They look funny. It's... They have robes on, white robes, and these hoods, and...Oh, I know what they are... Oh, no...

"They're dragging him right out of there... Oh my... he looks so small and... and afraid. And the one in the purple robe is yelling at him. He's saying... He's saying, 'Tell me what you did with him!' And Daddy says, 'Who? Who do you mean?' He doesn't know... He doesn't know, leave him alone! LEAVE HIM ALONE! DO YOU HEAR ME?"

"Mirabelle," Freud said gently. "They cannot hear you. They are not here. What you are seeing is like a movie. It cannot hurt you. Be calm and watch what happens."

"I... Yeah, I see but... There they are, right out in the yard. The man in the purple robe says, 'You know who I mean. What did you do to him? The Perrones are gone, nobody will protect you now. What did you do to my brother?' Daddy is shaking his head. he doesn't know. He didn't do anything to anybody. Why do they think he did?"

"Why would they?" Freud said softly. "Do you have any idea?"

"No, I don't... The purple man is... He's saying, 'You're a *Voodoo priest*, you black bastard. I know you did something to my brother to make him run away. He started coming here, to the Perrones' house two years ago. He came to this house all the time, and that was when he started acting funny. You put a spell on him, didn't you?' That's what the purple man is saying."

"Why would he think such a thing?" Freud asked.

"Well, Daddy used to... he did these little Voodoo things... He was a... not a bokor, no... Just a very minor little houngan... A dabbler, that's all. Lots of people used to do that. Still do... There's a man in the Woolworth's store... Lots of people do that... Little charms, medicines, you know... Cure some little ailment, make somebody fall in love with you... St. John the Conqueror root, things like that... It isn't harmful... It was just silly and I didn't like him doing it because it was... It was embarrassing... I was embarrassed and ashamed of him because of it... I shouldn't have... Oh,

"Just tell me what you see."

I'm sorry, Daddy, I didn't mean to say those things to you..."

"Be calm, Mirabelle," Freud urged. "Your father knows you did not mean what you said. Just tell me what is happening."

"And he just pulls the hood off of his head and sticks his face right in front of Daddy's face and says, 'You're too smart, nigger! Too smart for your own good! We know you know how to change people with that dirty nigger witchcraft of yours! Nobody wants a smart nigger around! You know what being smart gets a nigger? It gets him *dead*!'

"And they... They're putting the rope around his neck, and then they... Oh! They're... They're pulling him up, they're *hanging* him... There's no God to help him, there's no Voodoo loa... He's hanging there, by his neck, kicking and struggling and the purple man is just screaming and screaming at him. Then he... He's telling the others to let Daddy down again, and they lower him and his feet touch the ground. Oh, look at his eyes! They're so red, and he's coughing and trying to...

"I can't look at this... I'm rolling over onto the floor... Crawling up under my bed...That's what I'm doing, and... And the last thing I saw was that man's face, the man who hanged my Daddy and... Nothing else..."

She had begun to tremble all over and she was hyperventilating. Freud decided it was time to bring the session to an end. Almost. There was one more thing he had to find out.

"Easy, Mirabelle," he said soothingly. "It's over, dear girl. It is done. You don't have to look at it any more. Relax... Relax..."

He remained silent for a while, listening to Mirabelle's breathing. When it slowed to its normal rhythm he spoke again, as gently and calmly as he could:

"Mirabelle, you said the 'purple man' took off his hood. You said you saw his face."

"Yes."

"Did you recognize him? Do you know who he is?"

"I didn't... I didn't recognize him that night, but... But now, I..."

She suddenly opened her eyes. Somehow, she had brought herself out of the hypnotic state. She glanced around the room, as though to get her bearings, then looked Freud in the eye.

"Yeah," she said in a low, dark, frighteningly calm voice. "I know who it was."

CHAPTER TWENTY-FIVE
EXPOSURE

Gladys Turnbull had explored the Bay Phantom's secret headquarters, before creeping back up to the house and re-locking the door. She had made copious sketches and notes, but she knew she needed something more. She went home and lay for several hours on the sofa, unable to sleep or to do anything else but repeat to herself her list of justifications for what she planned to do.

Sigmund Freud went to bed at a little past midnight, turning over in his mind the things Mirabelle Darcy had revealed under hypnosis and afterward.

Mirabelle waited up for Perrone, but when four a.m. had come and gone with no sign of him, she went to bed.

Joe Perrone returned to Tull House at five-thirty, after another fruitless night, and went directly to his bedroom. There was much to do and much to consider, but he simply had to have some sleep before he tackled any of it. As was his custom, he switched on the radio and turned it down low before getting between the sheets.

Unknown to all of them, forces gathered, instructions were given and received, and things were set into motion that would not be stopped before a great deal of blood had been shed and a great many lives had been changed forever...

Mirabelle rose at 12:30, and found Doctor Freud in the kitchen, sipping tea that Beth Page had brewed for him. Mirabelle smiled at the new maid, grateful to have one person in the house who wasn't tormented by dark secrets. She joined Freud at the table and they discussed the revelations of the previous night, as Miss Page went about her duties in her quiet, efficient manner.

Shortly after one o'clock, Joe Perrone opened his bedroom door and shouted down the stairs: "Someone has blown up the Dauphine Royale Hotel! I just heard it on the radio! And there are reports of other explosions and disturbances! I've got to get downtown as quickly as possible!"

"Oh, Lord," Mirabelle said, dashing into the living room to switch on the big Philco set.

Perrone ducked back into his room for a few moments, then came hurtling down the stairs and into the hallway, swiftly unlocking the cellar door and heading on down, without pausing to secure the door again.

In the hallway, Gladys Turnbull knew that her moment had arrived. She ducked into the pantry, grabbed her Speed Graphic, and followed. She tiptoed down the stairs and saw that Perrone had entered the small dressing room on the right. She pressed herself against the wall and slowly inched her head around the edge of the doorway.

He had stripped to his underwear and put on the dark suit and cape. Now he was examining the inside of his mask before putting it on, probably making certain the lenses were clean and undamaged.

Without giving a single thought to what she was doing, Gladys stepped into the room, pointed her camera, and pressed the button.

Perrone looked up, startled by the bright flash. He was holding his Bay Phantom mask in his hands. The photograph Gladys had just taken would be beautiful. She could see it now, taking form in the developing tray.

"Well," he said. "This is rather awkward. Whatever are you doing, Miss Page?"

She said nothing. She couldn't speak, couldn't even move. *What have I done? He's going to kill me.*

"You know who I am then," he said as he pulled the mask over his head and adjusted it. "I don't suppose you wanted that photograph for your scrapbook."

She finally found her voice. "You're... not going to stop me?"

"What can I do?" said the Phantom, donning the slouch hat. "Take your camera away by force and destroy the film? You would still know what you know; I can't relieve you of that, short of killing you."

"I... I was, ah, kind of afraid you might." she said.

The Phantom shook his head. "And still you did it! You are either brave or foolish or both, Miss Page. But, no, that is not my way. The only other option I have is to imprison you here for the remainder of your life, and that presents insurmountable moral and legal difficulties as well."

"Uh... What are you going to do?" *What did I think he was going to do? Just let me walk out of here?*

He shrugged. "I'm just going to let you walk out of here. What *can* I do? I have work to attend to. So do you, I gather. That camera of yours is a brand widely used by journalists. If that is what you are, then you must do what you feel you have to. I believe in the freedom of the press, so long as it is not abused; and that would not be the case here. Joseph Perrone is in fact the Bay Phantom. It is the truth, and you have a perfect right to report it if you see fit. I haven't time to discuss it now. I'll give you a week's severance pay, but don't expect me to provide a reference."

With that, he pushed past her into the hallway, went to the tunnel access area, hopped onto one of the electric handcars, and was gone.

Gladys crept up the stairs, clutching her Speed Graphic to her breast. There was no sign of Mirabelle or Freud. They were probably in the living room, glued to the radio. Gladys slipped quietly from the house and got into her car. *I am not a contemptible traitor*, she told herself. *This is business. Hell, it's freedom of the press! Mister Perrone said so himself... You know, while he wasn't killing or imprisoning me...*

She waited for some response from herself, but there was only a frigid silence.

"Aw, to hell with you," she said out loud as she pressed the starter and put the car in gear. "You're too goddamn judgmental."

CHAPTER TWENTY-SIX
A PLAGUE ON ALL YOUR HOUSES

According to the information given to Caleb Carter, the attack on the Cathedral Basilica of the Immaculate Conception had been set for 2 p.m.

At three minutes past one o'clock, a series of explosions leveled the Dauphine Royale Hotel in downtown Mobile. Sixty-three people were killed. Witnesses said that after the bombs went off, the a man in a lab coat and a plaster mask identified himself as the "Black Embalmer," and claimed credit for the disaster, before heading off on foot in the direction of Cathedral Plaza.

The hotel was owned by Hector Sams.

At six minutes past one, sixteen blocks away, a huge blast ripped through the old brick building that housed the law firm of Jacob, Jacob, Jacob and Downey. Witnesses said that another "Black Embalmer" appeared and claimed credit for the bombing, before heading off on foot in the direction of Cathedral Plaza.

Jacob, Jacob, Jacob and Downey was the principal law firm employed by Hector Sams.

At 1:37, six large transport trucks, of the kind used by the military, entered the downtown area from six different directions, and started toward Cathedral Plaza. On the way, each truck stopped briefly in front of a business or office building owned by a member of the Carter family. A small squadron of men jumped from the rear of each vehicle and sprayed the front of each building with machine-gun fire. Witnesses said the gunmen were decked out in full Ku Klux Klan regalia; white robes festooned with arcane symbols, topped with white, pointed hoods.

In all, seventeen people were killed, and twenty-four were gravely injured. Half of the Klansmen got back into the trucks, which continued on their way. The ones who had been left behind started patrolling the streets. Several of them encountered men dressed as the Black Embalmer. Fierce battles ensued.

Soon, the downtown area was crawling with Klansmen, Black Embalmers, and innocent bystanders.

The annual Daughters of the Confederacy flower show had been underway for almost an hour in Cathedral Plaza, a small, grassy park across the street from the Cathedral Basilica of the Immaculate Conception, when the trucks arrived and started disgorging sheeted and armed Klansmen. They gathered in the plaza and stood in groups of three or four, weapons ready, facing the Cathedral. Some of the flower show attendees fled in fear, while others stayed where they were, regarding these newcomers with curiosity. News of the carnage around town had trickled in, but nobody had yet decided how to react. Several of the Daughters, decked out in colorful hoop skirts and wide-brimmed bonnets, clustered together behind one of the floral displays.

The Cathedral was a lovely example of Greek Revival architecture from the mid-Nineteenth Century, featuring a large portico with massive Doric columns. Twin towers rose more than a hundred feet into the air on either side of the facade.

As a nearby clock struck two, the crowd noticed something curious. Standing atop the Cathedral, just over the portico and midway between the towers, was a man in a lab coat. He had a plaster mask over his face and a megaphone in his hand.

"Good afternoon!" he said. "And welcome to the beginning of someone's end. Well, it actually began some time back, but I think of that as the preliminaries. Today you bear witness to the main event.

"Most of you have never heard of me. I am known as the Black Embalmer, for reasons I won't go into here. Just use your imaginations. I represent a certain faction that must remain nameless. These gentlemen arrayed in their white robes, Labor Day still being several weeks away, represent another. You may have noticed a number of individuals here who are dressed like me. They are my army, the Legion of the Deadly Departed. Our faction only wants to steal from you every so often, commit a few strategic murders from time to time, and to generally control what goes on in this city. In return, we supply you with one of mankind's most worthwhile discoveries: Alcohol. Also a bit of gambling and prostitution. You know; the things everyone craves but pretends not to.

"But this other faction, the one represented by these grim ivory specters, wants something very different. They want control, too. In return for it, they are prepared to offer you *nothing* in return. They serve a dim, confused ideology, rather than a straightforward and fundamentally sound economic agenda; much like the Russian Bolsheviks. We are progressive, but they wish to turn back the clock, to a time that never was, and restore a social order that didn't exist even if it did. Do you understand? They're crooks. We, on the other hand, are *criminals*. There's a big difference!

"And what do you suppose these cowardly, sheeted crooks plan to do? They're going to kill us! Yes, and they're going to take control of your society, your very lives! This cannot stand, friends, and my compatriots and I are prepared to shed our own blood, and anybody's else's, to protect your rights and liberties! My dear friends, I give you my Legion of the Deadly Departed; defenders of your freedom!"

The Black Embalmer paused in his oration while a dozen men dressed and masked just like him emerged from the front entrance of the Cathedral and walked slowly down the steps to the sidewalk. They, too, carried large and wicked-looking firearms. Several more of them trickled into the Plaza from all directions. It seemed that Downtown Mobile was suddenly infested with Black Embalmers.

One or two bewildered souls, stirred by the rooftop Embalmer's bombastic remarks, raised a cheer. It was feeble to begin with and quickly fizzled out.

Most of the civilians in the Plaza wore expressions of fear and anxiety. A keen observer might have noticed, however, that the hoop-skirted

Daughters were scowling fiercely, eyes narrowed, hands curled into fists. They looked more like Valkyries than Southern belles.

Rickey Harvard had been drunk almost constantly since the night he had seen the horrible black ghost in the Church Street Graveyard.

He was particularly plastered today, lounging around the front room in his father's house on Saint Francis Street, a block north of the Cathedral. He became aware of a great deal of noise and commotion outside, including what sounded like a peal of thunder. He staggered to the window to peek out. It was bright, broad daylight out there, no hint of rain. He scratched his head and went to another window. That was when he saw them.

Ghosts! Six of them, bold as brass, walking right down the street in front of his house! All white and billowy, with pointed heads.

"Oh, hell no," he said. "I ain't having this!" He rushed to the back of his house and grabbed his father's shotgun. He gulped down some bourbon and stormed out the front door. Looking up and down the block, he spotted the ghosts heading south, in the direction of Cathedral Plaza. He ran after them, catching up just as they reached Dauphin Street.

"Hey, you lousy dead sonsabitches! Get the hell off my street! Take this!"

He let loose a blast that cut down two of the white-sheeted ghosts. For spirits, they certainly contained a great deal of blood.

Rickey Harvard had just fired the shot heard 'round the world; or at least 'round Cathedral Plaza. Poor, misguided Rickey had let slip the dogs of war. As the Klansmen hit the pavement, the Plaza erupted.

The Bay Phantom had arrived downtown a few minutes earlier, having taken a tunnel that came out in the living room of a vacant house on Royal Street. Smoke hung in the air from all the explosions, and sirens wailed in every direction. He questioned a couple of passers-by, who told him of the ominous gathering at Cathedral Plaza. The Phantom proceeded to the little speakeasy that seemed to have become Louis Rickert's second home. Sure enough, there was Rickert, sitting at the bar, sipping a highball.

"Louis, it's mid-afternoon," the Phantom scolded, "and I need your help. Are you too intoxicated to accompany me?"

"Hell, you act like I'm a damn alcoholic," Rickert said indignantly, barely slurring his words at all. "I'm always fit and ready to serve, Boss."

They headed west on Dauphin Street, bound for Cathedral Plaza. The Bay Phantom was appalled at what he saw.

This was a war between two factions, one represented by the KKK, the other by the Black Embalmers. There were skirmishes going on all over downtown. The Phantom imagined that most of the Klansmen weren't genuine members, but hired hands. The same went for the Black Embalmers. Here were the missing bully boys he'd been seeking.

Ordinary citizens, too, had entered into the chaos, becoming involved in the wild melees. Some of them fought Klansmen, some fought Black Embalmers, and some fought one another. Old grudges had resurfaced to take advantage of the atmosphere of sudden, lawless violence. There were looters at work, too. The Phantom shook his head at this, more in sorrow than in anger.

"Attention, looters!" he said loudly as he made his way along Dauphin Street. "Many of you are no doubt caught up in the heat of the moment and are allowing yourselves to be carried away by your emotions! But a critical situation exists in this city, and your actions are not going to help restore order!"

There was a commotion in front of the little peanut shop that had been a fixture of the downtown area for many years. The proprietor of the shop had pursued a young man into the middle of the street, and was menacing him with a shotgun.

"What is this?" the Phantom asked.

"This little bastard snatched a handful of money out of my cash register, that's what!"

The Phantom looked at the youngster and said, "Is that true?"

The boy shook his head. "He's lying, mister. He must be crazy or something."

"I'm gonna blow his goddamn head off!" said the shop owner. "That'll teach all these punks a lesson!"

"I'm sorry," said the Phantom, "but I cannot allow bloodshed over crimes against mere property. And that language hardly does credit to a merchant whose clientele includes women and children."

"Then stop me," the man said defiantly, raising the gun and drawing a bead on the young thief, his finger tightening on the trigger.

"Very well," said the Phantom. "You're just too excitable right now. I'm sorry I have to do this."

He threw a short right jab at a spot just underneath and behind the merchant's ear, instantly rendering the man unconscious.

"Now," he said, turning to the young man, "I would appreciate it if you would give me the money you stole. You may go about your business, but I hope you've learned a lesson. I don't want to find you causing any more problems."

"No! I mean, yes, yes I won't cause no more nothing!" he dug down in his pants pocket and extracted two wads of bills. "Here, take it, Your Honor! Please don't hit me."

"I'm not going to hit you," said the Phantom, "but I want you to go right home and stay out of trouble."

The young man nodded wildly and swore to God he'd never even think of stealing again. He spun on his heel and dashed away.

The Phantom stopped down and took a ring of keys from the unconscious proprietor's belt.

"Louis, please go put this money back into the cash register, and lock the door when you come back out. And drag this poor fellow inside, where he'll be relatively safe."

As Rickert moved to obey, the Phantom addressed the crowd at large:

"I understand the seductive nature of temptation, especially at a time like this, and I'm not condemning any of you! Nor do I have time to stop you. But I urge you to do the right thing! If you are unable to stop yourself now, please give it some thought in the days to come! If you need to, please consult a clergyman or some other respected authority!"

Rickert had dragged the shop owner back into his shop and tucked him away behind the counter. While the Phantom was too busy orating to pay any attention to him, Rickert pocketed the money he had been entrusted with, then helped himself to what was left in the cash register. For good measure, he stuffed two bags of roasted peanuts into his jacket pockets.

And then the gunfire started.

"Dear Lord," said the Phantom, "that's coming from Cathedral Plaza."

When the boy who had fired the first shot saw what he had done, he screamed, threw his shotgun down on the sidewalk, and took off running. Most of the other Klansmen in the Plaza produced firearms of various kinds and opened up on the line of Black Embalmers in front of the Cathedral. The Embalmers returned fire. A few of them held the line, while the others retreated into the building.

The Embalmers were all equipped with bullet-proof undergarments, while the Klansmen were not. Several of the latter went down in the first barrage, white robes marred by large splotches of red. A couple of them realized what was going on and concentrated on the heads of the Embalmers. Two of them were killed, and the rest retreated into the Cathedral.

Meanwhile, running gun battles and brutal fistfights between Klansmen and Black Embalmers raged for blocks in every direction around the Plaza. The Embalmers had the upper hand in most cases, and a number of them broke off from their satellite conflicts and headed for the Cathedral.

A line of Embalmers quickly assembled on a side street and crept up behind the Klansmen who were still firing on the Cathedral, their bullets knocking chips out of the front steps and punching holes in the doors. They raised their weapons and were about to cut the sheeted men down when one of the Daughters of the Confederacy spotted them. She yelled at her sisters, and they all turned to face the would-be ambushers.

Three of them reached under their hoop skirts and produced sawed-off shotguns. One of the girls, an attractive redhead, took aim at the nearest Black Embalmer and fired, hitting the macabre mask dead-center. The Embalmer went down, his head exploding in a cloud of red-tinted plaster dust.

"What the hell!" Rickert exclaimed.

He and the Bay Phantom had reached Cathedral Plaza, and they were both having trouble believing their eyes.

"It's a proxy war," said the Phantom. "The real generals are hidden away safely somewhere, while their minions decimate one another's ranks."

The gunfire had petered out for the time being. Several Klansmen, Black Embalmers, and hapless citizens lay dead or dying.

"Very well!" yelled the real Embalmer from atop the Cathedral. "If these miserable would-be dictators want war, then war they shall have!"

With that, the Embalmer disappeared from view. Ten seconds later, one last transport arrived at the plaza, stopping in the middle of Dauphin Street. Two Klansmen jumped out of the cab and ran to the rear of the vehicle. They jerked the doors open and stood back.

A bulky, furry apparition jumped from the truck.

The Werewolf had arrived.

The monster bounded into the middle of a group of Black Embalmers and started shredding everything within reach. Ribbons of shredded lab coats and gouts of blood went sailing into the air. People started screaming.

And then the situation got worse.

Something stirred in the windows of both of the towers. Then came the sound and fury, in the form of a horrible, explosive chattering sound and a hail of hot lead. There were two machine-gunners up there, one in each of the twin towers. They had the high ground, and were taking ruthless advantage of it.

"Two more of those missing machine guns, I'd wager." the Phantom said. He was trying to formulate a quick plan when he saw something that instantly became his top priority.

Two children, a boy and a girl, had somehow managed to wander into the middle of the Plaza. They were standing stock still and obviously terrified. The trail of bullet impacts from one of the machine guns was moving along the ground, kicking up grass and dirt, heading straight for them.

The Bay Phantom sprang into action. He ran toward the children, dodging Klansmen, Black Embalmers and bullets. He snatched up the children and ran to the end of the Plaza furthest from the Cathedral. There was a good sized gazebo there, a few feet from the sidewalk. The Phantom raced around behind it and lowered the children to the ground. He instructed them to crawl under the gazebo, which was raised a couple of feet off the ground, and stay there until he came back for them.

The Werewolf went down under a hail of machine-gun fire. The Phantom didn't think any of the bullets had penetrated his armor, but the impacts would have caused a great deal of distress. The gunners were concentrating their fire on the huddled figure. Bullets were ricocheting every which way. Six Klansmen and four Black Embalmers went down with obviously fatal head wounds.

Patches of the Werewolf's fur had caught on fire from the sparks struck from his armor by the bullets. He heaved himself upright, howled, then dropped again and rolled across the grass, evading the gunfire and extinguishing the flames at the same time. He rolled behind the gazebo, out of the line of fire.

One of the Daughters of the Confederacy dashed around the other side of the structure and placed the barrel of her shotgun against the nape of the monster's neck. Evidently, she didn't know whose side he was on. Either that or she decided it would be a good idea to eliminate him regardless of affiliation. But before she could fire, the Werewolf lashed out. The first swipe of his claws shredded her pink hoop-skirt. The second laid her abdomen open from breastbone to groin. But she had hung on to the gun, and she used up what little life was left to her by trying to take a shot at her killer. It was a valiant effort, but her shot went wide. The Werewolf, on his feet again, kicked her in the face. She went staggering backward, leaving spilled entrails in her wake, before collapsing into a lifeless heap of blood, guts and ruined crinoline. The Phantom hoped those children hadn't witnessed that.

The Werewolf scampered off around the perimeter of the battle zone, slowing down now and then to disembowel one of the counterfeit Black Embalmers.

The Phantom wanted to pursue the monster, but the gunners in the towers were a much bigger problem. They were killing indiscriminately; their enemies, their comrades, and the handful of innocent bystanders who hadn't made it to safety were all fair game, it seemed. He needed a few seconds to think, so he ran over to the gazebo and ducked around behind it. Crouching down he peered beneath the structure and saw that the children seemed to be unharmed.

Rickert was already back there, crouched down, popping up now and then to take a potshot at an Embalmer or a Klansman.

The machine guns in the towers fell silent, but he knew they were likely just switching out belts. Handing him a loaded automatic, the Phantom told Rickert to try to circle around and get as close as he could to the tower on the left. Rickert nodded and took off.

The Phantom was steeling himself for a suicide run at the right-hand tower when he heard someone call his name. Whirling, he saw Mirabelle standing at the mouth of a narrow alley just across the street, not twenty feet away. She had on the black stealth suit she'd worn in New Orleans. A long, tubular apparatus was slung over her shoulder by a strap, and she carried a paper bag in one hand.

"Mirabelle!" the Phantom exclaimed. "What on..."

"*Shush*!" she interrupted. "Don't use my name! You don't want people to know I know the Bay Phantom. Hang on one second. I have an idea."

She put the bag on the ground and removed from it two odd-looking objects, which she shoved into her belt. She took a jackknife from a front pocket and cut two small holes in the paper bag, then pulled it over her head, adjusting it so she could see through the holes. That done, she dashed across the street, joining the Phantom behind the ruined gazebo.

"How did you get here?" the Phantom asked.

"One of your tunnels comes out under the Saenger Theater, remember?" She took the large, tubular apparatus off of her shoulder and handed it to him. "This is that thing I was working on, the rocket launcher. I'll load it for you. I only brought two of the projectiles, so make 'em count."

"How did you know I'd need this?" he asked.

"How the hell would you *not*? Let's do it."

The Phantom stood up and balanced the weapon on his shoulder. "I hate to do this to such a storied old building," he said, "and a cathedral at that. Those towers have been there since the 1890s. But this has got to stop."

He took aim at the right-hand tower and depressed the trigger. The projectile disappeared into the gloom behind the machine gun, then there was a flash and a terrific explosion. A plume of smoke rose into the air, and debris rained down onto the street and sidewalk.

Mirabelle reloaded the launcher as the remaining machine gun opened up again.

"Forgive me," the Phantom said sorrowfully as he fired on the left-hand tower. It reacted exactly as its twin had.

The children crawled out from under the gazebo.

"Hey!" said the boy. "Ain't you the Bay Phantom?"

"*Aren't* I the Bay Phantom," the masked man corrected him.

"You mean you don't know?"

"Who are you?" the girl asked Mirabelle, who was slinging the rocket launcher back over her shoulder.

She seemed startled by the question. "Me? I'm, uh... I'm Paper Bag Girl. This thing on my head is a paper bag, see?"

"I know what it is," the girl replied smartly. She appeared to be about six or seven years old, but there was something in her eyes that belonged to a much older person. "It says 'Piggly Wiggly' on the back. Are you the Bay Phantom's loyal assistant?"

"No," Mirabelle said dryly, "I'm his boss."

The children looked at one another.

"He lets a dame boss him around," the boy said with a snicker.

"So what?" said the girl.

"It's still dangerous out here, Mir... ah, *Paper Bag Girl*," the Phantom said. "Perhaps you should take these young people to a place of safety."

"Come on," said Mirabelle, taking each of them by the hand, "you can be my loyal assistants."

"Can I shoot off that big gun?" the girl asked eagerly.

"Hell, no!" said Mirabelle.

"Please, Paper Bag Girl... *language*," the Bay Phantom admonished her.

The Werewolf had completed his circuit of the Plaza, and was heading down South Claiborne toward Government Street. The Phantom caught up with Rickert, who had been searching for a vantage point from which he could shoot into the tower.

"It looks like the Werewolf's heading for the newspaper office," he told Louis. "That makes sense. If the Carters are his targets, he would certainly want to eliminate their pet editor, Mark Marvel. Let's go. We can still stop him."

The Phantom set off in pursuit. Rickert followed him for a quarter of a block, then slowed to a stop and turned around.

Damn if I'm going after that monster, he thought. *The Bay Phantom is crazy, and I'm not getting myself cut to ribbons on his account.*

He started back the way he had come. The fighting was almost over at the Plaza. There were no more gunshots, and a few cops had finally arrived. In all the chaos, the Bya Phantom had given little thought to the whereabouts of the police. Detective Tom Dart, who was known and disliked by Rickert, was supervising a squad of uniformed officers rounding up stray Klansmen and Embalmers. They had quite a collection of them at the north side of the plaza.

Rickert walked as nonchalantly as he could up Claiborne. He would pass right in front of the cathedral portico, which was now one of the few areas to which nobody was paying any attention. Once he crossed Dauphin Street, he could make it back to his apartment without any trouble. He was halfway up the block when a Black Embalmer came around the corner at the end of the street.

He spotted Rickert.

"Hey, you!" he exclaimed. "I saw you talking to that Phantom geek. You work for him!"

Rickert took to his heels. There was only one place for him to go; up the stairs and into the Cathedral.

"Now, where do you two belong?" Mirabelle asked as they left the battlefield behind. She was worried about Perrone, of course, but there was nothing more she could do for him, and these children needed to be returned to their families.

"We were staying in the Parlez Hotel," said the girl. "Me and my momma, that is. We came here so she could see that old flower show. She likes such as that, but I don't. I'm just a child, though, so I don't get to vote on where we go."

"Okay," said Mirabelle. "That's on the other side of Government Street. Maybe she went back there when she couldn't find you." She turned to the boy. "And what about you?"

The youngster seemed confused. Fortunately, his mother caught sight of the little group after they had gone two blocks. She was so overwhelmed with gratitude that she didn't mention Mirabelle's odd headgear. Having restored the boy to the bosom of his family, Mirabelle and the girl continued on their way.

As they were about to cross a street, a Black Embalmer lurched toward them and made a grab for Mirabelle or the girl or both. Mirabelle drew pistol from her belt and shot him in the chest. He wobbled for a second or two, walked backward a few paces, and toppled down onto the sidewalk.

"Wow," said the girl as they stepped gingerly over the prone form. "You drilled him good!"

"Oh, no," Mirabelle said, mindful of childish sensibilities. "He isn't dead. I just shot him with some knockout juice. You know, like ether."

"I don't believe that," the little girl said, "but it's okay. Looks like he had it coming. Some people would behave a lot better if they were about to be shot all the time. He looked funny, walking backwards like that."

If fact, the projectile Mirabelle had fired *was* a thin, hollow shell, and it *did* contain a fast-acting anesthetic. But there was no way this little wise girl would believe that.

"You know," the girl said, "I have a chicken that knows how to walk backwards. She's gonna be in a newsreel."

"Well, I'll be!" said Mirabelle.

"I like birds. I wanna get some big ones, like ostriches or something."

"Ostriches are unusual. And they aren't very pretty."

"That's true," the girl said, stooping to pick up a loose brick from the sidewalk. "I like pretty birds."

A Klansman, his white sheet smeared with dirt and blood, lurched out of an alleyway into their path. Stretching a hand in their direction, he said, "Hey!"

"Hey nothing," the little girl replied, beaning him square in the forehead with the brick. He staggered back into the alleyway, disappearing in the gloom.

"Nice one," Mirabelle congratulated her.

"Thank you. Am I your faithful assistant now?"

"Better than that. I'm stepping down. You can be the new Paper Bag

Girl. " She removed the bag from her head and handed it to the girl.

"Hey, you're colored," said the new Paper Bag Girl.

"That's right," said the former Paper Bag Girl.

"I don't got nothing against colored people. Most people I know think there's something wrong with y'all, and you're not like us white people. Even my momma says that sometimes. I don't believe it, though. I think colored folks are just as bad as white folks. Every bit as mean and crazy."

"I've always felt that way," Mirabelle said with a little smile.

"My momma said colored people aren't as smart as white ones. I don't believe that one, either."

"I'm one of the smartest people in the world, according to a test I took," Mirabelle said. "A doctor I know said there are only eight other people alive who are smarter than I am."

"Do tell! Who are they?"

"I never thought to ask."

"I'd find out if I was you," the girl advised.

By this time, they were only half a block from the hotel. A woman was standing on the sidewalk in front of it wringing her hands, talking to a man who was writing something on a clipboard. She looked frantic. But when she caught sight of Mirabelle and the girl, it loosened up. She shooed the clipboard man away.

The little girl waved. "That's my momma," she told Mirabelle.

The woman waved back, grinning and crying at the same time.

"Mary Flannery O'Connor, you come here this instant," she said as sternly as she could through all the emotions fighting for control of her voice.

"That's what I'm doing," said the girl, putting her new emblem of office over her head. "And my name is Paper Bag Girl now."

The Bay Phantom lost sight of his quarry when the Werewolf dashed through one of the large bay doors at the rear of the *Press* building. That would take him to the loading dock where the carriers received bundles of newspapers to be delivered. From there, he could go through the press room and on upstairs to the newsroom.

It was one of the imitation Black Embalmers.

"Oh, really!" the Phantom exclaimed. "I don't have time for this foolishness."

Okay, thought Tom Dart, as he stood looking up at the outrageously abused Cathedral of the Immaculate Conception, *that takes care of two more of those machine guns. There should be* one *left.*

He had just arrived at Cathedral Plaza and received a briefing from one of the cops that had made it into the war zone without being cut down.

The police had been instantly overwhelmed by the chaos that had erupted all over town. It had taken them a while to work their way to the center of the disturbance. Now that they were here, the tide seemed to be turning. The cop who briefed Dart said that someone who must have been the Bay Phantom had taken out the machine-gunners in the Cathedral's twin spires.

Dart had no doubt that the gunners had been using two of the three the machine guns that had been planted in Hector Sams' warehouse, only to be stolen back by the would be framers.

Then he saw something that caught his attention. On the roof of the Cathedral, directly between the towers was something that looked like an irregular lump of masonry. *That shouldn't be there*, he thought. It looked like the kind of large rock one saw out west. One did not see them on top of cathedrals in Mobile, Alabama, as a rule. As Dart studied the thing, it rose into the air, flattened out, and disappeared.

The "rock" had been a large, grey tarp, and it had just been pulled away by yet another Black Embalmer, to reveal what was concealed underneath.

The third machine gun.

"Thank you!" shouted the masked madman. "You've rounded them up for me!"

He swung the gun around and started firing into the mass of Klansmen in one corner of the plaza.

"Shit!" yelped Dart. He dived onto the ground and rolled, getting back to his feet in the middle of Conti Street and drawing his gun. He wanted to pick off the gunner, but he couldn't get a decent line of sight.

Well, now what? He thought. *I can't get to him from down here, and I don't have anything that can reach up there and...*

Wait a minute... Yes, I do!

He reached into his jacket and grabbed the hand grenade he'd been carrying since he found it in Simon Brickell's study. He hadn't wanted to leave it lying around at home or the office, and didn't want anybody else to know about it, so he had left it in his jacket until he could decide what to do with it.

That quandary had just been solved. He got closer to the Cathedral and shouted for the cops on the street to run to the other side of the plaza.

Bracing himself, he pulled the pin and lobbed the grenade onto the roof.

Two seconds later there was a massive explosion. The Cathedral groaned and creaked alarmingly, and several of the stained-glass windows shattered, but the structure held up. The same could not be said for the machine gun and its operator. There wouldn't be enough left of either one of them to fill a teacup.

Tom Dart looked upon his work with mixed emotions. The machine gunner had to be stopped, but it was a shame that so much damage had to be inflicted on this grand old building.

Rickert ran through the nave, the Black Embalmer behind him and gaining fast. He ducked between some pews and zoomed back and forth, keeping out of his pursuer's reach. When the masked freak stumbled and fell, Rickert hit the center aisle and ran for the stage, or whatever they called it. He was going to veer off to the side and dive through one of the doorways behind it, but he twisted his ankle and hit the floor right in front of the altar.

Looking up, he saw the lugubrious figure of Christ on the Cross. The Nazarene seemed to be looking reproachfully at Louis.

"*What*?" he snapped. "What was I *supposed* to do? Jeez, give a guy a break, wouldja?"

The Embalmer had gotten to his feet and was closing in on Rickert, limping slightly, but otherwise unhurt. Rickert didn't dare look back over his shoulder. Getting up onto his knees, he kept his eyes on the figure of Christ and said, "Listen, let's do a deal here. We need to talk this over, and we ain't got a whole lot of time. Get me out of this, and I swear I'll start going to church and I'll quit stealing, or whatever you want. I'll go help the Phantom, too. Honest! Whadda ya say, feller?"

The Savior made no reply. The footfalls that had been growing in volume stopped and Louis felt a hand on his shoulder.

"Okay," said the Black Embalmer. "Here's where you get yours."

At that moment, there was a terrible thunderclap that shook the whole building. Looking up, Rickert saw something that filled him with awe. He dropped to the floor and rolled away as Christ came hurtling down on top of the Black Embalmer, cross and all. Both the Redeemer and the Embalmer shattered into pieces, and a large pool of blood oozed out from beneath the rubble onto the marble floor.

"Damn," said Louis. "Thanks, I owe you one. I guess that means I've got to go help the Phantom, huh? Okay... but, you know, I'm thinking it would be nice if I got some kind of reward. You know, a little something extra for signing up?"

The city room was a study in productively channeled chaos. She saw a man she didn't recognize standing in Marvel's office, talking with the editor. Who the hell was this? He wasn't any reporter or photographer she'd ever seen. A free-lancer? He had some kind of a bundle underneath his arm, but it didn't look like a camera.

She went to her desk and put her camera down, then headed for Marvel's sanctum. She detoured around a distressed copy boy and almost collided with the sports editor, who seemed to be out of his depth today. By the time she reached Marvel's door, the man with the bundle was gone. Her eyes met the editor's, and she strode boldly into his office, teeth bared in an almost savage grin. Marvel sat there behind his desk like a malevolent little Buddha, trying to wither her with his gaze. She almost laughed. He was wasting his time.

"Hello, chief!" she said brightly. "How's tricks?"

"Why are you even here?" Marvel asked coldly. "You dodge your assignments, you phone in sick, you tell me you're working on the thing we discussed, but you produce nothing... You are *fired*, Miss Turnbull. You screwed up. I know a lack of talent and drive when I see it."

"Yeah, yeah," said Gladys. "Every morning when you look in the mirror, huh? Listen, Buster, wait until you see what I have in that camera of mine. And wait until you hear the story I have for you."

"What are you talking about?" Marvel asked, suddenly wary.

"Oh, nothing much. Just a picture of the Bay Phantom with his mask off. I know who he is, and I can prove it."

"Bullshit," Marvel said, but without the conviction he usually put into the word.

"Try me, then," Gladys shot back. "I'll take everything to the Biloxi paper; I know a girl there who is very interested in the Bay Phantom. Or maybe New Orleans. I'm sure the editor at the *Times-Picayune* would love to steal your thunder on this one!"

Marvel glared at her. She wondered if she had pushed him a little too far. You could cross the line, even with a wet rag like him, to the point where his lacerated male ego would override good sense. She didn't like what she was seeing in his eyes, and she wondered if all hell was about to

"...Christ came hurtling down..."

break loose in the midst of the storm that was already swirling around them.

As it happened, hell broke loose all right, but Mark Marvel was not the source. It came from the opposite direction.

Its arrival was heralded by a chorus of screams and shocked curses from reporters, editors and secretaries. Gladys whirled around and saw, standing in the newsroom doorway, a seven-foot-tall fur-covered monstrosity, a human-shaped wolf reared up on its hind legs. It stood surveying the large room, its huge head swaying back and forth.

"Oh, goddamn," she whispered. This must be the Werewolf she had glimpsed outside Brickell's house and heard Joe Perrone and Mirabelle discussing. Actually, rumors had been flying around everywhere concerning this creature, but she had taken them with a grain of salt. She hadn't had a good look at the monster herself, and figured most of the talk was just the typical feverish exaggeration.

If anything, it had been understatement.

The monster's head became still. Gladys noted, to her extreme discomfiture, that the furry snout was pointed directly at her, as were the baleful red eyes. That was the word that went through her head: *baleful*. She was pretty sure it was the first time in her life she'd ever applied it to anything. She wasn't at all sure it was the correct word.

"You," snarled the Werewolf. "You die!"

A brief speech, but an eloquent one. She was rather surprised that the thing could actually talk. As Gladys stood rooted to the floor, mouth hanging open, as the monster launched itself in her direction.

CHAPTER TWENTY-SEVEN
FIENDS IN THE CITY ROOM

The Bay Phantom threw a right cross at the faux Black Embalmer. It failed to connect, just as it had been intended to do. The Embalmer ducked underneath it, and right into a devastating left jab. The Phantom's blow shattered the plaster death mask and put its wearer on the floor, unconscious.

God alone knew how many Embalmer duplicates were running around loose today. The Phantom couldn't let them slow him down. The Werewolf had to be stopped. At least there was only one of *him*.

Three more "Embalmers" piled into the loading dock from the side street. They got between the Phantom and his goal and raised their weapons.

Two gunshots sounded from somewhere behind the Phantom and two of the Embalmers fell.

"Go, Boss, go!" shouted Louis Rickert. "I got this!"

As Rickert distracted the remaining Embalmer, the Bay Phantom cut around behind him and hit the stairs.

The Werewolf bore down on Gladys like a big, snarling, hairy freight train. She braced herself, which was all she had time to do. She couldn't even drop to the floor. The furry monstrosity filled her field of vision, she felt a breeze across her left cheek, and then... nothing. The only thing in front of her was the rest of the newsroom.

She heard a commotion behind her and whirled around to see the monster grappling with her editor. Mark Marvel had been the target! He was surely doomed. Gladys hardly knew which one to root for.

"Help!" Marvel squealed. "Goddammit, come out of there and *help* me!"

The door to Marvel's private washroom opened, and out stepped a man in a white lab coat. There was something over his head, a grey hood of some sort, and his face was covered by some morbid and disturbed soul's idea of a Mardi Gras false face. *Oh God, it's that freak I saw in the cemetery*! Gladys started backing away from the office.

"I thought you might show your ugly snout up here," said the Black Embalmer. "I only just arrived, and was taking care of some business in there. You have uncanny timing."

The Bay Phantom bounded up the stairs and through the wide doorway into the city room. The place was in chaos. He had to duck under and around all the people who were trying to flee through the doorway by which he had just entered.

When he got clear of the mass of frightened people, he saw an awe-inspiring sight. To the rear of the newsroom, in front of what must have been the editor's office, two outlandish figures were engaged in fierce hand-to-hand combat. One of them was the Werewolf. The other was the Black Embalmer.

This was the genuine article, the Phantom was certain. But he was not at all sure that the madman, lethal though he was, stood a chance against the Werewolf.

After a brief flurry of blows and claws, none of which appeared to have hit anything vital, the combatants stepped back and took one another's measure, slowly circling around the central point midway between them.

The Phantom bolted across the room and jumped on the Werewolf's back.

"Ha!" exclaimed the Embalmer. "Look who's here! It's a party now!"

"Keep him busy!" snapped the Phantom, as the Werewolf bucked and twisted, trying to throw him off.

"Gotcha," said the Embalmer. "My friend's enemy's best friend is my enemy's worst friendly nightmare."

The Bay Phantom hung on and went to work. He concentrated on finding the seam where the headpiece joined the rest of the costume. He found it and started working his fingers into the small gap.

The Embalmer danced around in front of the Werewolf, occasionally delivering a halfhearted punch. The Werewolf, ignoring the Phantom for the moment, aimed one swipe of his claws after another at the Embalmer. None connected.

"A few more seconds," said the Phantom through clenched teeth. "I've almost got it."

Wrapping his legs around the Werewolf's torso, the Phantom began tugging at the headpiece with both hands. It was stubborn, but he was sure it was starting to give.

Louis Rickert burst into the newsroom, having dashed up the stairs four at a time. He saw what was going on, though he couldn't quite process it. *Fight. Bay Phantom versus Werewolf.* He aimed his gun at the Werewolf's head and fired.

The impact caused the beast's head to snap to the side. His body jerked reflexively in the other direction, nearly dislodging the Phantom. The Black Embalmer seemed momentarily disoriented. The Werewolf regained his bearings almost instantly. Ignoring the Phantom on his back, he grabbed the Embalmer and lifted the madman into the air. Bracing his feet, the Werewolf reared back and flung him across the room, directly at the source of the shot.

The Embalmer struck Louis Rickert with considerable force, throwing him backward against the wall. Both of them fell to the floor in a heap, unconscious.

Meanwhile, the Phantom had nearly completed his task. Gripping the bottom edge of the headpiece in both hands, he gave it a shove, and felt it come loose from whatever moorings it had been attached to. He yanked it all the way off and tossed it aside. The Werewolf whirled around, and fixed the Bay Phantom with a fierce glare.

Here was the face of the Werewolf. It seemed familiar to the Phantom; he was sure he'd seen it before, in another place and time. But he couldn't pin it down, and he didn't have the time or leisure to search his memory.

The monster grabbed him by his upper arms before he could react. Since the strategy had worked so well with the Embalmer and the unknown gunman, the Werewolf lifted the Phantom over his head and hurled him across the room.

Gladys had made her way back to her desk. She was keeping an eye on the combat, and she saw the beast with the human head lift the Bay Phantom into the air and throw him… *right at her*!

She had to duck to avoid being hit. The Phantom bounced off the wall and hit the floor. Gladys, without thinking, rushed to his side and helped him to his feet. As she stood there, supporting him with his arm over her shoulder, two things happened.

One, the Werewolf jumped over a desk and began sprinting in their direction, claws outstretched. Two, the Bay Phantom turned his head to her. He started to say thanks, but his voice abruptly trailed off. And Gladys knew why.

She was looking at the Bay Phantom and he was looking at her. Presumably. She couldn't see his eyes through those blue lenses. Did he know who he was looking at? Did he recognize Beth Page? *Of course he did.*

He had a problem. And, very conveniently, the solution was approaching with the awful implacability of a hairy hurricane. He probably didn't mean all that stuff he had said to her after she took his picture. He had just been in a hurry. All he had to do now was stand still, and the Werewolf's claws would go right through Gladys Turnbull's throat. His secret identity would be safe. None of the witnesses in this room would know he'd let it happen on purpose. Nobody would blame him for her death. *Hell*, she thought, *even I won't blame him*. She just nodded and closed her eyes. "No hard feelings," she whispered. "My camera's on my desk."

She braced herself. It probably wouldn't hurt too much. One swipe of those claws would probably take her head completely off. She'd read somewhere that you lived for a few seconds after being decapitated, and she wasn't looking forward to that.

She felt a jolt and heard a hissing sound. *That must be my head coming off,* she thought. *Shit, here we go.* She felt a sickening sensation of motion, and waited for her head to hit the floor. But it seemed that her head was still attached to the rest of her body. She opened her eyes just as she bumped almost gently against the wall.

There was the Bay Phantom…Joe Perrone…staggering backward with the Werewolf's claws embedded in his left bicep. He had stepped in front of her and intercepted the killing blow, shoving her out of the way as the metal cut into his flesh and he hissed in pain.

No, Gladys thought. *He can't possibly be* that *goddamn noble.*

Then she had another thought. *I can't let this happen…*

"There comes a time in everyone's life," Roscoe Turnbull had told his daughter more than once, "when he, or she, is presented with a choice. And that choice will demonstrate once and for all what he, or she, is truly made of."

Gladys had regarded this as a rather cheap homily, a nice piece of well meaning, pseudo-profound bullshit of the kind her father had specialized in. But that time had come for her.

She watched for a second or two as the Bay Phantom struggled against the Werewolf. The monster had pulled his bloody claws out of the masked man's arm and was drawing back for a killing blow. Without hesitation, she snatched up her precious Speed Graphic camera, raised it into the air, and brought it down on the back of the Werewolf's head. Then she did it twice more. The camera was durable, but it couldn't survive that kind of punishment. It shattered into pieces, destroying the precious film sheet it contained.

Unfortunately, the blows had little effect on the monster. He noticed them, and glared at her for a second, before returning to the business of slaughtering the Phantom.

"Oh, no you don't, you son of a bitch," she said indignantly, hopping over to the nearest desk and lifting an Underwood typewriter over her head.

"Shrug *this* off, Fido," she snarled. Gritting her teeth, she flung the machine downward with all her strength. It smashed into the Werewolf's head, and he *didn't* shrug it off. He howled and slid from the prone form of the Phantom onto the newsroom floor, clutching his head in both clawed hands. The typewriter was still in one solid piece, more or less, though the platen had come loose and a dozen or so keys had gone bouncing off across the floor, so she picked it up again and slammed it down onto the monster's hands and head. The beast thrashed around and kept up an awful caterwauling. Breathing heavily, eyes gleaming, Gladys picked up the typewriter for a third time and delivered what she sincerely hoped was the *coup de grace*.

By now, the Phantom had managed to get to his feet. He was swaying like a drunk and blood was pouring out of his wounded arm like water from a fountain.

"I think that will do, Miss Page," he said, his voice surprisingly strong.

"My name is really Gladys Turnbull," she said.

The Phantom nodded.

"Jesus," she said, "you need to get to a hospital."

He shook his head. "It isn't as bad as it looks." He reached into his pants pocket and produced a jackknife, which he handed to Gladys. "I'd be obliged if you'd just cut off a strip from my cape and help me wrap it up."

"Yeah, sure I will," she said, quickly suiting action to word.

A few of the other people in the newsroom had roused themselves from their stunned paralysis and were moving cautiously toward the strange tableau.

"I saw what you did with your camera," the Phantom said in an undertone as Gladys wrapped his upper arm and shoulder in a long strip of black cloth. "Am I to assume that you've had a change of heart?"

"Hell, yes. What kind of a creep do you think I am, anyhow? Your secret's safe with me, even though it means I'll lose my job."

"Oh, I think not," the masked man whispered. "You just single-handedly subdued one of the worst mass killers this country has ever seen. If your editor were to fire you now, he'd look like the biggest jackass on the planet. After this, I daresay you can name your own salary."

She looked at him blankly for a moment, then a grin spread across her face.

"Goddamn," she whispered, "you're right!"

"Please, Miss Turnbull," said the Bay Phantom, "language."

He spared a few seconds to make sure the Black Embalmer and Rickert were alive and largely undamaged, then he knelt to examine the Werewolf.

"He'll live," the Phantom said. "He must have an extraordinarily thick skull."

The masked man reached into his jacket and produced a curious object. It was a furry, clawed glove, identical to the ones the Werewolf had on.

"This smacks of planting evidence," he said to Gladys, as he removed one of the Werewolf's gloves and replaced it with the one he had brought. "But since I'm only restoring this thing to its proper place, I suppose I can live with it. It has poor Simon Brickell's blood on it. When the police test it, I think my name will be cleared completely."

Then he went to Gladys' desk, picked up her phone, and dialed a number.

"Tom?" he said when he got an answer. "This is the Bay Phantom. Thank goodness I caught you in the office."

"Just barely," said the detective. "I came back for some more ammo, and I'm about to hit the streets again."

"Well, I have good news. Two of the authors of all this bloodshed have been neutralized. I'm in the newsroom at the Press, and the Black Embalmer and the Werewolf are here. I think..."

He was interrupted by an insistent tugging at his sleeve. It was Gladys Turnbull. "Look," she said, pointing to a spot near the door.

The Black Embalmer had gotten to his feet, and was on his way out the door.

"He never knows when to quit," said the Phantom. "Tom, the Embalmer's getting away. If he gets out of the building, I'll signal you when I catch him. Just keep an eye out for it. Goodbye and good luck!" He hung up.

"Please look after that man, Miss Turnbull," he said, pointing at the still-unconscious Rickert. Then he took off down the stairs after the Black Embalmer.

Most of the newsroom personnel had fled during the fight. The few that remained didn't seem to know what they ought to do, so they wandered about like bewildered children.

Gladys knelt down next to Rickert and put her hand on his forehead. "You look familiar," she said. "Where do I... Oh, shit! It's you!" She went to the water cooler, filled a paper cup, and threw it in Rickert's face.

He stirred, frowned, and started mumbling: "We had... deal... I went after him... where's my prize?"

Gladys got another cupful of water and splashed him again.

"Come on, buddy!" she said, slapping Rickert's wet cheeks. "Wake up, Fagin!"

He opened his eyes and said, "Who you calling a faggot?"

She laughed. "*Fagin* is a character from Dickens," she said. "He taught innocent little kids how to pick locks."

Rickert shook his head and blinked his eyes several times, then focused on the face of the woman kneeling beside him.

"Well, I'll be damned," he said with a grin. "You!"

"Yeah, me. My name is Gladys Turnbull, and I'm a goddamn newspaper reporter. Why don't you get up off the floor and have a drink with me? I've got a bottle hidden in my desk."

"Wow," said Rickert, looking up at the ceiling and the great unfathomable infinitude that lay beyond it. "I'm on a roll! What should I ask for *next*?"

The Phantom had been too far behind to nab the Embalmer before he could exit the building. He had followed the madman onto the street and was trying not to lose him. He had quite a time of it, since so many of the duplicates were still prowling around. He gradually closed the distance between himself and his quarry.

He followed the Embalmer all the way to Royal Street, and saw him duck into the little speakeasy that was the favorite haunt of Louis Rickert.

Before he entered the place, he drew a small flare gun from a special pocket in his jacket and fired a flare into the air; the signal he had promised Tom Dart. He hoped the detective saw it and interpreted it correctly.

Then he pushed the door open and entered the dimly-lit bar. It seemed to be deserted, but for the bartender, who stood in his customary spot behind the bar. It looked like the same man the Phantom had seen here before, but there was something different. He had evidently shaved off his moustache and dyed his hair.

"Excuse me," said the Phantom, "but did you happen to see a man wearing a plaster death mask come through here just now?"

"Can't say that I did, fellah. It's been mighty slow today. Is there a parade going on or something?"

"You mean you don't..."

That was when he noticed that the bartender had on a stained white lab coat just like the one the Black Embalmer had been wearing. In fact, it had the same pattern of bloodstains as the one the Embalmer had been wearing.

"All right," the Phantom said, drawing his automatic and pointing it at the man. "Come out from behind there, slowly."

"Or what? You're gonna shoot me in cold blood?"

"Well, of course not! But if you attempt anything foolish, I might shoot you in the arm or the leg."

"Did you follow me all the way here from the newsroom? How sweet! You didn't bring anyone else, did you?"

"Never mind all that. Just come around here, please. The Werewolf is out of commission and the police are rounding up both of the warring gangs as we speak. There's no reason for you to persist in this lunacy."

The Embalmer suddenly dropped out of sight. When he popped back up at the other end of the bar, he was wearing his mask. He hopped up onto the bar, then jumped to the floor on the other side. He held two long-bladed daggers, one in each hand.

"Come on," he said. "Let's you and me have a genuine barroom brawl!"

"Is this really necessary?" the Phantom asked in an exhausted, long suffering tone. "Have we not been through enough today? Why don't you just give up?"

"No, I want to fight you. You're very good, and I want to see if I can get the better of you. The first time we confronted one another directly, I kind of cheated; having my friend hit you over the head. Come on, just you and me this time, fair and square."

The Bay Phantom sighed. "Very well, if I must."

"That's more like it!" The Embalmer lunged forward, swinging one of the knives at his opponent. It wasn't a very artful attack. The Phantom danced backward, out of range. The Embalmer repeated his move, this time swinging the other blade. The Phantom eluded that one, too.

"Are you not going to do anything?" said the Embalmer in exasperation. "Do you want one of these knives?"

"I'm fine," the Phantom replied. "I can keep this up for quite a while, but not indefinitely. Neither can you. Surely we can find some common ground."

"We already did. I know you were Roy Markham. We talked about things, and you told me you understood, and you were telling the truth. I'm not going to give you a whole song and dance about how you and I are just alike, because we aren't. But you *do* understand, I know it. So you know what I'm about, and what I'm about is *not* sitting down and talking things over."

"I know, but..."

"But nothing!" the Embalmer spat. Then he was silent for a time. Perrone wondered what was going on behind that mask.

"Okay," the madman said at length. "Tell you what. Here." He tossed one of the knives onto the floor at the Phantom's feet. He placed the point of the other to his own throat.

"I understand you, too," he said, nodding his head. "I know how you think, what approach you take. So, either you pick up that knife and give me a good fight, or I'll slit my jugular. You know I'll do it!"

"Yes, of course, and you know I won't let you. Very well." The Phantom stooped down and picked up the knife. "Let's get this over with."

The Embalmer lunged again, and this time the Bay Phantom didn't move. Instead, he grabbed his opponent by the wrist, stopping the lethal blade in mid swing. He jabbed the Embalmer in the thigh with the knife he'd been given, but not very deeply. He wasn't interested in this kind of mayhem, and he didn't want to do anything that wasn't absolutely necessary.

The Embalmer twisted his arm and jerked his wrist free from the Phantom's grip. He swung the knife again, with no finesse whatsoever, like a small, awkward child playing with a badminton racket. The Phantom ducked it easily, and jabbed the Embalmer in the other thigh.

"Dammit!" said the madman. "You're not even trying! Haven't you ever heard of lethal force? Self-defense? Any of that stuff?"

"My life isn't in danger," said the Phantom. He had moved back to a distance of two feet. He and the Embalmer were facing one another, slowly moving around in a circle. "You're not good enough to get the better of me."

"Yeah," said the Embalmer, nodding, "You're the better man, all right. But I've got a secret."

"What's that?"

"Unlike you, I don't mind fighting dirty." He stepped back, dropped his knife, and removed a small black box from his pocket. He thumbed a little red switch.

Instantly, the Phantom felt an intense vibration in the hand that held the knife, followed he heard a crackling sound that issued from the hilt of the weapon. His body began to twitch. It looked as though he were trying to let go of the knife, and having no success.

"Inside the hilt of that dagger," said the Embalmer, "is just about the most powerful electrical battery of its size in the world. It won't kill you, though. That's my job, and I'm damned if I'll let a machine rob me of my occupation."

When the battery finally gave out, the Bay Phantom stood where he was, seemingly rooted to the spot. His body swayed gently back and forth.

The Embalmer stepped up to him and said, "Not very sporting of me was it?"

"I have a secret of my own," the Phantom said in a feeble whisper. "Do you want to know what it is?"

"Absolutely!" the Embalmer exclaimed.

"Come a little closer, please," whispered the Phantom.

"The Embalmer leaned forward. "Now, what is it?"

The Phantom took a deep breath and said, "I'm wearing rubber-soled shoes."

A powerful right cross put a long lateral crack in the Embalmer's death mask and sent the madman crashing through the front door and out onto the sidewalk.

The Phantom followed him out in a less precipitous manner and stood over him. "Are you ready to end this foolishness now?"

"Yeah, I guess so. You are *really* good at this stuff."

"Thank you."

The Phantom helped the Embalmer to his feet and was reaching for the handcuffs he carried in a side pocket when a voice rang out from halfway up the block:

"Hey! What the hell is this? What are you doing to him?"

The Phantom looked around to see Shorty Red, his head still swathed in bandages, approaching with great speed, an expression of pure rage contorting his face.

CHAPTER TWENTY-EIGHT
RESOLUTIONS

"Well, well," chirped the Embalmer, "If it isn't my old comrade Shorty Red! I'd say the balance of power just shifted dramatically."

"Yeah," said the giant, moving ponderously toward the two masked men. "I'd say so, too. I owe this guy right here, and I aim to pay my debt." He looked at the Phantom. "Are you okay?"

The Phantom nodded. "More or less, yes."

"Good." Shorty drew back a fist the size of a gallon bucket and delivered a crushing blow...

... to the Black Embalmer!

Shorty's fist slammed into the white plaster mask like a pile driver, cracking it in a spider web pattern. The Embalmer hit the sidewalk again, flat on his back, then quickly sat up. "Gobdabbt," he said, "you're hiddig duh wrog bad! Dad's duh Bay Faddum ober *dere*!"

"I don't quite understand this," said the Bay Phantom. "You hit him instead of me."

"Yeah," Shorty said, his voice softer than it had been. "I heard everything you said to me that night in Bayou La Batre. I didn't think much of it at the time, but after you and Rickert beat the crap out of me and I ended up in the hospital, I thought about it. I thought about it a lot. I figured I was gonna die. I had a few broken ribs and a collapsed lung, along with some other stuff. Big crack in my skull.

"Well, I pulled through the worst of it, but there was still a lot of mending to do, and a lot more time to think, so that's what I did. Penny Carter never came to see me. I thought there was something between her and me, but I guess..." He shook his head. "Well, the more I thought about what you said to me, the more sense it made. Why the hell was I doing all that crap to people? What good did it actually do me? I couldn't come up with an answer."

"Jeebeb Chrizzd!" exclaimed the Embalmer, rocking back and forth. "I dink you broge by doze!"

"I'm gonna break more than that," growled Shorty. He grabbed the Embalmer by the front of his lab coat and hauled him to his feet. He punched the madman again. More of the plaster mask disintegrated and a great quantity of blood spewed out from behind it. Shorty ripped away the mask and the gray cloth underneath, revealing the face of the Black Embalmer. What was left of it, that is; a mass of blood, loose teeth, and pulped flesh already starting to bruise. Both of his eyes were swollen almost shut.

"Oh, my!" exclaimed the Phantom, "Surely that's enough, Shorty! You've more than made your point."

Shorty nodded, a little regretfully, it seemed to the Phantom, and contented himself with maintaining an unbreakable grip on the battered lunatic's upper arm.

"I heard about all this shit going on down here," he said, "and I figured you'd be in the middle of it. I came to this bar hoping to find Louis Rickert. I heard he had practically moved in here. I thought he might be able to put me in touch with you. You were right, the Carters were exploiting me. When I was down, they turned their backs on me. I wanted to let you know that."

A police car whipped around the corner and screeched to a halt in front of the building. Tom Dart jumped out, gun drawn. A uniformed officer got out on the passenger side, his pistol at the ready. Right behind the squad car was an ambulance.

He looked at the Phantom and said, "Which one of these mugs should I shoot?"

"Neither," said the masked man. "The situation is under control. The injured man here is the Black Embalmer. This other fellow is... call him a good Samaritan who happened along and gave me a hand."

Dart glared at Shorty Red. "Yeah, I know all about this bird. He's a *real* good Samaritan all right. He'd be wanted for everything from jaywalking to murder one if anybody could prove anything."

"Which they can't," said Shorty Red. "Not that I'm proud of that. Not any more."

"Uh-huh," said Dart, utterly unimpressed. "Well, if the Phantom says you're okay, that's good enough for me. For now. I guess."

"This one, on the other hand," said the Phantom, hooking a thumb at the Embalmer, "should be removed from the streets forthwith. This is the Black Embalmer, Tom. It's good that you have an ambulance."

"I thought there might be a need. What happened to him?"

"I did," said Shorty.

Dart cuffed the Black Embalmer's hands and turned him over to the ambulance attendants, instructing the uniformed cop to ride to the hospital with them. They helped the badly battered madman onto a stretcher and started to slide him into the back of the ambulance. Before they got him all the way in, he made a noise and waved his manacled hands in the air.

"Waid!" he yelped. "I wadda say subthin tuh duh Faddom fore we go."

The masked man came to the rear of the vehicle, looked down at his recent opponent, and said, "Do you want to tell me something?"

"Yeh," the Embalmer said with a nod. "I do. Ibe gudda kill dese addedans ad edgape, den Ibe cubbin tuh ged *jew*."

"I beg your pardon?" the Phantom said. "Are you asking for a rabbi? I'm sorry, I just can't understand you. Perhaps one of these other gentlemen can help. Take care of yourself and cooperate with the officers and doctors. You'll probably spend a great deal of time in prison, if you don't go to the electric chair. I'm opposed to the death penalty in principle, and, confidentially, I think you are very ill. You know..." He tapped the side of his own head. "You may not be entirely responsible for your actions. It's nothing to be ashamed of."

The Embalmer tried to arrange his face into some kind of an expression, without success. It was just too dilapidated at present. He gave up and said,

"Yoo ah wud stoobid subbubbabidge, you dough dad?"

The Phantom shook his head apologetically and pointed at his ear. "Perhaps we can talk later," he said kindly.

Order was being imposed upon the recent, intense chaos. A veritable army of police, sheriff's deputies, and National Guardsmen were rounding up Klansmen and Black Embalmers, packing them into whatever vehicles they could scrape up. All available jail cells had filled up quickly, and arrestees were now being hauled them to a special temporary detention center at Bates Field.

Perrone was back home at Tull House. After assuring Mirabelle and Freud that he was fine, and that most of the recent difficulties had been solved, he stripped off the filthy Bay Phantom outfit and took a shower. After putting on some clean clothes, he went back downstairs and then into the cellar, where he found Mirabelle bent over a piece of equipment in her chemical laboratory.

"What are you up to, Mirabelle?" he said.

"I'm playing around with the gas ampoules you swiped from the Black Embalmer," she replied.

"Have you made any progress?"

"Not really," Mirabelle said. "I've attempted to analyze the gas, but it has defeated me so far. I took a chromatograph reading, and I thought I had the ingredients broken down. I know how it works, but when I tried to duplicate it, what I came up with was lethal. It shut down the autonomic nervous system along with everything else."

"My heavens," said Perrone. "If you can't crack it, then it is something very extraordinary indeed. I suppose that's what the Embalmer meant when he made that remark about showing me what I was really dealing with."

"Well, whoever made this is someone not to be taken lightly," said Mirabelle. "I emptied two of the valve equipped ampoules you swiped from the Embalmer and filled them with my own concoction. I wanted to see if there was something about the atomization process that rendered the lethal components inert, but no. I made two such ampoules and tested the first one. It was lethal, even after being atomized. The poison is very fast acting, and it becomes inert within seconds if it doesn't find its way into a nearby bloodstream. It has to be inhaled; it doesn't penetrate the skin via osmosis or anything.

"This is the other ampoule," she said, holding up the small, silvery globe. "A deadly little trinket. I'm going to put it in the upstairs safe. At the moment, I'm trying to think up some more tests to conduct, but..."

She was interrupted by the buzzing of the intercom. Perrone stepped over to the wall and pressed the button.

"Hello? Is that you, Doctor?"

"Yes," came the voice of Freud, issuing from the tiny speaker. "I think we may have some kind of a problem."

"What sort of problem?"

"There's somebody outside the house. I think it's a man, and he is dressed up as a purple ghost. He has two other ghosts with him, and they are of a more traditional hue."

"Doctor, don't move," Mirabelle barked into the intercom. "We'll be right there." She slipped the ampoule into her breast pocket and headed for the door.

"I don't think they are friendly," Freud added.

Mirabelle raced up the stairs, Perrone on her heels. As they reached the kitchen, they heard several loud reports coming from the front of the house. Just as they named it to the front room, the door gave way. Whoever was out there hadn't even bothered trying to knock and gain admission in a more conventional way; they had gone ahead and employed a battering ram first thing.

The stout wooden door, torn from its hinges, crashed to the floor. Perrone stepped protectively in front of Mirabelle and Freud, and watched as the Grand Wizard, arrayed in his gaudy purple, stepped into Tull House, flanked by two robed and hooded Klansmen.

"Good evening, Mister Perrone," said the sadistic cult leader. "You keep such charming company! A perverted Jew and a dirty nigger! And then there's that other thing."

"What thing?" Perrone said.

"You are also the Bay Phantom, are you not?"

CHAPTER TWENTY-NINE
GLAD TO SEE YOU GO

"It really wasn't necessary to ruin my door that way," Perrone said calmly. "Who's going to pay for it?"

"I have come to take some things from you," the Wizard said. "Those things are: the nigger you stole from me at the rally; everything in this house, especially equipment and other resources used by the Bay Phantom; and your life."

"You been stealing niggers again, Mister Perrone?" Mirabelle said. "Shame on you."

"I'm afraid I don't know what you're talking about," Perrone said to the Wizard. "What does the Bay Phantom have to do with me?"

"I figured out who you are," said the Wizard, "so don't bother with all that. I haven't come here to play make-believe, so you might as well know who I am before you die." Slowly and dramatically, he reached for his hood.

"Oh, you're Hector Sams," Perrone said, before the purple hood was halfway off. "I worked that out a long time ago."

Unmasked, Sams scowled at Perrone. "Well," he said sourly, "you at least admit that you're the Bay Phantom."

"How so? I said no such thing. Where did you get an idea like that? Did Penny Carter tell you something?"

"No, Penny was no help at all. I told you, I figured you out on my own. I don't know that she's even aware of your secret. She fed me a great deal of misinformation while pretending to be on my side. She started communicating with me some time back. She said she hated her family and wanted to see them broken. The hit on the Cathedral was her idea; she insisted that it was vital. She convinced me that if the assault were carried out at a particular time, it would open the door, thus making up for the loss of my nigger. She made it sound so plausible!

"All the while, she was acting as a strategist for both of the factions in the recent conflict. I only learned this after it was too late to do anything about it. She set us upon one another in the hopes that we would annihilate one another. It might have worked, but for the fact that I didn't put any of my real resources into the battle.

"Penny isn't dead, by the way. That was a charade to hoodwink her brother. I thought she was helping me because she hated him. What I didn't understand at the time was that she hated me, too. She hates everybody, and the only side she has is her own."

Perrone was surprised by the intensity of the relief he felt on receiving confirmation that Penny was alive. He felt a certain stirring that was utterly inappropriate under the circumstances. He had been almost certain that she wasn't dead, since the Grand Wizard had made no attempt to trade her for the man Perrone had liberated. As for the body that was found at Caleb Carter's house, there were a great many ways to arrange for the misidentification of a corpse. Whenever the face is obliterated, there's probably some skullduggery involved.

"I didn't need her to tell me anything," Sams continued. "I saw you in action at the rally in Bienville Square. I was in my office across the street, and I had an excellent view. It looked as though you were putting a mask over your head when you pursued the gunman into that alley. I thought it probable that you and the Bay Phantom were one and the same, and your performance at our meeting the other night reinforced this impression."

"Hmm," said Perrone, "I'll have to be more careful in the future."

"You won't need to. You don't have a future. No more than a few minutes' worth, at any rate."

"Dear me, that sounds dire," Perrone said. "So what happens now?"

"Now everybody here dies, except for me, and I take control of your resources. I'll bet you have all manner of things salted away here. Weapons, money, etcetera. All of that will help my cause. I really can't see letting any of you live. This degenerate Jew doctor is a blight upon the world, with his filthy scribblings. I'm not surprised you'd welcome him into your home, Perrone. You're a disgrace to the white race. I believe I'll kill the Jew first, then we'll see what develops after that."

"Let me do it, sir," said one of the white-robed goons. "I heard about him. He says little boys like to screw their mammas. That's sick."

Sams gave his henchman a blank look.

"Didn't you hear me? I said *everybody* here dies, except *me*." He raised the automatic and shot the man in the head, then did the same to the other one.

"This secret is mine alone," he said. "Now, where were we? Ah, yes. Perrone, would you like to live long enough to watch what happens to your little nigger whore, here?"

Perrone laughed grimly. "Mirabelle Darcy is worth a million of you, Sams, and you won't do anything to her. As for Sigmund Freud, I'm afraid he is too much of a titan to be extinguished by a flea like you. You placed your bet and you were wrong. Now you lose everything. I take no particular pleasure in what is going to happen, but it is necessary, I'm afraid. I am deeply sorry."

"Are you crazy?" shrieked the Wizard. "I have the upper hand, and I have history on my side."

"You mean the history in which your dreams and your way of life died decades ago?" scoffed Perrone.

"No, traitor. I mean the history in which my dreams and my way of life *endured*, in secret, until it was time for the faithful to take back everything that is rightfully ours. You, Mister Perrone, have no place in our world, so you must leave it. But first, you shall watch your friends depart." He gestured to Mirabelle with the barrel of his gun. "Come over here, little nigger. You obviously mean a great deal to this race traitor."

Mirabelle glanced at Perrone. A wordless communication flashed between them. She walked across the room to where Sams stood, stopping a foot in front of him.

"Do I kill you now?" Sams asked. "Or should I break your arms and legs and skull first?"

"You'd damn well better kill me while you can," she said, her voice hoarse. "Because if you stop at anything short of that, I am going to send your filthy goddamn redneck ass straight to hell, you shitbag."

"Mirabelle, please, language," scolded Perrone.

Sams laughed. "Are you trying to frighten me? Do you think you can trick me into sparing your life for a few more minutes? It would be fun, but... Suppose I don't do that? Suppose I just kill you right now?"

Mirabelle looked at Perrone again. They both knew what was at stake. Mirabelle was doomed, Doctor Freud was doomed, and so was the Bay Phantom. Unless... He nodded.

"In that case," Mirabelle said coldly, "I'd have to kill you first."

"And just how would you accomplish that, little nigger?" the Wizard asked.

"Good question. Give me a second to think about it." Mirabelle, a devout atheist, performed the sign of the cross, with special emphasis on the right arm. Then she closed her eyes and stood motionless and silent, not even breathing, for a quarter of a minute. Hector Sams looked on with a sneer, darkly amused.

Finally, she opened her eyes and said, "I reckon what I would do is expose you to an invisible poison gas. One that enters the bloodstream via the lungs and causes death in about a minute, but dissipates quickly in the open air. Then, see, anybody standing close to you who knew what was going on could hold their breath for about fifteen seconds and be perfectly safe."

"You've got quite an imagination!"

Mirabelle laughed sharply. "And *you've* got *none*. You're not paying attention, or else you lack the ability to put two and two together. Didn't you notice me holding my breath? Tell me, are you starting to get a headache?"

The Wizard sneered. "What's that got to do with..." A look of horror spread quickly across his face. His gloating turned instantly into animal fear.

"Yeah!" Mirabelle said brightly, clapping her hands together. "*Now* you get it, huh? Try moving your arms, or anything else. Kinda frozen, right? Total muscular rictus. Your throat will have seized up by now, and you probably can't breathe. To be honest, I think this is the best end you could have hoped for."

She had a few more things she wanted to get off her chest, but by this time, she was talking to a corpse. She reached over and, with a forefinger, gently pushed the rigid body of Hector Sams until it fell to the floor.

Doctor Freud cleared his throat. "Is this... this *thing* finished?" he asked, gesturing toward the body on the floor. "Are we out of danger now?"

"I believe we are," said Perrone.

"Oh, thank God!" the Doctor said. "For the past ten minutes I have been dying for a piss! Please excuse me. I know my way to the lavatory."

"It was the only way," Perrone said.

"Wait, are you trying to console me?" said Mirabelle with a strange looking smile. "Don't bother, because I'm not sorry. I feel good about it, in fact. Very good."

"Mirabelle..."

She shook her head. "It was a catharsis. This man here killed my father. Did you know that? Of course not. I didn't know it either. Well, I did but I didn't. I'll tell you the whole story later... Joe."

As she pronounced his name, she raised her head and looked him in the eye. The expression on his face made her laugh.

"Yeah," she said, "you finally got what you wanted. It was awfully damn expensive, though."

"Mirabelle..." he began, not knowing what ought to follow.

"But I get it now, Joe," she continued, looking down at Sams' body again.

"A look of horror spread...across his face."

"I really do. People like this, they have to be stopped. And the law can't do it."

She looked up at him, dry eyed, and said, "We're okay, Joe. We're doing what we should be doing."

He nodded, and the smile he gave her was both bleak and hopeful, in approximately equal measure. "Yes, Mirabelle, we are. I fear for us, but I believe we are."

She threw her arms around him and pressed her face against his chest. He held her tightly and kissed the top of her head.

"People like us have to get down in the muck," he said softly, "knowingly and without hesitation, so that the human race may one day leave it behind forever."

"I'm sorry I said all that damn stupid shit to you about how we aren't friends," Mirabelle said. "You *are* my friend. You're my friend and I care about you and I love you and we *are* friends."

She was sobbing now, and Perrone felt his own eyes beginning to water.

"We're more than that, Mirabelle," he said. "We're *family*. You know, many years ago, when we were no more than eight or nine, my Aunt Gertie visited us. Do you remember her? One day, she asked me if I'd like to have a sister. You know what I said? I told her I already had one."

"Now, that is what I call inspirational," came a voice from behind them. "Touching, too. Seriously." For a second, Perrone thought Freud had returned. But the voice was coming from the wrong direction and, though it was familiar, it wasn't the Doctor. He turned around.

"But, goddammit," said the Black Embalmer, pointing at Sams' body, "I wanted to kill *that* sonofabitch *myself*!"

"Oh dear," said Perrone.

"Oh *shit*," said Mirabelle.

The Embalmer still wore the filthy white smock, but he had not replaced the death mask. Huge purple bruises had blossomed on his jaw, forehead and cheeks, and his lips were grotesquely swollen. But he had evidently pushed his broken nasal cartilage back into place, because his speech was much clearer than it had been.

And, perhaps more to the point at this juncture, he was holding a very large, long barreled revolver.

"How come that asshole was here?" the Embalmer asked. "For that matter, where the hell *am* I? Who are you?"

"Let's backtrack a bit," Perrone said cautiously. "How did you come to be here?"

"Wait, I'm trying to think... Sorry, I've had a number of head injuries lately, and I'm having some trouble... Oh, I remember! I was in an ambulance, and I killed the attendants and the cop that was riding shotgun. Wrapped the damn vehicle around a tree in the process! That was my lesson for the day: Never strangle the driver while the ambulance is still moving! I extracted myself from the wreckage and hopped over to the Church Street Graveyard. Not long ago, I saw somebody lift up a grave marker and scamper down into the hole that was thus revealed. I intended to follow, but the cops came along at that moment, and it got complicated."

Mirabelle was staring at the Embalmer with an expression of utter bemusement, while Perrone regarded the deadly visitor with more curiosity than anything. Now was the time to be calm and show no fear.

"Do you need some help, sir?" Perrone said in a friendly tone. "Perhaps I could get you a taxi, or..."

"No, no," said the Embalmer. "I think I'm right where I wanted to be. I popped down the cadaver hole, followed the little train tracks down the tunnel, and here I am! You have *got* to be the Bay Phantom, right? This is your house? I kind of swore I was going to kill you. I do admire your taste in egresses, though. I have this kind of death fetish or something, and I'm a sucker for anything involving cemeteries and funeral parlors and the like."

"Very interesting," came a voice from the hallway. Doctor Freud stepped into the room. "It reminds me very much of a patient of mine back in Vienna, around the turn of the century. He disinterred his mother, disposed of her body, and slept each night in her casket, dressed in her shroud."

Mirabelle gasped and grabbed the doctor's lapels. "Sir," she said, "please get out of here and leave this to us." Perrone, for his part, had stepped protectively between Freud and the Embalmer, keeping a wary eye on the latter.

"Is that a fact?" the Embalmer said, sounding intrigued. He made no move to attack. "I don't suppose you'd have this fellow's phone number, would you?"

"Alas, no."

"You're a psychiatrist, then?"

"I am," the doctor replied with an old-fashioned courtly bow. "Sigmund Freud, at your service. Is there anything you'd care to discuss?"

There followed one of the lengthiest and most uncomfortable silences Perrone had ever endured. Finally, the Embalmer broke it:

"Sigmund Freud!" he exclaimed, sounding delighted. "Are you kidding me? I've read everything you've ever written! Aberrant psychology is my favorite topic. For me, it's more than just a lifestyle. When I was a child, Richard Von Kraft-Ebing's *Psychopathia Sexualis* was my favorite bedtime book. I still enjoy it when I'm in the mood for some light reading, but your work has so much more depth and insight."

"Thank you," Freud replied graciously. "Shall we have a talk, then? I would appreciate it if you would put away your firearm. Do you really need it? Sometimes a cigar is just a cigar, but a gun like that is *always* an attempt to compensate for something."

Detective Tom Dart had officially taken the Werewolf into custody. The maniacal killer had been stripped of his armored costume. During a brief press conference, Dart announced that it was now the opinion of the Mobile Police Department that the Werewolf had murdered Simon Brickell and the six police officers. The so-called Bay Phantom was no longer being sought as a suspect.

Two days later, it was announced that Thomas Victor Dart had been promoted to Detective Sergeant First Class.

It took time, but the Werewolf was finally identified as Gerald Sams, a young man who had gone missing more than a decade earlier. Where he had been since then, what had happened to him there, and who else might be involved, were unknown. As far as the Werewolf persona and suit were concerned, nobody was willing to speculate.

Mirabelle had disposed of the bodies of the two unfortunate Klansmen who had accompanied Hector Sams to Tull House. She assured her boss that she had arranged for the men to be given decent burials. Whether or not she actually did so would remain her secret.

Sams himself was returned to his home in the dead of night. The next morning, he was discovered in his bed by a servant. The official verdict was that Hector Sams had succumbed to a heart attack in his sleep. The lethal gas had left no traces for a pathologist to detect.

Shorty Red went on the Bay Phantom's payroll. Though the enforcer would not rejoin the ranks of Carter family underlings, he remained on the fringes of the criminal underworld. His wealth of knowledge and experience would prove invaluable, as would his prodigious strength. It was the Phantom's hope that he would be a positive influence on Louis Rickert, who was prone to backsliding now and then.

The election went ahead as scheduled, between two replacement candidates hastily selected by each of the political parties. Voter turnout was very low. The outcome made little difference to anyone, since both of the contenders were owned by the Carter family.

CHAPTER THIRTY
THE SISTER AT MIDNIGHT

Caleb Carter was sitting in his downtown office going over some rather mundane paperwork relating to one of his many enterprises. He would have to get together soon with the new mayor, a man whose name he couldn't quite remember, to sort out a few things. But that could wait.

On the desk in front of him was an urn containing the ashes of his late sister. He'd had the body cremated as soon as possible. Finally, the little hellion was under his complete control. It wasn't a cause for unbridled joy, though. He would miss her, in his way. She had been smart and she had been an asset to the organization he had built.

But he also knew that, had she lived, he would have been obliged to put her into this urn himself, sooner or later. He mourned her death, but he would not wish to undo it.

His grim musings were interrupted by a rustling sound from behind him. He swiveled his chair around and saw the drapes over the French doors moving.

"Who's there?" he said. "Come on out."

"Hello, Caleb," came a weird, muffled voice from behind the drapes.

"Who's there?"

"That's the funny thing. Something very ironic is about to happen."

From behind the drapes came a grotesque figure in a white lab coat and a bizarre plaster mask.

"Oh, God," said Caleb.

"Just like in a Greek tragedy," said the interloper, "you sowed the seeds of your own destruction when you hired the Black Embalmer."

"Wait a minute now," Caleb said. "There's no reason for you to kill me at all. I paid you off, and I can do it again. There's plenty of money in it for you. You've got no reason to do this."

"Oh, yes I do. There are some things you don't know. I'm not who you think I am, and I want to do things I can't do as long as you're alive. Your man downstairs saw me come in, but only from a distance. He wouldn't have noticed any discrepancies in my appearance. Later on, he'll tell the rest of the family what he saw and heard, and the Black Embalmer will be blamed for your death. Which is excellent, from my point of view."

"What? Who the hell are you, then? I don't understand. Whoever you are, the same deal still goes. I can give you money. Lots of it!"

"I don't want a little chunk of your money. Why should I, when I can get all of it? You die, I get rich!"

"I don't see how *you*... Oh. Oh my God, no. You're... Is that... is that *you*, Penny?"

A girlish giggle came from behind the mask. "Yep."

"You're alive? Oh, goddammit to... I mean...thank God you're okay!"

"I don't think you really feel that way, brother."

"Yes, I do. I was heartbroken, and I..." He shook his head. He wasn't buying it himself, and he knew Penny wouldn't. "How did you... I mean, whose body was it?"

"Somebody who used to look like me," said Penny. "I went to school with her, the poor thing. People used to get us mixed up all the time. Same hair color and everything. I've been keeping her on ice, literally, for months now."

"But the fingerprints..."

"I took those from the body before she went into the deep freeze. Put them onto a genuine official police department fingerprint card. It was very simple to replace the real one the cops had on file for me.

"You know, a pathologist would have discovered that she'd been dead for a while, if you hadn't rushed the whole thing through, as I knew you would. You were relieved I was gone, weren't you?"

Since they both knew the answer, Caleb didn't bother with it. "And you did this so that..."

"So that what *did* happen *could* happen. So that what is *about to happen* could happen. So that what will happen over the next few *years* could happen. Don't worry about any of that. You aren't included."

"For God's sake, Penny, I'm your brother!"

"I know. You'd think I'd feel bad about this, wouldn't you? I mean, I know you considered killing me, but you kind of had to. It was just business. Still is."

"Penny, you need help."

"No. I'm doing just fine. *You* could use some help, but you won't get any. You might be feeling a little woozy right now. That's because you've been breathing in a gas that is paralyzing your body. It's what the Black Embalmer uses. I also built this replica of that thing of his. Not the whole rig, just the harpoon. I'm going to jab this through your heart, and when they find you and ask the guard what he saw, the Embalmer will be blamed and I'll be innocent and rich and powerful."

She reached behind her back and produced a length of silver tubing. The tip had been filed down to a sharp point.

"I suppose the Embalmer is still out there," she said. "He's either dead or he isn't. I don't suppose he'll mind being given credit for your murder."

She giggled and raised the harpoon. Caleb said nothing. He knew it wouldn't make any difference now.

"I'm gonna have so much *fun*!" said Penny as she thrust the tube into her brother's chest.

The Black Embalmer was taken to the same sanitarium that was now home to the mysterious black man Perrone had rescued from the Grand Wizard. The Embalmer was kept under heavy guard, but had not shown the slightest inclination to escape, or to misbehave in any way.

Freud conferred with Atticus on both cases. The elderly black man was something of an enigma. He had apparently been drugged for a number of years with some unknown compound. He had begun to show signs of withdrawal, and Atticus was administering sedatives.

As for the Black Embalmer, he was the purest psychopath Freud had ever encountered. He was also the most cooperative. He seemed genuinely fascinated with the workings of his own mind, and participated enthusiastically in the doctor's attempts at diagnosis. However, he refused to give specific details of his personal history. He would not reveal his true name, his place of origin, or any information about his family.

It was Freud's professional opinion that the Embalmer was a hopeless case in terms of genuine rehabilitation, but an absolutely mesmerizing object of study. Unfortunately, it would likely take many more years than he had left on this earth to unravel even the smallest part of the puzzle.

It was his personal opinion that the Embalmer was intelligent and charismatic, with a good sense of humor. He was also one of the most dangerous individuals currently inhabiting the planet, and should be securely locked away for the remainder of his life. The Embalmer's unofficial presence at the clinic, outside the aegis of the judicial and medical establishments, presented little in the way of ethical problems, since the man remained there of his own free will, and agreed to be kept under lock and key. For the time being, it seemed that Joe Perrone had a much better chance of keeping the Embalmer on ice and out of lethal mischief than did any of the duly constituted authorities.

Doctor Atticus, after examining the anonymous man as thoroughly as he could over a period of several days, telephoned Perrone with a report.

"You may think I'm nuts," he said, "but I believe this man is a zombie."

"I beg your pardon?"

"I know how it sounds. Look, I'm not talking about the kind of zombie you see in movies or horror stories. You may not know this, but 'zombification' is a genuine phenomenon. There have been documented cases, mostly in Haiti. They aren't dead people who've been returned to life; they're people who have been drugged with a compound that makes them appear to be dead. After the victim is interred, the Voodoo practitioner exhumes him, revives him, and keeps him drugged with another compound that saps his will and turns him into a sort of automaton. The victim can be kept in that state indefinitely, and used as slave labor."

"What can be done to help him?"

"Nothing that I know of. But the effects of the 'zombie drug' disappear after a while, if no more is administered. We'll just have to keep him comfortable and wait."

Recalling Mirabelle's account of her hypnosis session with Freud, Perrone asked a question:

"Does that man have anything on his neck that might be a rope burn?"

"As a matter of fact, he does. There's also evidence that his neck was broken at one time. Ten years ago at least, maybe closer to fifteen."

"And there isn't any way to establish his identity?"

"Not that I can think of. I'm sure he looked a lot different ten or fifteen years ago than he does now. I doubt he's ever been to a dentist, and if he wasn't a criminal, his fingerprints aren't on file anywhere."

Perrone said nothing of this to Mirabelle. He disliked keeping things from her, but this was a potential bombshell, and would have to be handled with care.

"We need to discuss something," said Mirabelle.

"What?" Perrone asked. "If you want to talk about hiring another girl, I'm afraid I..."

"No, not that. About your wounds. Mainly the ones the Werewolf gave you, but everything else you've been through lately as well."

"Why, the wounds I sustained battling the Werewolf are virtually healed already."

"I know."

"They must have been less severe than I thought," Perrone continued. "I don't think they'll even leave scars."

"I know that, too," Mirabelle replied, nodding.

"And those three puncture wounds in my arm; they bled a great deal when they were fresh, but there doesn't appear to be any lasting damage."

"Exactly. Listen, I saw those cuts when they were still relatively fresh. The bicep was split nearly to the bone in three places! Deep muscular lacerations. You should have lost the use of that arm!"

He stretched the arm out in front of him and turned it this way and that by way of demonstration. "There's nothing wrong with it at all, Mirabelle," he said. "See? Full range of motion, no pain."

"Right," she said. "And that should not be."

"I've always been a quick healer," he offered.

"Please," she said, making a face. "This goes way beyond quick healing, and nothing in modern medicine can explain it, either. The antibiotics I gave you didn't do it. I don't know what did, and it bothers me."

"There's nothing unnatural going on," said Perrone. "I take good care of myself, I eat properly and get sufficient rest, and I…"

"… *and* you constantly throw yourself in front of maniacs with blades," Mirabelle interrupted. "They carve you up like an Easter ham, and you walk away from it like you hadn't gotten anything worse than a paper cut."

Perrone shook his head. "I think you're imagining things. I've been getting a great deal more exercise recently, and that's bound to have a salubrious effect on my constitution."

"I'm not going to discuss it with you any further," Mirabelle said, "since you seem also to have become incapable of listening to the slightest degree of reason. Consider the subject closed for now. But I am going to run some blood tests, and if they don't tell me anything, I'll think up some other tests to run. And you have no choice in the matter. Something funny is afoot, and I don't know what it is, and there is nothing I hate worse than not knowing what something is."

CHAPTER THIRTY-ONE
OF FISH AND FIRE

"Tell me about yourself and Doctor Piranha," said Sigmund Freud.

"What, specifically, would you like to know?" Joe Perrone asked.

Perrone had realized that there must be more to his own story than he was aware of, and he was eager to discuss it with Freud. When would he ever have another opportunity like this? He had the feeling that this was the kind of thing Gandhi had advised him to be on the lookout for.

And if that weren't enough, Mirabelle had insisted on it. Actually, it was more like an order.

It was not a formal psychoanalytic session. He and Freud were sitting in armchairs in the living room at Tull House. Mirabelle was on the couch. They had discussed Perrone's early life, the incident that had led to the creation of the Bay Phantom, and many of his experiences since then.

"That's up to you," said Freud. "We have discussed everything else, and I sense that your encounter with him three years ago is a pivotal point in your history. Just tell it in your own words. Talk freely. Be as brief or as long-winded as you wish."

"Well," said Perrone, "Doctor Piranha was the worst of criminals; the kind with no discernible motive. With most of them, the motive was glaringly obvious; profit. But Piranha? He just wanted to destroy. He didn't benefit financially from any of it. It was his only apparent purpose in life.

"I hadn't been fighting crime for very long. I had spent time in a boarding school until I came of age. Of course, I had been educating myself secretly, learning things I thought I would need to know. Detective work, you know, forensics. And various exotic fighting styles.

"It was a boom time. Prosperity seemed to attract... unusual criminals. I had noticed them becoming more... colorful. Oh, I had some grand adventures! At some point, though, people in general became more desperate and more aggressive. I was kept very busy for a few months. Piranha started up in April of 1928. He specialized in blowing things up; banks, railroad bridges, shipyards. Most of them belonged to the Carter family. This was a full year before the Depression set in, but there were, as they say, clouds on the horizon. Many people were angry at the 'haves.' Piranha didn't stand out. But, that summer...

"He dropped on Mobile like a nightmare. In June, he stepped up the pace, blew up more buildings, and hijacked radio broadcast signals to gloat over what he had done. And the chilling thing was... he made no demands.

"One day in August, he announced that he had planted huge caches of explosives all over the city. It was his intention, he said, to erase Mobile from the map. There was a deadline, and it was very near.

"I didn't even attempt to find the explosives. It was hopeless, really. I assisted in the evacuation. When the first blasts went off downtown I assisted the police and firefighters.

"Earlier that day, he had kidnapped Abelard Carter and his son, Jeremiah. Abelard was a grand old man, the unofficial mayor of Mobile. A businessman, a landowner. Kidnapping him was a nasty slap in the face to this city. Abelard Carter and my father had been great friends, known each other all their lives. They had extensive business and personal connections. At the time, I never suspected the Carters of the things I now know to be true.

"We saved a few lives...too few. When Piranha came on the air to announce the abduction and execution of Abelard Carter, I used a device I had created to trace the location from which he was hijacking the broadcast signals.

"I caught up with him. I was just in time to witness the murder of Abelard Carter, and too late to stop the explosions. So much destruction! Only the center of the city escaped total devastation.

"I did save Jeremiah Carter, and I captured Piranha. I handed him over to the authorities, but not before I..." His voice trailed off.

"Yes?' Freud prompted. "Not before you..?"

"Not before I came to within a hair's breadth of killing him. I found him and I tore off that mask he wore, that ugly rubber fish head. I couldn't even look him in the eye. I just started punching him. He didn't fight back. I recall breaking his nose and doing something to his jaw. Then I got my hands around his throat and squeezed."

"What made you stop?"

"I... I don't know. I can't remember. I just recall dragging him out of his headquarters and throwing him into the trunk of my car. I drove to a police station and dumped him in the lobby.

"You know, I was part of the reason he didn't get the death penalty. I couldn't very well testify in court to what I knew. Even if I had revealed my true identity, any good defense lawyer could have torn me to shreds on the stand. And that was fine with me. At least I had stopped him, and he would never be free again. They managed to cobble together enough lesser charges to get him what amounted to a life sentence in a federal prison."

Freud was silent for quite some time.

"Those were the mechanics of the thing, Joseph," he said. "And they are all but irrelevant. What concerns us here is what lies beneath them. I think we must go even further back than Doctor Piranha, to the night your family perished.

"You knew it was not any ordinary burglary. There was a mystery there, one the authorities never even acknowledged, much less solved. That's how you felt, wasn't it?"

Perrone nodded. "I didn't even realize it at the time."

"You sensed something unseen, some force behind the men that killed your family. This, I think, is why you felt compelled to wear the mask. The dark presence behind your tragedy had no face. Therefore, in order to properly confront it, you had to be the same way. No face, no past, no explanation. Ordinary policemen could never find it or come to grips with it, but you had to do this. So, in effect, you eradicated your own face and identity, so that you might learn to move in the same circles as your nebulous enemy.

"And still you could not find him. You spent some time finding and punishing substitutes. Not necessarily a bad alternative and it might have sustained you. But the coming of Doctor Piranha robbed you of that sustenance. Why? That is what we must learn.

"This desire to penetrate the unknown is also what ties you to Charles Fort and his neverending catalog of enigmas. You've an insatiable desire to lay bare every mystery you become aware of. The paradox here is that you can never know *yourself.* Your quest precludes this. You join the ranks of the enigmas."

"Am I hopeless?" Perrone asked.

"Not at all," Freud said. "I have a suggestion. Hypnosis was a great help to Miss Mirabelle. Would you be willing to try it yourself?"

Perrone nodded.

"I'd like to be present," Mirabelle said.

"I've no objection to that," said Perrone. "Your insight will be invaluable."

Freud helped Perrone into the hypnotic state, and sat next to him with his hand on the man's forehead.

"Relax, Joseph," said the doctor. "You are in no danger. You are just an observer. Go back, into your past, and see what is there. Try the night your family was killed. I know it is upsetting, but nothing you see can harm you now."

"Yes," Perrone said in a strange, dreamy voice. "That night... I woke up... I don't know what aroused me, but something... I hear noises and smell smoke, and I have the sense that... My brother. My brother is there. What is he doing? What is he *doing*?"

"Tell me," said the doctor. "Tell me what you see. Don't worry about what it means."

"Anthony got out," Perrone said. "He *didn't* burn. I... I saw him strangle a man and... And I helped him... He switched clothes with the man, then heaved the man's body back into the bedroom... And then he... He gave me something... Injected something into my arm, and..." He shook his head. "I can't remember anything else. Not about that night, but... Anthony... He had done that before, given me a shot of something... He said it was vitamins, I think... More than once... I was so young... And he... He told me it would be okay, that I wouldn't... That I wouldn't remember what he had done, because... I don't... I don't remember why, but he didn't make me promise... He did something..."

"What did he tell you?" Freud asked gently. "The night of the fire?"

"He told me... He was very calm, even after he killed that man and he said... He gave me that shot and he said, '*That's the last one you'll need, Joey. You'll be okay now.*' He seemed sad, and I... I had never seen him sad before... Or happy or mad or anything else... He was always just..."

"Cold," Mirabelle whispered, too softly for anyone else to hear. "Cold as a fish."

"And he said something else," Perrone continued. "I didn't understand it, but... he asked me how many burglars there were and I told him four. He looked at me and said, '*No, Joe, there were only three. Only three burglars.*' I knew that was wrong, but I nodded, and I... But there *were* only three, that's what I always thought... But that night, I counted them... I saw three of them downstairs, but there was the one Anthony... The one he..."

Mirabelle leaned over and whispered something to Freud.

"Are you sure, my dear?" the Doctor replied. "If you think it best, I shall trust your judgment."

Mirabelle just nodded, a faraway look in her eyes.

"Joseph," Freud said, "I will soon bring you out of the hypnotic state. When I do, you will remember nothing of what we have discussed here. Do you understand?"

"Yes," said Perrone. "I understand."

The time came for Sigmund Freud to leave them. Perrone and Mirabelle took the doctor to Bates Field, for the first leg of his journey back to Vienna. He would travel to New York by airplane, then board a ship to cross the Atlantic. They walked into the terminal with him.

"Be careful, Doctor," Mirabelle said. She held his hands in hers and looked into his eyes. "I'll miss you. You've done so much for me..."

"You did it yourself, my dear," said Freud. "I merely helped you navigate the Inferno."

"Nonsense," said Perrone. "We both owe you a great deal, Doctor. I've learned a lot from you."

"And I from you," said the doctor. "For example: Sometimes a hot dog is just a hot dog. Unless it is a machine gun."

The three of them laughed, Mirabelle the loudest and longest. Then she started crying. Overcome by emotion, she kissed Freud on the cheek, excused herself, and returned to the car.

"You didn't tell her it was me that asked you to come, did you?" Perrone said.

"Of course not," said Freud. "That will be our secret. Believe me; I would have come anyway, had I known how much distress she was in. I am grateful to you, Mister Perrone."

"And I to you, Doctor."

He wondered if these two extraordinary people were fully aware of how extraordinarily fortunate they were to have one another. He doubted it. People so seldom were.

A voice over the loudspeaker system announced that the flight was now boarding. Freud shook hands with Perrone.

"Take care of yourself, Joseph," he said. "And take care of Mirabelle, too. And let her take care of you when it is necessary. You are two of the most extraordinary people I have ever met. If I can be of further help to you, do not hesitate to summon me."

"Thank you, sir," Mirabelle said into the telephone. "That's all I needed to know. Goodbye."

She sat at her desk for almost an hour, pondering the notes she had made during her conversation with the staff physician at Leavenworth Penitentiary.

Prisoner #10121963, aka "John Doe," aka Doctor Piranha, had sustained a wound a year ago during an altercation with another prisoner. The wound should have been fatal. The other prisoner's makeshift stiletto had pierced Piranha's heart, of that, the physician was certain. Piranha had bled profusely, and required a blood transfusion. The transfusion, the physician had confided to her, was something of a hopeless gesture, as it had seemed certain the patient was doomed.

But Piranha had pulled through, and it hadn't taken him very long at all. Exploratory surgery revealed no puncture wound to the heart, though there was a small area, the size and shape of a pinky finger nail clipping, that looked like scar tissue. A week after the incident, there were no scars to be found on Piranha's chest. The original puncture caused by the shiv and the incision made by the physician were both gone, leaving no trace.

That couldn't happen. It was as impossible as the rapid disappearance of the deep gashes the Werewolf had given Joe Perrone.

What the hell is going on here?

She said nothing of this to Joe Perrone. She disliked keeping things from him but this was a potential bombshell, and would have to be handled with great care.

EPILOGUE ONE
UNITED STATES FEDERAL PENITENTIARY
LEAVENWORTH, KANSAS

"Do you need anything else, sir?" asked Warden Seymour Pallas.

"Not at present, Warden," said Doctor Piranha, placing particular emphasis on Seymour's new title. "Nothing but a bit of privacy that is. You make an excellent administrator, Seymour. It's a pity your predecessor met with that... accident. But we were fortunate indeed that you could step into his shoes."

Pallis nodded.

"I love what you've done with this office," Piranha continued. "It's a lot more... *earthy* than it used to be. Now, if you'll just leave me with the telephone for a few minutes..."

"Yes, sir," Pallis said obsequiously.

When he had stepped out of the room, closing the door behind him, Piranha lifted the receiver and dialed a number.

"Hello to you," he said when the other party answered. "Things went smoothly, I gather, since I'm reaching you at this number... Of course, I was quite sure you would... I will never make the mistake of underestimating you... Yes, I heard about Sams... Shame about him *and* his brother... Well, I may have done. I was quite the little experimenter in my youth. It took him a while to blossom, but the results were both gratifying and timely... Drugs and hypnosis merely allowed certain existing proclivities to flourish... I just helped him discover his true identity... No, mine was a foregone conclusion from the start; I needed no encouragement, not even from myself... The Bay Phantom is off limits. His intervention prevented the recent business from becoming even more of a bloodbath than it was. I have my own plans for him, and I believe I made that quite clear... Well, that is the question, isn't it? Do you? Well, please handle it with care... You are in an excellent position now, and you and I are much closer to having what we want... Indeed there is, and I am pleased to leave the bulk of it in your capable hands... Do keep me posted. I'll have some new designs for you presently. Things should be easier for me, as I have engineered a favorable change of regime here, thanks to your efforts... We'll speak again soon.... Goodbye."

EPILOGUE TWO

Penelope Carter wandered around her new office in the penthouse of the nameless hotel, admiring the décor she had selected.

"You did good, Hillyard," she said to the man sitting in the leather chair in front of the big desk that had once been her brother's. "I appreciate your help with Caleb."

The lawyer shrugged. "I like to back winners. Caleb was getting too conservative. The world is changing, and you seemed like the one best able to keep up with it."

"It's going to change even more," she said. "I predict a rash of unusual accidental deaths among some of Mobile's more prominent citizens in the months ahead. I have the list right here." She tapped her right temple with an index finger. "I recognized quite a few of the faces I saw at that Klan rally. I don't think we're going to have to worry about any more challenges from that quarter. They managed to amass a great deal of money and power. Their political takeover of the state might have succeeded, and the blight would have spread. It might have come down to a new Civil War! Well, that's not going to happen now."

"There's been another change in what you might call our infrastructure," Parnell said. "We can't count on Mark Marvel any more. The publisher made Gladys Turnbull associate editor. Theoretically, Marvel is still in charge, but I gather Miss Turnbull will be the one actually calling the shots."

"Well, we can deal with her if we need to," said Penny. "I've already spoken to Mister Capone's people in Chicago. As you know, Big Al was a little leery about my taking control of the operation here, but he's got plenty of troubles of his own right now. I wouldn't be surprised if he went away for a while. Always pay your taxes, Hillyard! Mister Nitti and Mister Ricca are a lot more amenable."

"My God, Penny," said Parnell. "You didn't have anything to do with... Never mind, I don't want to know."

Penny giggled. "Now," she said, "what about my official resurrection? I need to come back from the dead, you know."

"Oh, yeah, that's no problem. I mean, you *are* Penny Carter, obviously. Once our guy switches those fingerprint cards back, all the cops will have is a mystery they can't solve. Your poor double's body has been destroyed. If there are any loose ends we can blame them on the Black Embalmer, the Werewolf or the Bay Phantom. We're spoiled for choice, really. I've already set the process into motion."

"So you won't need to do anything else?"

"Not me personally, no. I did my part. Now all we have to do is wait. Everything will take care of itself."

"That's very good, Hillyard," Penny said. "I owe you big. How will I ever express my gratitude? Ah, I know!"

She pulled open a desk drawer, reached in, brought out a little silver .22 pistol, and shot Hillyard Parnell in the forehead.

"The reason I did it that way," Penny said to the corpse, "is because if I had given you a chance, you'd have started blubbering and begging and humiliating yourself. I wanted to spare you that, because I really *do* owe you. But you never would have understood. The Good Old Boy Network is coming down. This is a girls' club now!"

Penelope Carter basked in the glow of the things she had wrought, going to and fro in her new office and walking up and down in it. After a time, the telephone on her desk rang. Smiling, she lifted the receiver.

"Hello? Ah, I was wondering when I'd hear from you... Oh, yes, just like clockwork. I've just clipped off the last irritating loose end, and good riddance... No, you're much too smart to do that... I guess you know by now what happened to the big irritant and his boy's club... They're exactly where they belong now. Did you have anything to do with that Werewolf business? I mean from the beginning... I see... The same way you discovered your own? No, I don't suppose you did. And what of this Bay Phantom? He was actually quite helpful, but now he'll probably set his sights on torpedoing my family's business... Yes, you did, and I intend to respect that. You wouldn't happen to know who he really is, I suppose... Well... Maybe I have an idea... Of course, Doctor... Indeed we are, and there is much work to be done... Oh, I'm looking forward to it... I will... I'm glad to hear that... We certainly will... Goodbye, Doctor. Take care."

She hung up and turned her attention to the stack of mail on the desk. She selected an oversized envelope and slit it open, removing a greeting card.

Dearest Penny:

Hope this finds you well. You may have been wondering about my fate. Rumors of my demise are as exaggerated as reports of your own death. Nice one, by the way! You make me proud!

Anyhow, I have retired from my active practice for the time being. I had not intended to, but I was unexpectedly presented with an opportunity that I simply could not refuse. This came courtesy of our mutual friend, the one with two faces. You figured him out, didn't you? As for you and me, our business relationship has been mutually beneficial, I think, and we might want to think about resuming it whenever I tire of this sabbatical. I'll keep in touch. Until we meet again, I remain,

yours sincerely,
The Bad Egg

Penny chuckled and set the card aside. He was a real character, all right. She would certainly make further use of him in the future.

For now, though, she had a card of her own to write, as long as she was thinking about it. She opened a fresh box of greeting cards, selected one, opened it on her desk blotter, and began to write:

Dear Joey:

You've heard that I'm dead, right? Well, it ain't necessarily so. I want to see you again, very soon. You have my phone number, and I suggest you use it. This isn't a threat. I would never harm you. I think I may know something about you, something you don't want other people to know. Don't worry, I will never breathe a word of it to anyone. I think we are more alike, you and I, than I ever dreamed when I first met you. Things are changing. I foresee a wild ride ahead, Joey. We are young and we are free to do absolutely anything we want to. Are you with me?

All my love,

Penny

THE END

ABOUT OUR CREATORS

AUTHOR -

CHUCK MILLER - was born in Ohio, lived in Alabama for many years, and now resides in Norman, Oklahoma. He is a Libra whose interests include monster movies, comic books, music and writing. He holds a BA in creative writing from the University of South Alabama.

He is the creator/writer of TALES OF THE BLACK CENTIPEDE, THE INCREDIBLE ADVENTURES OF VIONNA VALIS AND MARY JANE KELLY, THE BAY PHANTOM CHRONICLES, and THE MYSTIC FILES OF DOCTOR UNKNOWN JUNIOR. He has also written stories featuring such classic characters as Jill Trent: Science Sleuth, Armless O'Neil, The Griffon, and others.

Miller received the BEST NEW WRITER OF 2011 Award from Pulp Ark. His first novel, the critically acclaimed "Creeping Dawn: The Rise of the Black Centipede" was published in 2011 by Pro Se Press. The second installment in the Black Centipede series, "Blood of the Centipede" was published in 2012. "Black Centipede Confidential" is slated for release in 2013. Also due in 2013 is "Vionna and the Vampires," the first installment of "The Incredible Adventures of Vionna Valis and Mary Jane Kelly."

http://theblackcentipede.blogspot.com/

ARTIST –

ZACHARY BRUNNER – graduated from the School of Arts with a degree in filmmaking. Upon gradution, he realized that he would rather pursue a career in illustration, needing a more creative job than the high-stress environment of film production. He began working with comic writer Jim Krueger on two graphic novels, "The High Cost of Happily Ever After," and "Runner." "High Cost" is currently available at Amazon, "Runner," is expected out this year.

While studying at SVA, Zachary worked as a concept artist on an animated film called "Brother," directed by Sari Rodrig. The short film went on to win countless awards all over the world, having been shown at festivals such as Cannes and the Student Emmys. Zach currently is working on Sari's second short animated film, "Essence."

For the past year, he has also worked as a storyboard artist for Torque

Creative, the in-house advertising agency for Mercedes-Benz. He is also currently working on several storyboards for short independence films.

Other print projects included "Christopher Rising," "Penny Dreadful" and "The Poisonberry Fortune" and "Foot Soldiers,Volume 1." He planes on furthering a career in concept art and in the comic book industry.

A Son's Revenge

Veteran Police Sergeant Clarke is gunned down by hoodlums, shot in the back of the head. As he lay dying, a rush of blood to his face formed a macabre mask, a crimson mask! When his son, Doctor Robert "Bob" Clarke, saw that strange stigmata he interpreted it as a sign, inspiring him to become his father's avenger, the Crimson Mask!

Once again Airship 27 Productions digs into the dusty vaults of long forgotten, second tier pulp heroes to revitalize another great character in brand new, exciting adventures. Writers J. Walt Layne, Terrence McCauley, C. William Russette and Gary Lovisi took on the challenge of creating new, bizarre mysteries for the pharmacist turned crime-fighter and in doing so have put together a terrific collection of fast paced pulp action echoing the thrills of the original classics.

Aided by retired Police Commissioner Warrick, his former college roommate David Small and lovely nurse Sandra Gray, the Crimson Mask must hunt down the villainous distributors of tainted heroin, stop an invisible thief, learn who ignited the latest city gang war and solve the mystery of a killer targeting his father's allies.

Hold on to your fedoras, jump on the running board and get ready for blazing thrills galore, pulp fans, as the Crimson Mask is back!

AIRSHIP27HANGAR.COM

NEW PULP

PULP FICTION FOR A NEW GENERATION!

CHECK AVAILABILITY AT: AIRSHIP27HANGAR.COM

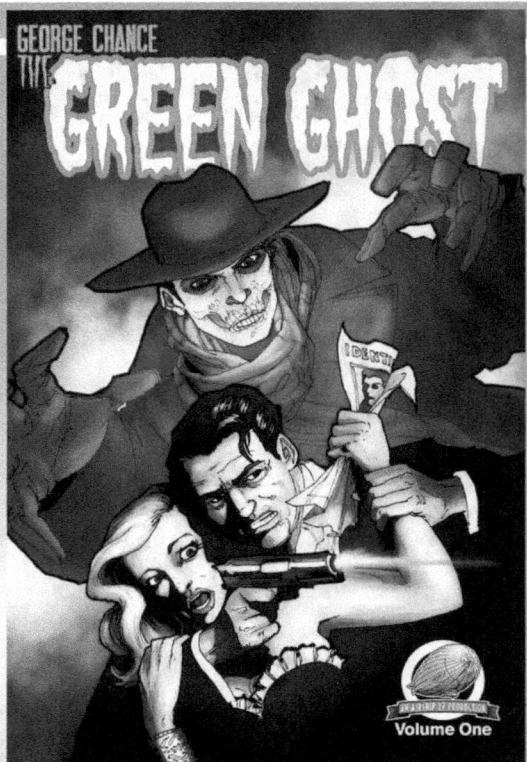

www.ingramcontent.com/pod-product-compliance
Lightning Source LLC
Chambersburg PA
CBHW071237250626
47163CB00001B/217